W9-BUP-384

COVENTRY PUBLIC LIBRARY

RENEGADE

Also by Kerry Wilkinson

RECKONING

LOCKED IN

VIGILANTE

THE WOMAN IN BLACK

THINK OF THE CHILDREN

PLAYING WITH FIRE

COVENTRY PUBLIC LIBRARY

Kerry Wilkinson

RENEGADE

ST. MARTIN'S GRIFFIN NEW YORK

This is a work of fiction. All of the characters, organizations, and events portrayed in this novel are either products of the author's imagination or are used fictitiously.

RENEGADE. Copyright © 2015 by Kerry Wilkinson. All rights reserved. Printed in the United States of America. For information, address St. Martin's Press, 175 Fifth Avenue, New York, N.Y. 10010.

www.stmartins.com

Library of Congress Cataloging-in-Publication Data

Wilkinson, Kerry, 1980– author.
   Renegade / Kerry Wilkinson. — First U.S. edition.
      p. cm. — (The Silver Blackthorn trilogy ; 2)
   ISBN 978-1-250-06133-1 (hardcover)
   ISBN 978-1-4668-3855-0 (e-book)
   1. Escapes—Fiction. 2. Survival—Fiction. 3. Kings, queens, rulers, etc.—Fiction. 4. Fate and fatalism—Fiction. 5. Social classes—Fiction. 6. England—Fiction. 7. Science fiction. I. Title.
   PZ7.W6515Ren 2015
   [Fic]—dc23

                                                      2014032295

St. Martin's Griffin books may be purchased for educational, business, or promotional use. For information on bulk purchases, please contact the Macmillan Corporate and Premium Sales Department at 1-800-221-7945, extension 5442, or write to specialmarkets@macmillan.com.

First published in Great Britain by Pan Books, an imprint of Pan Macmillan Ltd, a division of Macmillan Publishers Limited

First U.S. Edition: July 2015

10   9   8   7   6   5   4   3   2   1

RENEGADE

1

It is one of those beautiful late-summer mornings where the sun is high and warm, even though it's not yet midday. The sky is endless and blue, the grass lush and green, the clouds white and fluffy. In the distance I can see fields of pink, yellow and red flowers. Everywhere I look, there is a different colour: a canvas of lavish paints stretching in all directions.

'We're never going to make it there.'

I don't need to turn to know that Opie has his arms crossed, wanting to take control of the situation.

I stay sitting on the grass bank that overlooks my home village of Martindale on one side and the flourishing landscape on the other, sensing him standing over me. Beyond the grass, the flowers and the trees is a hill that stretches high into the blue of the sky. My father once told me we'd walk there when I was old enough but that was before he died.

I put on the voice I always use when I want to get my own way: 'I want to try walking there.'

'You'll get tired after a few hours and I'll end up giving you a piggyback home,' Opie replies.

'It's only across a few fields. I don't want to go *up* it – just reach the bottom.'

'It's a long way, Silver.'

'We can do it next summer when we turn fifteen. We'll take a picnic and set off early. It'll be fun.'

'It won't be fun when I have to carry you back.'

I turn, grinning, expecting to see Opie's sandy hair and half-smile, ready to dive at his legs and roll around in the dirt. Instead, I'm blinking up at Imrin's face, his black hair and dark skin the opposite of what I expected.

This time it is Imrin's voice speaking, saying my name softly.

As I drift back to the present, I remember the rest: being chosen as an Offering and taken away from my family and friends. Imrin and I were effectively prisoners of the King, at his mercy, knowing each day could be our last. We did the only thing we could to avoid a certain fate – we escaped.

I screw my eyes tighter together, trying to picture Opie's face and the woods outside Martindale – my woods – but everything's a grey haze, like a dream you can't quite remember.

The air feels uncomfortable as the thin moisture clings to my throat, making me want to cough. I force myself to swallow, listening to the rain tenderly caress the outside of the building. If I had been thinking straight, I would have made sure that some bowls or cups were left outside to capture the water but I am too tired to do anything about it now. My shoulders and arms ache from the way the Kingsmen shunted me around and my legs are tired after our escape from Windsor. My thigh begins to cramp painfully and I shake my foot in an unsuccessful effort to clear it. Instead, the pain grows until I find myself flailing involuntarily.

'Are you all right?'

Imrin's whisper is both reassuring and startling. His voice has that soothing feel, as if he is telling me a story, but I can also hear the edge of concern. The very fact I am waking up to him is a reminder of everything we have been through in the past few months.

'It's just cramp,' I murmur, trying not to unnecessarily wake any of the other escapees. There are twelve of us in total and we are all tired, cold and hungry.

Imrin places a hand on my face, his gentle fingers tracing from my cheek to my chin. A tendril of moonlight snakes through a gap in the roof of our makeshift shelter, illuminating his dark skin and darker hair. 'What do you want to do?' he whispers.

It could have been any of us asking that. Between Imrin and myself, we managed to mastermind the escape but hadn't planned what to do afterwards. I have felt the others looking at me, asking that same question. We may have been imprisoned but at least there was food, water and shelter. We are all teenagers but now they look to me, expecting answers.

I do not reply, instead continuing to rotate my ankle and wiggle my toes until the pain has gone. My eyes feel raw and sleepy but I know I'll not be able to rest for any longer, so haul myself into a sitting position, peering at the cluster of bodies clinging to each other for warmth under the threadbare blankets we stole away with us.

Imrin sits up and stifles a yawn, before offering me his blanket: 'Are you cold?'

I shake my head, looking instinctively towards my thinkwatch with its orange face and lightning bolt imprint. We have grown up using them for everything from knowing daily schedules to communicating with each other. And, of course, telling the time.

Everyone takes the Reckoning when they are sixteen, a test that determines our place in society. An Elite means just that. If you become one, the face of your thinkwatch turns black with the faint symbol of a crown to show that you belong to the top section of society. If you are a Member, the front becomes orange with a lightning bolt, to symbolise industry and productivity. Inters have blue watch faces marked with a sword, while those in the lowest band of society – the Trogs – have yellow watches inscribed with a small sickle.

The last occasion on which I managed to send a message on my thinkwatch was the eve of our escape. Using codes stolen from the Minister Prime, I bypassed the security devices around Windsor Castle that blocked us from contacting the outside world and messaged the families of the Offerings, telling them to get to safety. None of us know if it got through.

I thought that our thinkwatches would begin to function normally outside the castle walls, but instead they have all been disabled remotely. I wonder if that is partly where the disorientation comes from. When you spend a lifetime relying on something and it suddenly stops working, there is bound to be a sense of confusion. Aside from being unable to communicate, mine is the only one that still functions. The countless times I took it apart, replaced bits and tinkered seem to have paid off.

Luckily, it still has the one thing that might offer us a way out.

I flash through the screens as Imrin's yawning becomes infectious and I find myself trying to stop my mouth from opening. He is grinning as my eyes water and I return his smile before looking back to the watch. Before we escaped, I copied maps from the Home Affairs Minister's thinkpad onto my watch. The screen is a lot smaller, but through trial and error I have just about figured out where we are. After our escape, we crossed the remains of a wide, broken road and settled in a partially collapsed building on the edge of a small town called Beaconsfield. On our first night we heard Kingsmen trooping through, shouting and demanding anyone in hiding to show themselves. None of us dared move, even during the day, but tonight it has been still aside from the rain.

Or, perhaps, because of it.

Included with the map was intelligence about pockets of resistance. The locations are general and spread out and the King doesn't seem to know specifically where they are.

'How far away is that?' Imrin asks as I show him my watch, indicating the nearest area where rebels might be.

'At least twenty miles. Maybe more?'

'That's going to take us at least a day.'

'We should go at night,' I reply. 'We have to stay out of sight and we're not going to be able to make it in one go anyway – not with Hart the way he is.'

As I mention his name, I glance across to where Hart is sleeping. He comes from Martindale and was taken to the castle two years before the rest of us. He is easily the largest of our group and although he should be the strong, powerful one, he was beaten while covering for me. Blood comes up every time he coughs, which happens a lot, and I am almost certain his ribs are broken.

Imrin nods in agreement. 'We need to find something to

eat before we head out. There's no way we'll get all that way without food or drink.'

He's right but it is easier said than done. I edge across to the broken door he has wedged in the middle of a half-buckled wall. From the outside, it looks like a partly collapsed building, although inside we are sleeping in a deceptively large area. Carefully, I move the wood to one side and peer out into the still-dark early morning. The rain has slowed nearly to a stop but the biting breeze is vicious, making the hairs on my arms stand rigid.

'We could go into the village while it's still dark,' I say, checking my thinkwatch instinctively for the time. With the Kingsmen last night and the rain this evening, we haven't dared leave our hideaway.

Imrin gently rocks Pietra awake and tells her what we are doing. On the other side of her, I see Bryony – the girl Pietra reported for hoarding food at the castle and could have had killed. I haven't noticed them speaking to each other yet but the fact they can be so close together shows that things have changed. Our only light comes from the moon shining through cracks in the wall but I can see Pietra's wide eyes looking towards me, asking silently if it's a sensible plan. I try to shrug but my shoulder is still hurting and I end up wincing with pain.

I don't want to wake the others, so hold my hands out palms-up, indicating we don't have a choice. She nods, understanding, before Imrin eases the door out of the way. With barely a sound, we are outside and I pull the blanket tightly around my shoulders, climbing over the rubble of what was once somebody's house. Imrin reaches out to hold my hand but I act as if I haven't noticed, knowing I am going to have to get used to relying on myself.

As the wreck of concrete, brick and tile evens out onto the dusty street, I'm amazed by the sheer destruction in front of us. The Civil War ended seventeen years ago but many places were either abandoned then or in the years since. The King urged his subjects to congregate into larger communities, where it is easier to help each other – but also where we are simpler to keep track of.

The night is fighting to keep its hold on the morning. It's as still as it is cold, yet the crisp air feels heavenly in my lungs – a constant reminder that we were so close to never experiencing the outside world again. We stop and listen for nearby movements but there is nothing aside from the gentle rustle of wind.

There are a few smaller buildings around, but Imrin points towards a scorched sign on the ground that has a painting of a lion-like animal on it and the words 'The Red Griffin'.

'It's a pub,' he says, pointing towards the crumbling remains of a doorway.

We have to shift more rubble to enter and inside it is

shielded from the moonlight by a roof that is almost intact. Broken chair legs plus ripped patches of carpet and cushions are scattered around our feet.

'Have you ever been in a pub before?' Imrin whispers.

'We have an inn in Martindale but my mum never lets me go near it. There's this older guy called Mayall. He drinks a lot and sleeps on the streets when the Kingsmen aren't around. He's always in the alley at the back.'

We make our way to a large circular bar in the centre but that is where most of the damage has happened. The roof has caved in, allowing a small shaft of light to illuminate us but blocking any way through.

'There's probably a kitchen through there,' Imrin says, pointing towards the pile of bricks.

As he begins to pick aimlessly at the debris, I walk around to the far side, scuffing past patches of broken glass until I find a small hole in the wall where it looks like there was once a serving hatch. Wallpaper has peeled away from the surface around it, leaving patches of crumbling brick-work visible. One of the hatch's wooden doors is hanging limply from a single screw and it falls to the floor the moment I touch it. At first I think I cannot fit through the gap but it only takes a glimpse of my bony arms to remind me how thin I now am.

I call for Imrin and within moments he is next to me

again, asking if I am okay. I have to tell him to stop worrying, else he is going to drive me crazy.

He supports my feet as I heave myself through the hatch, using my hands to feel my way into the darkened space. There are lots of rough edges as I clamber to my feet and try to find my way around. It is very dark, with the only light coming from the hatch, but I can tell from the echo of my footsteps I am in a large room.

As I turn, I bump into a tall fridge. Stupidly, I open the door, before quickly slamming it as the smell of something rotten makes me heave. I have no idea when this place would have last had electricity but in the subsequent years whatever was left inside has putrefied, leaving nothing but the foul stench of time. I have to take a few deep breaths before I can clear my head.

Everything is covered with a thin layer of dust but the room is surprisingly well-ordered as I trace my way around the edges. I identify a larger cooker as well as two more fridges and a bank of sinks on the far wall. At first I ignore them, focusing on what might be in the cupboards, but then the memory of running water floods into my mind and I find myself turning the taps in hope more than anything.

At first there is a sputter, followed by a creak of pipes and suddenly there are splashes of water bouncing from the metal sink, sloshing over my clothes. I shiver uncontrollably but it feels wonderful as I let it flow, turning the taps as far as they can go and giggling in childish satisfaction.

It may only be a small victory, but it is still a victory.

I use my hands as a cup, allowing the liquid to soothe my raw throat and drinking so quickly that I end up coughing uncontrollably.

After turning off the taps, I hunt around the cupboards until I find one that is full of saucepans. The first is so heavy that my shoulder aches but I force myself not to drop it, filling it with water and carrying it across to the hatch for Imrin.

He drinks greedily and then soaks his hands before using the water to scrub his face.

'Did you find anything else?' he asks.

'Not yet. I didn't expect the water to be on.'

'Is it clean?'

'I'm not sure; it's too dark. I let it run for a while before drinking.'

When it comes to easing the thirst that has been consuming us, I don't think either of us is too bothered how clean the water is.

I tell Imrin I will find some more containers and then head back to the cupboards, pulling out as many as I think we can carry and filling them with water. We could bring everyone here and get them to help dig through the rubble – or fit a few of the girls through the hatch – but I don't think we should all be out together unless we have to be. I take the pots to Imrin, who heads off towards the exit as I return to check the rest of the cupboards.

In the darkness, I nearly cut myself on some knives in a drawer but carefully find the sharpest ones and tuck them into my belt. In the furthest corner of the room is another pile of debris, smaller than the rubble blocking the entrance. I can vaguely see the outline of a doorway and pull away the slabs of concrete I can lift until the space is clear. Imrin is by the hatch picking up more water but he doesn't call for me, so I trace the outline of the wood until I find the empty space where the door handle should be, reaching through with my fingertips and trying to pull the door towards me. Even though my fingers are small, it is stuck firmly in the frame.

I am not sure why but somehow I know there is something useful beyond. I think about calling for Imrin but it is still quiet on the other side of the room. Without a handle, it is hard to get any sort of grip on the door and it refuses to budge as I wrench it with the ends of my fingers. It is only when my foot slides across the tiled floor on a loose rock that I realise I haven't cleared all the rubbish away. I find myself yawning again, my throat sore.

After using my hands and feet to clear away a selection of small stones from underneath the door, it swings gently towards me with the creak of a rusty hinge. The air smells musty and dry but as I reach forward, my hands close around what are undoubtedly tins of food. There is not enough light to see what might be on the label, but my mind swims with thoughts of sweet, juicy fruits or rich, creamy soup. I take the two tins closest to me, excited to see what Imrin will say, and then cross back towards the hatch.

There is no sign of him but the rest of the water has been taken. In the few minutes I have been away, the light has changed from the dark blue of moonlight to the first traces of morning sun. After finding food and water, a little warmth would be very welcome.

As I lean through the hatch, I spot Imrin's silhouette pressed against the wall opposite. He is breathing heavily and I open my mouth to tease him about how unfit he is. It is only as the first squeak of a word escapes my lips that I realise it isn't Imrin at all.

2

The figure is too tall and wide to be Imrin. At the sound of my voice, he turns towards me and a man barks: 'Who's there?' The voice is gruff and stern: demanding, not asking.

Quickly but carefully, I slide the top half of my body back through the hatch until I am lying flat on my back underneath the hole in the wall. He repeats his question but I remain silent, fighting the sudden urge to cough. I place the tins on the ground and cover my mouth, forcing myself to stay quiet as I hear him moving around. Twice, he says 'hello?' and I know he hasn't seen me. Each heavy thump of his leather boots on the concrete sounds like a clap of thunder. There is a trickle of stones as he steps closer and I don't need to see him to know it is a Kingsman – the way he is moving and the harsh tone of his voice gives him away.

I wonder what has happened to Imrin. All of the pans filled with water have gone and I didn't hear any commotion, so he must have returned to our hideaway at least once. I try to calm myself but my worst fears are flowing: that I have led all these people to their deaths and I'm going to end up on my own.

I stare directly up and, although I cannot see the Kingsman, I sense him close to the hatch. The mist from his breath spirals through the air above me and for a fraction of a second I smell the faint odour of wine. It feels as if I am in a battle to see who can stay the most silent. If he had thought the noise came from a rat or other creature, he would have already walked away. I push myself even closer to the wall, hearing the sudden scrabble of movement before a pair of gloved hands reach through the hatch. There is no way he can fit through the space – but this is also my only way out.

The Kingsman's hands paw at the inside of the walls and instinctively I flinch, staying tight to the ground, thinking he is grabbing for me. I want to race away but he is fumbling in the dark, wondering what is on the other side. He grunts and there is another thump as the front section of a sleek black helmet pokes through the space.

Kingsmen act as the King's guards, both an army and a police force. They each have identical armour made from a black metal named borodron. It is thin and flexible but – as far as I know – impossible to penetrate. The material is rare and was used to allow access to certain areas around Windsor Castle. The man is so close that I can see the smooth curves of his helmet as a thin stream of sunlight arcs around the non-reflective surface. His head twists one way then the other as he struggles to pull himself further into the room. I stay completely still, the pain in my shoulder suddenly stabbing as my body betrays me. I can see the shape of his square rigid jaw as his nostrils flare, as if he is trying to smell me out.

I count the seconds until his jaw relaxes and then allow myself a small breath as his head disappears back through the hatch. His hands scratch at the underside of the hatch as he withdraws, sending a crumble of plaster on top of me just as I am breathing in. There is a fraction of a second where I feel myself panicking before I inhale the dust. I try to stifle it but it is too late as I sneeze involuntarily. Above, there is a moment of confusion followed by a flash of movement as the Kingsman lunges back through the hatch.

This time he has no doubt where I am, launching himself as far through as he can, his arms stretching towards the ground. Despite the agony in my arm, I am too quick for him. I roll away as his hands brush the tiles, and then I pull the kitchen knife from my pocket, lunging upwards and plunging it into a gap between his armour and helmet, deep into the side of his neck.

In the instant his mouth curves into the word 'you?', I realise he is the first person I have ever killed. As we escaped the castle, I led the people chasing us away from the main group. I have never asked what they went through to get out but the chances are someone in the group had to become a killer.

The Kingsman's body goes limp, hanging through the hatch, a trickle of blood oozing from his wound onto the ground. My hand is shaking in shock but my head is telling me to concentrate on whether there is anyone else nearby.

I pull the knife from his neck, wiping the worst of the blood on the wall, before placing my hands on top of the guard's head, pushing as hard as I can until he slides awkwardly through to the other side. I try to ignore the trail of crimson, throwing myself through the hatch and edging around to the front of the pub. *Don't look at him*, I tell myself. *Don't look*.

There is no sign of Imrin but the hole in the rubble we created to enter the pub is now larger. I creep towards the gap and peer outside, my heart thundering.

I've killed a man. Maybe he had a wife? Children? A daughter who'll never see her daddy again?

Stop.

In the time I have been inside, mist has settled across the village, dousing the patchwork of destruction in a crisp frost that signals winter is on the way. My hope that the sun would bring warmth is quickly forgotten as a few drifting rays of sunlight sparkle through the fog, making me feel colder. Pulling my blanket tighter around my shoulders, I notice flecks of the Kingsman's blood along the lining and shudder, remembering the way the blade felt slicing into his skin.

He would have had a daughter, like me. Another young girl without a father.

Outside, there is no movement and the only sound is the faint call of a bird somewhere in the distance. I brace myself to start running, knowing I could be back at the hideout in a couple of minutes but then rock backwards on my feet, wondering if perhaps I could end up leading enemies to everyone else.

As I try to decide what to do, footsteps crunch across broken bricks. I duck out of sight, peeping through the rubble as Imrin saunters across the bank of debris on the far side of the street. There is a blanket tied around his waist and his hands are tucked into the folds like they are pockets. He is mumbling something to himself, grinning as if he doesn't have a care.

When he enters the pub, he jumps in surprise as I grab his arm and pull him into a corner.

I try but fail to keep my voice calm. 'Did you see anyone out there?'

Imrin seems confused. 'No, it's just us.' We hurry around to the hatch where the Kingsman is lying in a pool of his own blood. I don't want to look but force myself – there is blood everywhere, ruby spatters and oozing pools creeping across the floor.

I did this.

Imrin gasps in shock: 'Where did he come from?'

'I don't know, I thought he was you at first.'

He stumbles over a succession of words before finally saying something that makes sense: 'What are we going to do?'

I know this is my life now, making decisions for everyone. I want to tell him about the guilt I feel at killing. Was the Kingsman forced into this job, or did he do it willingly? Did he hunt and hurt people because he wanted to, or because the King would do something horrible to his family if he didn't? Did he have a daughter?

I hold my quivering hand behind my back, blinking away the dark thoughts and trying to act as the leader Imrin needs me to be. I speak with as much authority as I can muster: 'There could be other Kingsmen nearby. We can't stay around here any longer in case anyone comes looking for him.'

I slide the thinkwatch from the Kingsman's wrist. The thinkwatches of adults who have not taken the Reckoning stay a dull white-grey colour. I throw it to the floor and stamp on it as Imrin looks on, mouth open. 'We don't know if theirs contain trackers,' I add. 'There are tins of food inside the kitchen that will keep us going for a while. Let's get everyone here quickly – we can stock up on food and drink and then we've got to go.'

Imrin is rooted to the spot, staring at the body. He has seen death before, so it is not a fascination with that. I think he is shocked at how close the guard came to me, which is altogether more worrying. I need him to think of himself, of the group, not just me.

'Let's go,' I say, clapping my hands and shunting him back to the present.

We hurry across the rubble until we reach the hideaway. Inside, everyone is awake and Hart is sipping water from one of the saucepans. His lips are crusty and sore but he smiles in gratitude, as if I have somehow rescued everyone instead of leading them into greater danger. Jela and Pietra are sharing another pan of water, while Faith is fully dressed and ready for action. It looks as if she has cut her tousled blonde hair even shorter, standing with the aura of someone who will do anything it takes to keep our group safe. Out of us all, she is the person who amazes me the most. In our society, she is a Trog, the lowest of the low, and yet she has fought for those who would have spent their lives exploiting her. Jela, Pietra, Imrin and Hart are Elites – the highest level in our society – while I am a Member, the next category down, indicated by the orange of my thinkwatch. Most people end up as Inters, while a few are Trogs. I am not tall but Faith is shorter than me, feisty and desperate to make an impact. Out of everyone, even Imrin, I trust her the most.

The water and full night's sleep seems to have cleared everyone's exhaustion but Faith knows something is wrong.

'We have to go,' I say, as everyone turns to face me. 'There's at least one Kingsman out there. I've dealt with him but there could be others. We found tins of food and there are a few houses we can raid clothes from. We've got to move quickly and then get out.'

I already knew Imrin, Faith, Jela, Pietra, Bryony and Hart before we escaped but there are five other Offerings with us who I don't really know. One of the boys, Frank, asks where we are going.

'We have to make a decision,' I reply. 'We know roughly where the resistance movement is. We can either try to find them, stay here and hope for the best – or we can all go our separate ways. We have to decide now because there is a dead Kingsman out there and sooner or later he'll be noticed.'

I am forcing my hand not to shake at the memory of the blood and notice Jela looking at me knowingly. The reaction of the others is mixed. Faith is already by my side as Hart slowly pulls himself to his feet. Frank looks as if he wants to ask more questions but everyone else has flocked towards me and he is left with no choice. They have made their collective decision to follow me in the same way that I have allowed myself to become their leader. I'm not convinced it is any of our preferred choices.

Being outside during the daytime is what I wanted to avoid but we have to move in case more Kingsmen are on their way. If anyone is watching, it will be better if we're not a single target, so we separate. I tell Faith about the tins of food in the kitchen, knowing she will have the stomach to ignore the Kingsman's body, and send her to the pub along with Hart and the other boys.

The streets are as empty as they were before but they feel more dangerous as the cool autumn sun begins to burn through the mist. I lead Jela, Pietra and two other girls to a row of houses on the far side of the pub. We ignore the properties that are damaged the most and target the ones where the roofs have not fallen through.

The first home is a mess of shredded furniture, curtains and carpets: a family's life destroyed by war, famine or both. After wrenching some wood away from an inner door, I tell Pietra and the others to try their luck upstairs as Jela and I move to the next place.

The rejuvenating effect of the water is wearing off as I drag my weary limbs over the fence and kick a pile of bricks away from the door.

'Did you sleep?' Jela asks, her voice soft and concerned.

'A little.'

'You look so tired.'

I shunt a piece of wood to the side and slide into the house, reaching for Jela and pulling her through with me. Despite our escape and lack of nourishment, she is somehow as naturally pretty as she always was. Her long blonde hair is tied in a loose ponytail, framing her high cheekbones and smooth skin. Her brown eyes shine with a hope I'm not sure she should have. I am almost envious until I remember the way she was taken by the King before being returned to us as the shell of the person she was. Somehow, even with everything that has happened, she has come out the other side.

'We're looking for clothes, bags and blankets,' I say firmly, being the leader. 'Anything that is light and easy to move.'

Jela nods as we skim through the house, climbing across shattered frames that hold photographs of other people's memories, battered furniture and remnants of technology long since forgotten. We help each other to climb the stairs, hopping across splinters in the wood and balancing precariously in the areas where the handrail has collapsed. The bedrooms are surprisingly intact and the layer of dust is the only thing indicating everything is not as it should be. First, I check a wardrobe, finding a pair of rucksacks at the bottom, plus rows of woollen jumpers and trousers hanging tidily above.

Jela is looking over my shoulder and reaches for one of the sweaters. 'What do you think happened to the owners?'

'My mum told me there were evacuations during the war where everyone had a few minutes to grab anything they could before having to leave.'

Jela puts on a green jumper that looks good with her eyes. I hand her a different one. 'This is darker,' I say, and then pass her two others. 'Put those on underneath. It's going to be cold.'

She nods acceptingly, taking the first sweater off. 'How long do you think we're going to be on our own?'

'I'm hoping we can find one of the resistance groups.'

'What then?'

I pull out a similar selection of clothes for myself, taking the smallest pair of jeans and four tops which I layer over each other. 'I don't know. If things went to plan, everyone should have seen on screen exactly what the King is like. They will have watched him forcing Imrin and me to fight, taunting us with food and generally abusing the people everyone thinks had gone off to serve the country. Anything could be happening out there.'

Jela opens a second wardrobe and pulls out a pair of heavy walking shoes that are far too big for either of us. 'Did the Kingsman say anything?'

I'm surprised by my own coldness: 'I didn't give him the chance.' Do I mean it? I'm not sure.

As we continue hunting through the clothes, stuffing the rucksacks full of anything that could be useful, there is an uncomfortable silence until Jela breaks it: 'Is this what it's going to be like?' The gentle way she speaks reminds me of the girl I was, not the woman I am becoming.

I stop for a moment, taking a breath. 'I hope not.'

Jela is fascinated by the contents of the second bedroom, where there is a selection of soft toys in the shape of various animals. Inside the wardrobes are children's clothes far too small to be of use but she isn't focused on them. Instead, she sits on the bed and begins to sort through the dust-covered creatures. At first I want to take charge and tell her we don't have time but there is a part of me that wants to forget our problems and enjoy the simplicity of a different age.

'That's a giraffe,' Jela says, handing me something with brown spots that has a long neck. I turn it over in my hands, before noticing something else at the bottom of the pile.

Jela smiles as I pick it up. 'What's that?'

'It's a tortoise. There was one in the King's zoo at the castle. Imrin told me a story about one. He wanted me to take things slowly and not rush in but I couldn't stop thinking of how the King had taken you. The fact it could happen to anyone made me want to get everyone out as quickly as I could.'

Jela nods but there is a telltale swallow and I wish I'd never mentioned what happened to her. 'What's happening with you and Imrin?' she asks. 'Are you . . . ?' I try to stop myself showing surprise at her question but it is too late as she adds: 'Sorry, you don't have to answer . . .'

I stumble over my words, embarrassed at how uncomfortable I feel. The truth is that she probably deserves to know who I am. She and the others have entrusted their lives to me, after all.

'It's complicated,' I reply.

'Is that because of your *friend* back home?'

I have told Jela all sorts of things about life in Martindale but have always been careful not to be specific about people. I suppose it didn't take too much to put two and two together.

'He's called Opie . . . Opie Cotton,' I stammer. 'We grew up together but then there was the Reckoning and the Offering.'

Opie and Imrin are opposites in so many ways; their skin and hair colours are different, Imrin thinks first, Opie acts. But they both look at me with the same desire to take care of me. Opie and Imrin: I am the only person who knows the full extent of the mess I have got myself into.

'You won't tell Imrin, will you?' I add.

Jela pushes the giraffe into the top of her bulging rucksack, smiling. 'Of course not.'

I run my fingers across the softness of the tortoise, rubbing away the dust. 'I didn't plan it like this. I didn't think I'd ever get out of the castle and then, with Imrin, we started planning together and everything happened from there. Now we're all outside, I don't know . . .'

Jela takes the tortoise and puts it into my rucksack. 'I knew you wouldn't take it otherwise.' I stand but she stops me, placing a hand on my arm. 'I don't think I ever said "thank you". After everything with the King, no one wanted to talk to me but you not only did that, you got me out too.'

Before I can reply, she is on her feet, heading for the door. It is a good job because I had no idea how to respond.

As Jela leads us down the stairs, I spot a dark red hat buried under a collapsed banister and crouch to pick it up. The dead Kingsman's final word was 'you?' It doesn't take a lot to guess how he recognised me. I scrape my hair with its distinctive silver streak backwards, pulling the hat down tightly and checking with Jela that it is out of sight. The hat is made of wool, with flaps that cover my ears, and I tie it under my chin before we head out into the cool morning, our bags full of supplies for the journey ahead.

3

Between us, we check a few more houses before returning to the pub, where Faith and Bryony have been organising all the boys, including Imrin. I am barely through the gap in the wall when she hisses at someone to push a piece of board into place across the opening. The tins of food have been neatly divided into different stacks and Faith points to one underneath a boarded-up window.

'Those are all fruit,' she says, before pointing to other spots around the room. 'We've got meat there, beans and vegetables there and everything else on the far side. It's all out of date but it's better than nothing. We can open them with knives. I also found a few plastic containers at the back of the cupboard and we've filled them with water.'

I tell her she's done a great job as the rest of us begin to unpack clothes from the bags. In only a few minutes, we are all wearing clothes more suited for the weather. Hart is a completely different person in clothes not spattered with blood. Faith is transformed – entirely in black, looking ominously like a smaller version of the Kingsman who lies dead around the corner.

After one final glance towards the man I killed, one more gulp in which I tell myself I had no choice, we leave the pub together and head towards the woods at the edge of town. Once we are beyond the initial line of trees, I stop to check my thinkwatch. The orange face swirls into a map but the screen is so small that it is not easy to understand the lines and shapes. The position of the sun reveals the east, from which I can figure out the broad direction we should be taking.

As everyone passes around a container of water, I take a deep breath and talk loudly enough for them to hear. 'I don't want any of you to think I'm forcing you into something. If you want to, you can take food, water and the clothes you have and head off with no problems.'

No one moves.

I nod largely in relief and then continue: 'We are heading roughly north west. The map I have shows rivers and the old roads, so we should have some idea of where we are. We've got around twenty miles to go but we can't be seen. I'm going to scout ahead with the rest of you hanging back. I need someone to . . .'

Before I can finish, Faith cuts me off. 'I'll do it.'

Her eyes are fixed on me, utterly serious.

'. . . I need someone quick to come with me who can run back to the rest of you if necessary. We'll try to stay out of sight in woods and along hedges.' I turn back to Faith. 'Are you still happy to do that?'

'Yes.'

I turn back to the others. 'Everyone else has to stay together. Faith and myself will make sure we regularly check behind, so if you have any problems, find shelter and stop. Don't call out and don't do anything stupid.'

'How do you know the rebels will want anything to do with us?' Pietra's question is so quiet, it is almost lost on the breeze. 'I don't want to cause trouble,' she adds nervously.

'It's fine,' I say. She isn't asking anything that I haven't asked myself. 'Honestly, I don't know – but I don't have any better ideas. The only other thing we can do is continue to hide and hope we eventually find a safe place.'

It is not the answer everyone wanted but it is truthful.

When there are no other questions, we pack the water away and Faith and I begin to head through the woods. The only sound is our feet cracking the frost-covered twigs and the faint rustle of animals somewhere in the undergrowth. In Martindale, Opie and I taught each other how to catch the squirrels and other creatures that lived in the woods outside the village. It is where I felt most at home but this is more of a densely packed forest. There are a few berries clinging to the bushes and trees which are alien to me.

'You should probably take this,' I say, pulling out the kitchen knife from my pocket and handing it to Faith.

She glances sideways at me and it is only then I realise how quickly her legs are moving to keep up. She grins and reaches into a pouch that is clipped to her belt and pulls out a knife of her own that is sharper and longer than the one with which I killed the Kingsman.

'I got this from the kitchen,' she says. 'There's another in my sock, too.'

It makes sense, but it is hard to forget the sweet girl who once told me how she had been ill and that was why she had been categorised as a Trog. Somehow I have helped to turn her into the soldier she now is.

* * *

As the day wears on, the faint wisps of fog continue to hug the ground as the sun does nothing other than threaten to break through. We avoid any areas that look as if they could be filled with civilisation, mostly staying in fields.

The rest of the group remains a steady few hundred metres behind us, with Faith and I keeping a careful watch. Each hour, we stop for a brief respite that allows me to check the direction in which we are heading and gives the rest a chance to have something to drink. I had been worried about how Hart might fare but he seems to be holding up and we are moving quicker than I imagined. I am fairly certain we are on the right course but don't know for sure. Even though Faith is from the Southern Realm, she says her home is much further north than where we are right now – closer to Middle England where the four Realms of the Kingdom intersect.

As the sun begins to set, we reach a patch of woodland. We should now be in the general area where one of the rebel groups is based but there is no specific location on the map.

Faith and I wait for the others to catch up. When they do, Hart is holding a hand across his chest, trying not to cough. It is good to see there are no new blood marks on his clothes but he needs medical help soon.

We huddle together surrounded by a copse of bushes but even with our warmer clothes, the evening air is biting as the light begins to disappear. I am wedged between Hart and Jela as we pass a container of water around and I point to the far side of the woods.

'The map says the rebels are in that direction. I have no idea what we're looking for but if they were out in the open, the Kingsmen would have gone after them. I don't know if that means the rebels have moved on, or if they're hiding.'

A burst of wind skims through the trees, the chill hurting my lungs as I pause for breath. 'We're all tired so we can either use our blankets to camp here for the night and try to stay warm, or we can carry on through to the other side of the woods. There might be somewhere with a roof, or we could stumble across the people we're looking for.'

The only consensus is that people do not want to go too far. Given the trek we have already made, plus the temperature, I don't blame them. According to the map, there is nothing here except for the woods, a river which we have followed and a village. That seems to be our best bet, so we wrap ourselves in blankets and edge through the trees together.

Although I am used to the woods at home, the nervousness of the others adds to my unease. The clouds are still low, the dipping sun and high moon offering little light through the trees. Every squeak and crackle in the undergrowth sets a ripple of apprehension running through the group as I realise hardly anyone is used to the outdoors in the way I am.

Imrin reaches out to hold my hand and I let him, knowing it is for his benefit more than mine. Faith creeps ahead stealthily until we are within sight of the edge of the trees.

'Stay here,' I whisper to Imrin, releasing his hand. 'Keep everyone as warm as you can. We'll be right back.' I see his eyebrows rise in confusion until Faith appears by my side. 'Her clothes are darker,' I say, knowing that isn't the true reason why I want her to be with me. The alternative is to tell him that I need someone who can look after themselves as well as Faith can. Not only that, I need a respite from the way he fusses over me.

His eyes flicker sideways and, for a moment, I think he is going to insist upon coming. Instead he nods. 'Once everyone is settled, I'll scout around the area in case there's shelter.'

'Good idea,' I say, meaning it.

As he turns, Faith and I move past the tree line, to where a ridge overlooks the village. The mist has lifted slightly, allowing the moonlight to offer a small amount of illumination.

'What can you see?' I ask as we stand together. It is too gloomy for me to be sure of my own thoughts.

'That looks like a church,' Faith says, pointing towards some debris on the far side of a field. I squint through the murk and it is hard to tell if she is right. At the edge of the village closest to us is what could be a large arched window frame but the only indication of a spire is a pointed piece of rubble in the distance.

She leans further forward. 'Above the window, it looks like a cross. Do you reckon there's anyone in there?'

It is more of an indentation with different coloured bricks but she is right.

'I don't know, probably not,' I reply. 'I can't see any areas that haven't been flattened. If it is a church, surely that would have been the first place the Kingsmen checked if they came through here?'

Faith hums an agreement as we carefully slide down the bank, skimming along the edge of a hedge until we are near to the building. I don't need to say anything as Faith nods and points to the near side of the rubble as I head to the other. It is scary how we seem to be on the same wavelength.

I watch her crouch as she disappears into the darkness while I stare up at the cross. Any glass that was once in the window has gone but the cross embedded in the wall above it is unmistakeable. Faith was right.

Quickly and quietly, I clamber over the piles of stone. At the peak, I stop to peer into the distance where there is nothing but rows of flattened houses. If anyone is hiding, they are doing a very good job of it.

At the far end, I see that the demolished pointed section is definitely a spire. It is hard to tell exactly what happened, but it seems to have collapsed in on itself, leaving the tall pyramid-shaped part jutting out from the large remains of what would have once been the rest of the tower. I stare up at a second cross on top of the roof and realise how little I know about the war. Everything we have been taught has either come from our parents, who would have only seen it from a personal point of view, or from information fed to us by the King. I find it hard to imagine what could have caused this type of destruction and why a village of this size would be targeted. Could an army have done this, or would it have been a bomb either dropped from above or triggered under the village?

I am brought back to the present as Faith hisses my name, the sound amplified by the silence around us. I move around the spire until I see her standing at the edge of some rusted gates. 'Did you find anything?' I call.

'Just this graveyard. I climbed as high as I could but there are fields and the woods in one direction and bricks in the other.'

The cemetery has long since been abandoned to weeds, with grass that is almost as tall as us poking through the metal fence.

'We could come back during the day?' Faith says. 'Perhaps one or two of us at a time?'

I shake my head. 'We'd be in the open too much. There's no cover because everything is so flat.'

'We'd be able to see from a distance if there were Kingsmen or anyone around.'

'True, but they'd be able to see us too. Let's stay together and try a few streets over.'

Faith doesn't query me, following as I manoeuvre into a side street that is relatively clear of clutter. We keep carefully to the shadows, moving in single file. If anything, the buildings are in a worse state the further we venture. At the other side of the village is a sign thanking people for driving carefully but there are no other indications of civilisation. Apart from the semi-collapsed church, the rest of the area has been levelled.

'You were right,' I say. 'We'll have to come back tomorrow in case we've missed something. Perhaps we could come with Imrin or Pietra for a fresh set of eyes?'

We turn to head back to the woods, my legs ready to give way.

I stifle a yawn as Faith asks the question I suspect she has wanted the answer to all day. 'What was it like, killing the Kingsman?'

'I didn't have time to think about it,' I reply, trying not to remember the bloodstains on the bottom of my blanket. 'He was reaching for me and the knife was in my hand and then his neck before I knew it.'

Faith's voice sounds higher, cracking slightly as she replies. 'Do you feel guilty?'

'It was him or me . . . I've been telling myself I didn't have a choice.'

For a few moments she doesn't respond but then she replies through choked tears. 'There was this man at the castle when we were escaping. I don't even think he was a guard. Imrin told us you were leading the Kingsmen in the opposite direction but we couldn't get through the door at the medical bay quickly enough and this guy came out of nowhere. I'd grabbed a sword from the ground as we were running and could barely lift it. He took me by surprise and the next thing I know, he was on the floor with blood everywhere.'

I reach out and take her freezing hand. 'It's not us that made this happen. We'd be back in our towns and villages with our parents, brothers and sisters if we hadn't been brought here to serve the King. We're doing what we must to stay alive.'

For the first time, I realise that Faith's bravado is fear. The only way she can deal with the terror inside her is by pretending she's the strongest of us all. 'It would be nice to see my mum and dad again one day,' she says. 'I don't have any brothers or sisters and never had many friends. It was just the three of us. After I was chosen, I thought they'd at least get extra food with me gone.'

As she talks about her family, it makes me think of my mum in Martindale and my brother, Colt. The cobbled streets seem farther away than ever. Hopefully they got my warning message before we escaped and are hiding somewhere in safety. I always knew that by escaping there was a chance they could be punished. This is the guilt I have to carry: that I might have chosen my own safety over theirs.

We loop around the front of the church and help each other over the stile before heading along the line of hedges. The silence somehow seems worse now I know Faith is faking things as much as I am. Neither of us is as strong or as confident as we pretend, so what does that say for the others?

The moon bursts through the clearing clouds as we cross the fields, suddenly illuminating our muddy surroundings and giving us an uninterrupted view towards the trees. It feels as if the temperature has dropped by a degree or two as I pull my hat tighter over my ears. On the far side of the field is a second stile. Faith begins climbing first but slips, her muddy boots sliding from the wood as I step forward to support her. Her entire weight crunches onto my good shoulder and I try not to wince in pain but she is already apologising.

Before I can tell her she has nothing to say sorry for, our eyes lock in a moment of terror as a male voice screams in agony from the trees high above.

4

The aches and pains from a day of walking evaporate as I hurl myself over the stile and barrel up the bank. I can hear secondary follow-up whimpers echoing around the outer forest but it is hard to tell who the noises are coming from. Getting down was easy but the slope is more mud than grass and for every half-a-dozen steps I take forward, I slide at least half that amount down again. Faith has no such worries, clambering on all fours up the incline as if she has been doing it all of her life. When she reaches the top, she lies flat on her belly and stretches down until I am close enough for her to haul upwards. I have no idea how some-one so small can be so strong but her grip is solid and she isn't even out of breath as I finally fall over the top of the verge, collapsing face-first in the mud.

My feet slide along the first few steps until we cross the threshold of the trees where a blanket of leaves provides solid footing. Still the cries bounce around the woods, soft moans of pain that I can feel as much as hear. There is a smattering of rucksacks and clothes where we left everyone but they've all gone. Panic is building in my stomach – they are all my responsibility.

We follow the moans deeper into the woods, looking for a trail of blood or anything else that might give us a clue about what has happened.

As we reach an area where the trees are thicker, the sounds intensify. I round the corner of tightly packed bracken into a small clearing and realise too late that if there is some sort of trap, I have dashed straight into it. The plants are dense and I take a few moments to adjust to the lack of light. A female voice says my name, setting off a succession of people who sound relieved that I am there. Shapes gradually drift into focus, with Imrin crouched on the ground looking towards me, asking what he should do. I struggle to catch my breath as I approach, turning to take in the scene.

There is a semi-circle of people standing around, all looking at me. Frank is next to Imrin flat on his back, his leg a mangle of blood, material and flesh stuck in the vicious jaws of a spring-loaded animal trap.

The first time I ever saw one was in the woods outside Martindale with Opie. We had spent months trying to create our own snares and traps from pieces of rope and various wooden crates that we chopped up and rigged to capture squirrels inside. Anything we caught would be a supplement to our meagre rations but we weren't very good. Weeks passed with us catching nothing until Opie clumsily pounded through the trees one day in the way he always does. Underneath his arm was a thick metal semi-circle, which he said he'd discovered at the back of one of his father's friend's houses.

It wasn't huge but when he dropped it on the floor it left an indent in the grass, before he showed me how it worked. There was a catch on the side that he pressed down and then we wrenched the thick triangular teeth apart together until it was lying flat. He wanted to leave it out overnight to try to catch something we could eat, but I couldn't let him. I eventually taught myself how to tie a knot properly, allowing us to set better traps, but there is a big difference between that and the cruel sharpened claws which have sliced through Frank's leg.

'I gave him something to bite on,' Imrin says as I notice that Frank has a thick twig in between his teeth.

'Why?'

Imrin's voice wavers in panic. 'We were looking for somewhere to sleep. It was sheltered here but it's so dark. I saw the trap just before he stepped in it. He was screaming and I didn't know what else to do. I couldn't get the trap open.'

I take another quick glance around the semi-circle and realise that no one has a clue. Partly because of where and how I grew up, the outdoors almost comes naturally to me but none of the others seems to have those instincts. Most people grow up in cities.

With as much authority as I can manage, I tell everyone except for Imrin and Faith to stand back. Crouching on the ground, I can see Frank's jaw straining against the wood, the muffled cries of pain cutting like a knife through me.

I brought us here.

I run my fingers along the rusted edges of the trap until I find the concealed button underneath and then count to three before telling Imrin and Faith to pull as hard as they can. Slowly they yank the jaws apart before I tug Frank's leg out and place it carefully on the floor. I can't help but brush my fingers across his flesh, making him cry out again. It feels like the remnants of a boiled egg: wet and squishy, unnaturally soft.

I lean in to take a closer look but don't even know where to start. It is hard to distinguish what is leg and what is material, with the wound marked by mud and grass. There is a murmur of voices behind me but I cannot hear anything over Frank's moans.

As I am about to turn to the others to see if anyone has any ideas, a steady orange haze of light appears around us. Everyone looks towards me as if I can offer some sort of explanation but I can only watch as a figure approaches from behind everyone. One by one they turn to stare as the silhouette gradually becomes the shape of a man. He isn't particularly tall, but his shoulders are broad and his hands are huge. He carries himself with an air of authority and danger.

At first I think he is a Kingsman but, as he nears, I can see he is wearing heavy black boots and a pair of jeans. Instead of a helmet, his shoulder-length hair is loose and blowing behind him in the breeze. As everyone else notices him, they seem entranced, stepping to one side, allowing him to continue moving as he ignores them, heading towards me.

He is so close, I can see scuffs of mud on his knuckles as he glances towards Frank, and then looks directly at me. 'Who are you?' he asks, his voice deep and intimidating.

'Just travellers.'

The man nudges open his long coat, revealing a lengthy knife clipped to his belt. 'Who are you?' he repeats.

'Travellers. We were looking for somewhere to stay for the night when my friend accidentally stepped on the trap.'

The man peers towards Frank again before his eyes flicker back to me. He nods over my shoulder at the ring of fire. 'Every spot of light you see is one person who is armed. You have ten seconds.'

I feel everyone breathe in at the same time as I realise he isn't messing around.

'We're travellers,' I insist. 'We're moving north but got a little lost.'

The man scratches the stubble on his chin, narrowing his eyes as he tries to figure out if I am lying. 'What's your name?'

'Olive.'

It is my mother's name and the lie comes instantly. I still don't know if anything was broadcast from the castle on our final evening. Silver Blackthorn could be either a nobody or the most wanted person in the country.

'You know transporting people across Kingdom borders is forbidden?' He isn't asking a question, merely telling me what we all know.

'So is carrying a concealed weapon.'

I reply instinctively, matching his aggression with a small amount of my own. I did not expect to intimidate him but I did think I'd get more of a reaction than the nothingness he offers.

'Why are you here?'

'We're passing through. It looked as if there might be somewhere to shelter.'

'Where have you come from?'

'Beaconsfield.'

It is a risky lie but I cannot think of anywhere else in the South other than Windsor. He is unmoving.

'You don't sound like you're from the South.'

'My father wasn't from around here.'

The man nods slowly, although his eyes are narrow and untrusting. His eyes flicker towards the ground. 'Who's he?'

'That's Frank. He really needs some help.'

For a few seconds, nothing happens but then the man stretches out his arm and clicks his fingers before letting out a low whistle. Half of the lights around us are instantly extinguished and then there is the clump of footsteps until two more men join us in the clearing.

'What do you reckon?' the first man says to the other, motioning towards Frank.

'We'd have to move him quickly.'

'Will he live?'

'No idea. He might lose the leg.'

The way they speak is so casual that it is as if they haven't noticed Frank is a person in pain. The first man glances between me and Frank before making a decision.

'Okay, take him,' he says.

The other two put their heads under Frank's armpits and haul him to his feet. He shrieks in agony as the wood that was in his mouth drops to the floor. I start to step forward but realise they are trying to help him. One of them supports his damaged leg, the other taking the rest of his weight. Together they carry him out of the clearing.

'Where are you taking him?' I ask.

The man has his knife out of his belt and is twirling it between his fingers. 'Somewhere he'll be looked after.'

'Who are you?'

'You tell me and I'll tell you.'

He could be one of the rebels I am looking for, or part of a localised militia group. One of the girls in the dormitory at the castle told us that she had not seen a Kingsman until she was twelve years old. Instead, a group of local men kept peace in the area. If they had any problems, they could call Kingsmen in. Telling this man the truth is not a risk I can take, not with eleven other people's lives in my hands.

'We're travellers,' I repeat. It isn't even a lie.

The man whistles a second time and the rest of the flames disappear. More people emerge through the dense mix of bushes and trees. They edge closer until our group tightens, completely surrounded. The strangers are dressed in clothes suited for outdoors, each carrying a knife. The man nods towards Faith. 'Where have you all come from?'

Apart from the rustle of the wind, there is silence. I can tell from her face that she can't remember the answer I gave. In my head, I repeat the word 'Beaconsfield' over and over but the way Faith's eyes dart from side to side is enough to make my hand flash towards the knife on my own belt. Before I can touch the handle, the man's arm shoots out, grabbing my wrist, before he viciously twists me around. I screech involuntarily, pain ripping through my already damaged shoulder. In a flurry of movement, I look around to see everyone from our group being held by someone bigger and stronger. Faith's legs are flailing but she is being restrained by the biggest person I can see.

Before I can try to fight back, my head is wrenched backwards with a sharp tug of my hair. My ears are bitten by the sharpness of the breeze as my hat tumbles from my head. The knife is yanked from my belt and the jagged edge is pressed against my windpipe.

'Last chance,' he hisses in my ear. 'Who are you and what are you doing here?'

I have no option but to tell the truth but before I can speak, there is a collection of gasps as a man's voice sounds nearby. 'She's Silver Blackthorn.'

5

The grip on me is instantly released as I am pushed forward and peer up to see the man staring at me in shock. With my hat on the floor, my silver streak of hair is hanging across my face until I push it behind my ear. There is a murmur of recognition around the circle as the other strangers say my name.

'*You're* Silver Blackthorn?' the man says suspiciously, his bewilderment unmasked.

'Yes.'

'*The* Silver Blackthorn?'

'I suppose so, how many do you know?'

The man again glances towards my hair before he nods to the person closest to him. 'Blindfolds. Let's go – we'll take them to him.'

He grabs me again, this time slipping something around my eyes and fastening it tightly, before pulling my hair back and tugging the hat over my ears. There is nothing I can do.

'Get their bags,' he adds, and then we are marched away in the darkness. At regular intervals someone tells us to stop, before we are turned in a different direction and told to start again. Whichever route we are taking, it is not the one Faith and I took towards the village. I can feel the softness of the grass and mud under my feet long enough for us to have covered the full length of the woods. Under the bottom of the blindfold, I can see the faintest sliver of light but it is not enough to be able to get any sort of bearings. The only sounds I can hear are the murmurs of our captors, repeating my name in hushed, worried tones.

I am not sure what to make of the fact they know who I am. If it was a really bad thing, I would surely be dead already, but that could mean that Kingsmen are on their way. The only thing I can have any degree of certainty about is that at least some of the final banquet from the castle was broadcast.

Eventually the ground becomes solid, with the footsteps of a couple of dozen people reverberating around concrete streets. Under my blindfold I can see the grey of stone but there is nothing that tells me where we are. We are told to stop walking and I hear a clatter I can't identify before someone tells us to move slowly. Gradually we edge down what sounds like a set of stone steps.

'Are you going to seal it?' a voice asks behind me, before someone else queries where we should be taken. When the floor levels out again, I feel a hand on my arm guiding me quickly until I realise too late that I am being led away from the sound of the others.

I fight to yank my arm away but a hand grips me tighter, making me gasp and telling me to keep moving.

'Where am I going?' I ask.

I recognise the man's voice as the same one from the woods. 'Keep moving.'

'Where are my friends being taken?'

He doesn't reply but a gentle push in the bottom of my back is enough to keep me walking. I hear a door being opened and can tell we have entered a large room because the echo of our footsteps lasts for a fraction of a second longer.

Through the gap at the bottom of my blindfold, I can see a faint glow of orange light on a floor I think is wooden. The man who has been guiding me moves away, before there is a second male voice. 'I thought I told you to deal with it?'

'They were just kids and said they were travellers. One of them was caught in one of our traps, so we brought him here. We were going to send the others on their way after scaring them a bit.'

There is a sigh before the second man lowers his voice and hisses aggressively. 'So why did you bring them here?'

I feel a hand on my head as the hat is wrenched away.

My hair is uncomfortable as I shake my head, disorientated from the blindfold.

'Is that . . . ?'

'She says her name is Silver Blackthorn,' the voice from the woods says. 'There are twelve of them in total, so the numbers are about right.'

There are faint whispers but nothing I can hear clearly. Suddenly the blindfold is pulled away, leaving me blinking painfully into the light of the room. The dazzling green stars take a few moments to disappear as the shapes of two men slowly swim into focus. I can see the man from the woods more clearly in the light, his eyes a piercing brown in a face lined by zigzag scars around his ears. The other man is taller and less well-built, with blond hair and blue eyes. He is smiling.

'*You're* Silver Blackthorn?' he asks.

My legs sag uncontrollably at the knees as I struggle to remain standing. The dark-haired man scrapes a wooden chair along the floor, placing it next to me. I can't control my sigh of weary relief as I finally lean back and take in my surroundings. The room is square with a low stone roof and a thick wooden table pushed against the far wall. Lining each side are wooden chairs like the one I have been given. It smells of damp, like the back room of Opie's house where the ceiling leaks.

'Yes, I'm Silver,' I reply.

The blond man is trying to control his excitement but failing. 'So you actually escaped?'

'What gave me away?'

'I'm sorry about the blindfolds,' he says. 'It's a necessity – if people knew where we were, we wouldn't be around any longer.'

'Who are you?'

The two men exchange a look, before the blond one nods slightly. 'I'm Knave and this is Vez. We have our own community underground here.'

'Where are we?'

Knave points to the door behind me. 'Back there is the original crypt from a village church. Overground it's covered with rubble – you'd never know we were here. There was a large cellar and a few other basement rooms in which we now live.'

I start to speak but the words get stuck on my tongue as I realise the significance of what he said: 'Your name is Knave?'

'Yes.'

'You escaped too.'

Before we left the castle, Hart helped me access the Minister Prime's office. I stole the list of the names of every Offering that had been made to the King. Everyone was categorised by where they were now. Most were dead but one name was marked as 'AWOL'.

Knave looks at me, his head tilted in confusion. 'How do you know that?'

'I read your name on a list in the Minister Prime's office.'

His eyes narrow in suspicion before I tell him the story of how I managed to see the names and how we escaped. I miss nothing out, telling him about Hart, Imrin, Jela, Pietra, Faith and the parts they all played.

'You worked together?' he eventually says.

'It was the only way.'

Knave turns to Vez and touches him on the arm. 'Can you give us a few minutes? Check on the others and make sure the injured one is all right.'

Vez nods and strides past me, closing the door behind him.

'Where are my friends?' I ask.

'Vez thought it best if we talk to you directly, rather than have everyone else involved. He's right.'

'What about Frank? His leg is really bad.'

'We have a few medical experts and some meagre supplies. We'll do what we can.'

I nod, relief spreading. 'How did you get out?'

Knave takes a chair from the side of the room and sits opposite me. At first he just stares, eyes scanning me up and down. He begins slowly: 'It was on the supply train that comes once a week. I worked in the kitchens and figured out the schedule. Each week, I would sneak out when we were busy and go to the door that leads to the platform. One day it was left open slightly. I didn't know if there were going to be Kingsmen at the bottom of the steps but didn't really care. There were only three of us lads left by then – everyone else had been killed or traded. I ran and hid in a sack at the back of one of the compartments.'

I can't hide my surprise: 'That was our first plan but someone else got there first. He was caught and I've never seen him since.'

Knave apologises. 'I suppose they started checking when they realised how I got away. I waited for an hour and then jumped as soon as the train reached a patch of grass that looked soft enough to land on. I broke an arm falling but at least I was out.'

'How long ago was that?'

'Four years.'

He looks a lot older than twenty, lines already wrinkled around his eyes. 'Who are you people?' I ask.

It is hard to tell whether I should trust him – or whether he trusts me. We both have our secrets. He ignores my question and asks his own. 'Did you come here by chance?'

I'm not very good at trusting others and know I potentially have the fates of so many people in my hands. For a few moments neither of us says anything but he continues staring at me, his blue eyes hardening.

'When I found everyone's names, there was also a map,'

I say. 'It showed locations of rebel groups. I didn't know if it would be useful but downloaded it onto my thinkwatch. We didn't know where else to go after we got out so headed here.'

Knave's top lip twitches as he tries to figure out if I am telling the truth. 'Show me.'

My arm is aching but I raise my watch for him to see and flash through the screens until I find what he wants to see. His fingers are warm on my skin as he holds my wrist and zooms in and out.

'Why does your watch still work?'

'I don't know.'

It is a half-truth – I don't know exactly why but suspect it is because I have taken it apart so many times, replacing parts and experimenting with the technology.

He skims through the areas of the maps that show other rebel strongholds, muttering under his breath and then unclipping the watch and taking it from my wrist before I can react.

'Hey!'

'You can have it back in a minute.' He crosses to the table and picks up a thinkpad, pressing the two devices together and then returning my watch.

'The Kingsmen caught some of our men overground a year or so ago,' he says after sitting down again. He is staring at the pad, not at me. 'They killed them on the spot but we always assumed they would think there were more of us nearby. We have scouts out by the woods and Kingsmen come past every now and then. They have never found us. We've thought about moving a few times but have a lot of what we need here – and as long as we're sensible, we should be safe.'

'I didn't see anyone in the woods.'

Knave smiles. 'You wouldn't have but they saw you. You're lucky we found you and not the Kingsmen.'

'Where are you from?'

Knave stands and reaches out a hand. 'Come with me.'

Before I sat, my knees were hurting but now my thighs burn with exhaustion and flames dance along my lower back. Knave reaches out to support me, gently holding my upper arm and asking if I am all right.

'I'm fine,' I reply, shaking him off and forcing my body to obey.

Knave leads me into a corridor. 'I think this was an old study,' he says, closing the door behind us and moving ahead. Everything smells stale and damp and there are spots of water dripping from the arched stone overhead.

'After I jumped from the train, I was on my own,' he says. 'I come from the East and initially had the idea of returning home. I spent my first night in a hollow underneath the train tracks and realised it would be the first place Kingsmen would start searching. I created a sling from branches and vines and followed a river until I found the village above us.'

Knave is walking slowly, peering over his shoulder every few seconds to make sure I am still there. At an intersection, he leads me left. 'It was a small community at the time, perhaps a couple of hundred people, but there were farms on the outskirts that provided food and small industries such as bakeries that kept everyone well fed. I slept in someone's barn for the first night and then went into the centre of the village the next day. I didn't know it then but everyone knew everyone else, so I stood out instantly. This old guy ushered me into the back room of an inn and told me I was asking for trouble. I was ready to fight my way out but he laughed and told me not to be so silly.'

We reach a large wooden door and Knave stands next to it, turning to face me. 'No one ever asked any questions about who I was but within a day, someone had looked at my arm and someone else had given me a room to sleep in.'

'Did they know you were an escaped Offering?'

'I don't know how they would – they just weren't bothered. A few weeks later, the person I was living with took me to a meeting in the village hall late one night. I hadn't known it before but they said they were a resistance group, opposed to the King. They didn't know what was going on at the castle but had been unhappy since the end of the war. They could see through Victor and the broadcasts but they were completely disorganised. They had no weapons, no knowledge of any other rebel groups and didn't know what they wanted to do. I think they found comfort in small acts of defiance against the Kingdom and that was their way of rebelling.'

'What happened?'

Knave pushes the door open, leading me into a large room where there are beds, blankets, cushions, pillows and other comforts dotted around. We stand in the doorway as a dozen or so people turn to face us.

'This is where most of us sleep,' Knave says. 'There are just over thirty of us in total. This is the crypt but we managed to dig through one of the walls to make it bigger. It's more comfortable than you might think, plus we manage to stay warm, even in winter.'

I feel everyone's eyes on me and turn to leave. Knave follows, closing the door. 'When you are living like the village was, it is impossible not to be noticed,' he says, leading us back the way we came. 'We still took our rations, but whenever the Kingsmen would bring them around, they couldn't help but notice we were doing well anyway. One day, a lot of them came. There was no warning, no orders to get out; they came with swords, spears and fire. Some of us ran for it but others . . .'

He doesn't finish his sentence as we stop at the inter-section.

'Even the children?' I ask.

Knave nods. He licks his lips, gazing into the distance and takes a second to compose himself. 'Some of us hid in the woods for a few days until we were sure they'd gone and then came back. The way it is now – piles of rubble – is pretty much how it was then. They destroyed the church and everyone's houses, burned the crops and then left as if we had never been here. In the space of a day, they wiped the village off the map.'

I can barely begin to comprehend the brutality, although his story explains why places such as Beaconsfield are now abandoned, even though they probably survived the war.

I ask the question, even though I know the answer: 'Why?'

'It's all about control. If we are huddled together in the cities, they control the flow of food and the rations. Hungry, thirsty people only rebel if they believe they have anything to fight for.'

I think of Martindale and wonder if that's the fate that could one day befall my village. Perhaps it already has.

'There weren't many of us left afterwards but we banded together and salvaged most things that were worthwhile. Every now and then, other people will stumble across the area and we either ignore them and let them move on, or we bring them down here if we think we can trust them. We set up a radio communication system. Initially, it was for trying to listen into broadcasts that no one else is supposed to hear. Mainly for things such as schedules for the ration trains – nothing very interesting. Then one day, we came across a broadcast on a different frequency from a rebel group asking if there were others out there. We didn't know if it was a trap, or something the King's people could be intercepting, but we have some clever people here and found out where they were broadcasting from. I won't bore you but, in short, there are other rebel groups around the country. Slowly, we're becoming more organised as we salvage weapons and supplies from other abandoned towns and share information.'

'How do you know the King won't find you?'

Knave shrugs. 'We don't, but what choice do we have? We cover our tracks as best we can and we're careful with our broadcast codes. We all know we could be found at any point.'

'What are you planning?'

I realise instantly it is a question too far. If they have anything in mind the last thing they should do is share it with a stranger. Knave ignores me. 'Recently, our comms went down. Everything we do is triangulated through an area around Middle England but we haven't been able to raise them, so we can't talk to anyone else. It's happened before intermittently but never for this long. We've been cut off for almost a month and all we get are the standard screen signals everyone else does.'

'Is that how you know who I am?'

Knave's eyes narrow – he is worried. 'You mean you don't know?'

'Know what?'

He takes my hand, guiding me quickly along the tunnels into a room that reminds me of Kingsman Porter's office in Windsor Castle. It is packed with jumbled heaps of electrical items; broken thinkpads and tatty cables mixed with watches and pieces of metal that look almost new. On the wall ahead is a row of screens and he approaches the first one, playing with a dial underneath until it fizzes to life.

In the centre of the screen is my face, the location instantly recognisable. The image has been taken from the security camera outside Porter's office at Windsor Castle. My face is staring directly into the camera, my silver streak of hair brushed to the side. Above my image is one word in large capital letters: 'WANTED'. Underneath are three more that send chills through me: 'DEAD OR ALIVE'.

6

My response is pathetic: 'I'm wanted?'

'That's been on a constant loop in between any other programming for the past three days,' Knave says, nodding at the screen. 'You were lucky it was us who found you.'

'Why?'

'The other evening, our screens turned themselves on. It was hard to see what was happening because the footage was from security cameras. It has never happened before but we couldn't hear anything anyway. There was a flash of people fighting but it was really hard to make out and then the last thing we saw was the King choking on something before the screen turned itself off.'

I tell him I had set those cameras to broadcast and then about my imprisonment and the way I was made to fight Imrin, before we eventually escaped.

He shakes his head. 'That's not what it looked like. We couldn't tell what was going on but the next day, the King was on camera saying that the traitor Offering Silver Blackthorn had tried to kill him. They showed footage of him choking and you running away.'

'That's not what happened. We knew someone would help the King before the fruit killed him. It was meant as a distraction.'

Knave shrugs. 'It doesn't matter what happened – that's what everyone saw. The whole country thinks you're a traitor. Not only that, but the King offered a year's rations for the capture of you or anyone associated with you. Last night, there was a programme showing capture squads searching for you around Windsor – small groups of men with weapons. I thought you knew – when Vez said it was you, I assumed you were hiding from the capture squads.'

I shake my head, partly in disbelief but mainly in fear. 'I didn't know . . .' I reach for a chair and collapse into it, the weight of everything feeling too much.

'I'm sorry,' Knave says, but it isn't his fault. He asks if I want something to eat or drink. Or somewhere to sleep. I barely know what to say but ask him to take me to Frank.

I don't even try to memorise the layout as he leads me through more tunnels into a stone room he calls the medical bay. There are two beds and some equipment against the back wall. One of the beds is empty but Frank is asleep in the other, his leg covered by a sheet.

'How is he?' Knave asks a man I assume to be a doctor.

The doctor rubs something away from his eyes and stifles a yawn. 'I've sedated him so he can sleep and done what I can but I'm not sure yet. If the leg is infected, he might lose it because I don't have everything I need here. I'll know more tomorrow.'

Knave turns to me. 'Is that all right?' I nod, satisfied that Frank's getting good care, but the doctor's yawn is infectious and my body is aching. 'The others have been given a room to share. We brought your bags and made sure there were plenty of blankets and things for you to make yourselves comfortable. We didn't think it was fair for you to have to mix with us on your first night.'

I ask him to lead me there and he takes me back into the corridor. 'Can I ask you another question?' Knave goes on.

'Okay.'

'What is it you actually want? You came to find us but never said why.'

I am so tired that I can't hide it any more, speaking through a yawn. 'There was this lad named Wray. We're all the same age but he was smaller and more vulnerable than the rest of us. The King killed him on our first night, just because he could. So many of us have died, names you wouldn't know. Others, like Jela who is with us, have survived but he took something from her. One way or the other, with or without you, I'm going to do something about it.'

Knave laughs gently but not in a mocking way. He understands. 'Do you have a plan?'

It is my turn to laugh. 'Not yet. You?'

'I have an idea or two. First we have to fix our communications devices.'

We reach a door, which Knave tells me is temporarily our room. I reply that we'll talk in the morning and then enter the room. Almost everyone seems to be asleep but Imrin has stayed awake for me. I say I'm fine and kiss him on the forehead, before taking the soft tortoise from my bag and curling up into a ball.

* * *

I sleep more peacefully than I have in a long time and the next thing I know it is morning and Imrin is shaking me awake. His breath tickles my ear as he asks what happened the night before. I keep my eyes closed, enjoying the way they feel shut, and tell him everything that Knave told me. As I talk, Imrin gently strokes my hair, smoothing it to my head, his lips brushing the back of my neck when he speaks. We have cuddled together before, usually in the hidden passageway that connected our dormitories, but this feels more natural. Even though I can sense the others around us, we may as well be on our own because it is only his voice I sense; his breath, his hands.

He tells me they had their blindfolds removed after being brought to the room and that they were given something to eat and drink. We both understand why they couldn't show us the route into their hideout and no one seems to have been hurt. It is nice to hear him speaking without that speckle of fear under his words – but then he spoils it by asking if I think my mother is safe. I sit up and open my eyes, telling him that I think she and Colt are fine, but it is Opie who falls into my head. His hands, his arms, his eyes.

Opie and Imrin.

The others are either asleep or pretending to be as I pack the tortoise back into my bag. 'It's from your story,' I tell Imrin when he questions why I have it. At first I think he is going to say something else but he smiles in the way he used to when we first met. The way that makes me feel as if I am the only person who matters.

Imrin and Opie.

'I have to find Knave,' I say. 'Stay and tell the others that we're safe here. Frank is being looked after but he's not in a good way. I'll be back later.'

I wonder if he is going to ask if he can come but he nods and ties my bag shut. 'I'll look after the tortoise for you,' he says with a grin.

The corridors are empty but it doesn't take me long to find the intersection and I trace the steps back towards the room where I was first introduced to Knave. He is there with Vez as I knock and let myself in.

'We have water if you want to wash,' Knave says.

'Do I look that bad?'

Even Vez smiles. 'It's the smell I was worried about,' Knave replies, winking.

Vez apologises for how we were treated the previous evening but I tell him I understand. Of the two, Vez seems more like the adult but it is clear from the way he looks at Knave that the blond man is in charge. There are more questions as they ask how I slept, before offering me some water to drink, which I greedily accept. It is only when Knave asks how my body is feeling that I realise my legs do not hurt any longer. The dull ache in my shoulder is still there but I have become so used to it that it barely registers any more.

Eventually, Vez pulls the table away from the wall and we sit next to each other looking at two connected think-pads.

'These don't work on the regular network of thinkpads,' Knave says, pointing towards a red spot on the screen. 'This is your map. There are eight other rebel groups marked on here but we only know of five of them. I'm not sure if that means there are more of us than we thought, or if the Kingsmen captured or killed someone acting individually and mistook it for something it wasn't.'

'They're all in the South,' I point out.

Vez nods. 'There are other rebels around the country

but it's better if we don't know too much. If someone is captured, they have nothing to tell.'

The two men look at each other, before glancing back to me. 'I know you were scared by the coverage I showed you last night,' Knave says. 'But we also think it could be an opportunity. We are slowly getting organised but people are worried for their families and themselves. It isn't easy standing up against the King.'

I shake my head, missing their point.

Vez leans across the table, his voice low. 'You're the person who can bring us all together.'

'How?'

'Everyone thinks you tried to kill the King.'

'But I didn't.'

They glance at each other again before Knave replies. 'No one else needs to know that. As soon as we tell the other rebel cells that we have Silver Blackthorn on our side, they'll know that we stand for something.'

I look from Knave to Vez. Their eyes are fixed on me expectantly. 'I'm not who you want me to be. I'm a sixteen-year-old girl.'

Their excitement is unaffected. 'You're already who you need to be just by being here,' Knave replies.

The red dots on the screen blink hypnotically as I sense Vez and Knave's expectation.

'I'm not going to do it,' I say as firmly as I can.

For a moment, neither of them says anything but I look up to see the same fire in Vez's eyes that I saw before I knew his name. The danger from when he was in the woods, asking who I was. 'Why not?' he asks.

'Because I don't want to. I didn't come here for me – I came because I wanted everyone else to be safe. You haven't told me a plan, all you've said is that you have people who want to fight. But what's the point in fighting when the King has men and weapons that can wipe out entire towns and villages? This isn't a war you're going to win by fighting. I thought you'd have a plan that was . . . *different*.'

Vez starts to speak but Knave cuts him off. 'Do you have a better idea?'

I pause, thinking, wishing I did. 'Not yet.' I don't want to give either of them time to contradict me, so add quickly: 'What's the problem with your communications?'

Vez is angry but trying to hide it and Knave answers. 'We don't know. We usually have test signals once a week, which are designed to let each other know we're still here. We've not heard anything in four weeks. Sometimes there are glitches and certain pockets are cut off but we haven't heard anything from anyone.'

'Did you say everything was centralised in Middle England?'

Vez turns to Knave, apparently annoyed he has given up the information, but the blond man ignores him. 'We have a contact in the North building at the Middle England junction. Their code name is Rom.'

'You don't know who it is?'

'No, it's safer that way. They help our groups talk to each other but we've not been able to contact them either. We think there's a problem in Middle England, as opposed to with the other rebel groups, but we don't know for sure.'

'I'm good with electrical things. If I go to Middle England, I can try to fix it after finding your Rom.'

Vez laughs dismissively but Knave remains silent.

'Where I grew up, there were all sorts of abandoned electrical items,' I add. 'I learned how electronics worked and built things of my own. In the castle, I set up that broadcast and helped to get everyone out.'

They don't seem as impressed as I'd hoped.

'Do you trust me?' I eventually ask.

They both shake their heads. 'It's not about trust,' Knave replies. 'A lot of lives rely on people like Rom. We don't know who he or she is, so why would you be able to find them, let alone sort out our problem? For all we know, Rom is dead.'

I'm not sure how to reply but Vez cuts in. 'If she can't be who we need her to be, then an enemy's enemy . . .'

He could be saying that we should be allies but I understand what he means underneath that – if I won't do what they want, then I am disposable.

I stand, knowing there is nothing more to be said. I only know what I have seen on screen and in the brief moments I passed through on the train. Middle England is perhaps the most defended place in the country after Windsor Castle and isn't a place where we'll be able to keep a dozen people safe. 'Will you look after everyone I leave behind?'

Knave nods.

'We're happy to share what we have with you,' I say. 'But any food you can spare for us to take would be appreciated. I'll see you in an hour.'

*　　*　　*

As I re-enter our room, half-a-dozen people start chattering at once. They want to know if I am okay and if we are safe. I tell them everything I know, saying that I think we can be secure here but that if anyone wants to leave, they will be allowed to as long as they don't mind being blindfolded as they are led out. Nobody moves, which in one way is flattering and wonderful but in another again makes me realise quite how much responsibility I have for everyone.

Nobody says it but there is the obvious question hanging between us: what now?

I don't tell them about Knave and Vez wanting me to be their figurehead; instead I say that I am going to Middle England and that I need a small team of people to help me.

Everyone volunteers to come but I don't need to be particularly adept at reading expressions to know that some
would much rather stay in the relative safety here. Faith and
Imrin are my obvious companions and Jela is someone who
is hard to turn down. She more than anyone has a score to
settle with the King but taking her means it would be tough
to say no to Pietra. I tell Hart he should stay to recover
but he assures me he is fine and says he will follow anyway.
The fact he stifles a cough while replying isn't convincing
but he leaves me little choice.

I tell Bryony that she should stay safe and she nods an
acceptance I know is also relief. She takes Pietra's hand,
hugs her tightly and tells her that she is forgiven for her
betrayal at Windsor Castle. Pietra hugs her back, tears
streaming down her face.

After that there is nothing more we can say. Pietra dries
her eyes while the rest of us pack our bags and head
through the corridors.

Knave meets us at the intersection but there is no sign of
Vez. Instead there are two others I don't recognise. They
help us fill our bags with food and water, before Knave
presses my knife into my hand and offers the others their
choice of blade.

'We don't have much,' he says. 'But you can bet most
people out there will have some sort of weapon.'

He tells me again about the capture squads, that there

was more about it on the screen last night and that we shouldn't trust anyone. I tell him we will wear blindfolds on the way out if he wants us to, but he shakes his head.

'You'll need to find us again when you return,' he adds with a smile.

He leads us up a narrow flight of steps which seem different to the ominous echoes under the blindfold from the night before. At the top is a hatch that he unbolts and pushes upwards with his shoulder and a grunt of exertion. One by one everyone steps outside until it is just Knave and me.

His blue eyes look at me crookedly with fascination. 'Do you know how many times I've left this village since the day I arrived?' he asks.

I shake my head.

'Not once. I've stayed here and tried to make things happen from this little hole in the ground. You've been here less than a day and already you're happy to trek across the country to benefit people you don't even know.'

I feel awkward standing slightly below him on the steps and shrug because I don't know what he wants me to say. He opens his arms and, without thinking, I find myself embracing him, letting him hug me.

'Good luck, Silver Blackthorn,' he says. 'I'll see you again soon.'

7

As the hatch is slammed behind me, I look down at what appears to be a patch of rubble. A thin layer of gravel and a few larger stones have been stuck to the exit. Even close up, it would be hard to detect this was anything but another patch of debris. I peer around to see the remains of the church and realise I probably stepped on this exact spot when I was here with Faith. Even though they took us a longer route in the blindfolds, it was simply to hide their real location.

It's not the best disguise but I scrape my silver streak backwards and pull the hat down until my head is covered and then we start to head north.

With a smaller group, I am happier about us travelling together but as soon as we cross into a field with a large overgrown hedge shielding it from the road, I tell everyone that I want to wait here until it is dark and that we should travel at night and rest during the day.

'How far away is Middle England?' Jela asks.

'Probably three nights depending on how quickly we go. If we're walking at night, we won't have the sun to guide us, so we'll have to be smart. My watch is working, so we can look for landmarks such as rivers.'

'We're going to be walking close to my village,' Faith says, but doesn't specifically ask if we can make a detour.

'We can't risk being seen by anyone that might recognise you,' I reply. 'Everyone knows you escaped with me and they'll assume that if you're around, then so am I.'

'You sent messages to all our parents about getting to safety before we escaped. I know where mine would have headed and they won't be with other people. If they got it, we'll know that everyone else's family should be safe too.'

I take a moment to consider this and can't fault her logic. It would be nice to know that my mother and Colt got my instructions. The worst case scenario is that Faith's family didn't get it. From what Knave told me, none of our families has been paraded on screen, which would surely have happened if they had been captured. In the faces of Jela, Pietra, Hart and Imrin, I can see they would like to know if their loved ones are safe.

'You'll have to direct us on our final day,' I say. 'We'll have to be careful.'

I catch Hart's eye as he coughs and covers his mouth with his hand. I start to ask how he is and then remember how annoying it is when Imrin keeps asking me the same thing.

I tell everyone that even though it is daytime and we

have slept recently, they should try to rest as much as they can. I then divide us into watch teams, pairing Imrin with Pietra – knowing she is the weakest and he is the strongest – and Faith with Hart, thinking that her common sense will compensate for his injury. I take the first shift with Jela because I know she won't want to talk about what could happen next.

While the others nestle themselves into the tallest clumps of grass, Jela and I edge along the hedgerow until we are at the top of a slope where we can see for a few miles in each direction. The sky is mottled with a grey haze of cloud that bobs gently in the breeze. We flatten a patch of grass and use the remaining tall stems to shield us from view. I check the stream that runs along the length of the field against the map on my thinkwatch, making sure we are still heading towards Middle England and telling Jela which direction we should take that night, if only to clarify my own thoughts.

'How do you do it?' she asks as we settle down to keep watch.

'What?'

'All of this. If I had everyone waiting for my next instruction and hanging on my words, it would drive me crazy, but it doesn't even faze you. One minute we're being led into that place under the church blindfolded, and the next you have the main guy giving us food and wishing us well. That took less than a day.'

When she puts it like that, it does sound impressive.

I shrug, unsure what to say. 'I don't know. I'm just me.'

Jela smiles and lies on her front on the grass. 'Exactly. *You're* the reason.'

I feel embarrassed because it is something I would rather not think about and we break into an uncomfortable silence.

'Will you tell me a story?' Jela asks softly.

'What about?'

'Tell me about Martindale.'

After Jela returned from the King's company, she didn't speak to anyone. I would sit with her, telling her stories about my home and have shared memories with her I've never thought about telling anyone before.

'Do you remember Opie?' I ask.

'The other Imrin?'

It shouldn't be funny but for some reason it is. As Jela giggles to herself, I find myself joining in until we end up shushing each other, which leads to another cacophony of stifled laughs. It's nice to feel young.

'Yes, the other Imrin,' I concede, still smiling. 'My earliest memory of him is from when we were about five or six. There were a bunch of us all roughly the same age in a field on the edge of the village playing this game where someone is "it" and the rest of you have to get away. You just run and shriek and then, eventually, it either gets dark or your mum comes over telling you it's time to go home. I was watching "it" chase Opie but then, as they were running, Opie's shoe came flying off. He kept running for a bit as if he hadn't noticed but, because it was summer and the ground was hard, there were all these little stones and he ended up hobbling around. The grass wasn't like this but it was still long and as he stopped and got tagged, he turned around to look for his shoe. He was trying to retrace his steps but couldn't see it.'

Jela picks a small white and yellow flower from the ground and pushes it into her hair. 'Do you have daisies in Martindale?' she asks.

'Fields of them.'

She grins. 'I'd love to see them one day. Anyway, what did you do to him?'

I try not to grin but the smell of the grass has brought the memory to the front of my mind. 'I saw exactly where it was and picked it up and lobbed it in a bush when he wasn't looking.'

Jela splutters in outrage. 'Why?'

'I don't know, I was just a girl and he was this big lad who lived down the road. Do you remember being young when you really liked someone?'

Jela grins. 'Maybe.'

'I think I knew then that he was someone I liked. You don't know what those feelings really mean, so you end up annoying the other person instead. Our families always knew each other. We would hang around as really young children, being naughty and getting into trouble. Our house was bigger and we'd celebrate birthdays and things like that together. Then there was this period where I must have annoyed him every day for about five years.'

'Really?'

'I'd pinch him on the arm and call him "Dopey". I would move all his things around at school, just to see if he noticed.'

'What happened?'

I feel a lump in my throat thinking about him and his younger brother Imp. 'I think I grew up. One day he was someone I was bugging, the next we would be out in the woods together, running, climbing, hunting and talking. It was as if there was no middle ground.'

Jela sighs wistfully, as if I am telling her something she already knows. 'Do you remember when I told you about my friend Lola when she ate some of the tan fruit and was paralysed?'

'Of course.'

It was her story that gave me the idea of how to escape the King. While he was temporarily crippled from the fruit juice, we ran for it.

'The lad who found her was called Ayowen. He's my Opie. It was really small where we lived and he was this lad

I'd seen around the village but I was too young to know who anyone was. One day I asked my mum who the kid playing in the mud was and she said "Ayowen". I don't know if it was the way she said it, but I couldn't get it out of my head for the rest of the day. I lay in bed that night saying it over and over: "Ay-o-wen". After that, he wasn't just the kid that always had dirty hands, suddenly he was Ayowen.'

'What happened?'

'I didn't have the courage to speak to him for a year!'

I am used to my chest and ribs hurting but this time it is because of laughter as I cannot control myself. Suddenly, I am no longer Silver Blackthorn: Offering and renegade. I am Silver Blackthorn: immature teenager. It feels good to let go.

'What happened when you spoke to him?'

'He mispronounced my name. He called me "Jel-Ah", instead of "Jee-lah". I was so pleased he said something to me that I didn't bother correcting him. He called me the wrong name for about three years.'

I cannot stop myself from laughing again and it feels good to be talking about something that isn't the King.

'What does he look like?' I ask.

'This is going to sound strange but the main thing I remember are his eyebrows.'

'*Eyebrows?*'

Jela shrugs. 'I'm not sure. They're really symmetrical and when he smiles they angle up in this way that fits with the rest of his face.'

I still don't understand. *Eyebrows?*

She sniggers: 'I know it sounds stupid. Anyway, what does Opie look like?'

'He's a little like Knave: blond and messy. Before I left, he'd started growing this little piece of stubble just because he could. It looked like he'd glued bristles from our sweeping-up brush to his chin.'

Jela giggles but the way she sounds so girly reminds me of Opie's brother Imp, when he once asked me why I wasn't like a proper girl. In the past I have sometimes wished I could be that person others expect me to be but now I'm not sure I will ever get that chance.

'You missed something out,' Jela says, sitting up. 'What happened to Opie's shoe?'

I smile as I remember. 'He spent about forty-five minutes looking for it and was getting angrier and angrier. He kept turning to the other lads, saying: "One of you must have taken it". The whole time, he refused to take the other one off in case that went missing too, so he was hobbling around in one shoe before he gave up and limped home. When everyone had gone, I sneaked out and fished it from the hedge, before leaving it on his front porch when it got dark.'

'Ah, so you were good to him after all?'

'Well I did spend the next few years calling him "Dopey", "Mopey" and "No Hopey", so I could have been a bit nicer.'

We share some water and talk more about our upbringings until it is time for Imrin and Pietra to keep watch. Because it is light, I think I'll struggle to sleep but after resting my head on my blanket and cuddling my tortoise, it feels like only seconds until Faith is nudging me awake, pointing to the dimming skies and saying we should start moving.

Walking at night is better from a safety point of view but the natural beauty of some of the scenery is lost without the light. Despite many of the villages being destroyed, there are still vast green fields and glistening lakes that would have been magnificent during the day. Until the Offering, I had barely left Martindale and can tell from the others' reactions that few of them have seen anything other than their home towns and villages.

We stop to eat and rest every few hours and even though we have cans to eat from, Faith catches squirrels with basic snares and her knife so effortlessly that it is as if she has been doing it forever. We light fires within tree lines and use our blankets to stop the orange glow from giving our position away.

At the end of our second night of walking, we find the

remnants of another battered, abandoned town and sleep in a partially collapsed house, taking it in turns to share a real bed as the others keep lookout. Over the course of the journey, I realise how everyone's skills are working together for the group. Faith can do almost anything physical; she never runs out of energy and can climb and hunt. Imrin is terrific with directions. I thought I would be able to follow the map at night but get lost too quickly. He instantly seems to know where north is and finds safe spots that allow some of us to sleep as the lookout pairings are able to see for miles. Jela has become a nurse of sorts to Hart, who cannot hide how much he is struggling. He doesn't cough as often as he did but there are blood speckles on his clothes again where he cannot control himself. Pietra, meanwhile, just listens and watches. She knows she doesn't have the natural ability Faith does, but she takes everything on board and is able to offer ideas.

Midway through the third night, Faith tells us we are close to the edges of her home town. Middle England, Rom and the broken communications are in the distance but she leads us onto a ridge overlooking the area in which she grew up, before we find a spot to settle. Although it is more dangerous to be out during the day, Faith says her parents will be in a cabin a few miles away, a spot where they spend a few weeks each summer. She insists no one else knows about it.

RENEGADE

There is glee in her voice as we plan to set off as soon as the sun rises. I am pleased for her but can feel something deep in my stomach, knowing that if her family aren't around then there is a reasonable chance my mother, Colt and Opie are in serious danger.

8

Travelling as a group of six during the night is one thing, but having our sought-after faces in the open during the day is a risk too far. As soon as the first wisps of sunlight begin to appear, I ask Imrin, Pietra and Hart to wait and then Faith, Jela and myself head down the brow and trace the line of hedges until we are on the outskirts of the town.

It is a strange thing to notice but Faith walks differently as she leads us around the edge of the town and across a cobbled bridge before we reach a large field. There is almost a skip to her step and she cannot stop smiling. 'This is the long way round,' she says. 'There won't be anyone who sees us this way, so we'll be safer.'

I ask her to tell us about the cabin.

'It's on the edge of a lake not far out of town. It was built by my dad's dad and was handed down. We save up our food and sneak there every summer for a week or so. As long as we're back to collect rations, no one notices. We've never told anyone about it because, well, you don't, do you? It's not good for people to know you have something they don't.'

She's right about that.

'You don't have any brothers or sisters, do you?' I ask.

'No, it's just me.'

As Faith leads us over the top of the field, we emerge into a small patch of trees that overlooks a lake. The water is a deep blue as the sun twinkles from the surface. There is a thin strip of brown sand around the edge and a smattering of wooden shacks in various states of disrepair close to a muddy trail.

'Does anyone else stay here?' Jela asks.

'Not at this time of the year. There are a few people when it is summer but we all keep ourselves to ourselves. It's not good to ask questions.'

Faith is keen to knock on her family's cabin door but I sit on the ground and tell her we should wait. After thirty minutes of no movement in or out of any of the shacks, the sun has fully risen and the frost that made the ground crackle under our footsteps now makes our descent to the lake a perilous mixture of sliding and grabbing onto tree trunks for support.

Faith is in her element and if I hadn't shushed her, she would be shrieking with pleasure.

The cabins back onto another area of woodland, so we dash across the trail and stay within the tree line until Faith points us to the one that is theirs. It is the largest one and I am annoyed at my own prejudice. Because she is a Trog, I expected something run-down.

'I have my own room at the back,' Faith says, sounding pleased with herself. 'It's probably the same size as our actual house.'

There are windows that look out towards where we are but neither of us can see any movement. Ideally I wanted to see a sign that Faith's parents are here and then make our approach. I know that she wants to say hello and spend some time with them but the longer we stay somewhere like this instead of moving on, the more chance we have of being found.

After another ten minutes, there are still no signs of life and there is only one option to find out if anyone is in. Faith is understandably delighted as we walk around to the front of the cabin, facing the lake, and she raps loudly on the wooden door.

My throat is dry and I find it hard to swallow as the knock echoes around us before being replaced by a serene calm. I try to picture my mother's face as Faith reaches forward and bangs louder on the door. Again there is silence and I see visions of my mum and Colt being led away by Kingsmen. I think about the families of the rest of our group and how I have put them all in danger because I didn't find a way to check if my warning message got through.

As my hands begin to shake, there is a scratching on the other side of the door. I try to stop her but it is too late as Faith says, 'Mum, it's me' loudly enough that the syllables seem to bounce around the water.

More scratching and then the door swings inwards a few centimetres.

'Mum?' Faith's voice cracks as she takes a step forward and the door opens the rest of the way.

There is an instant resemblance as the woman in the doorway stares curiously at her daughter, arms hugging across her own chest. Facially, Faith and her mother are incredibly similar, but there are also clear differences as the older woman has long dark hair and doesn't have the same athletic body Faith does.

'It's me, Mum,' Faith repeats, opening her arms.

The woman continues to stare at her, eyes wide in surprise. It is only with her expression that I realise this is the first time any Offering has ever returned to his or her parents.

'How . . . ?' the woman says.

It is only one word but it breaks Faith completely. Suddenly the young woman who has been so resourceful and grown-up is reduced to a girl crying in her mother's arms. I watch her blonde mop of hair bob up and down as she sobs, before I hear Jela next to me choking back a tear too. Before I myself crack, Faith's mother waves us all into the cabin, locking three bolts across the inside of the wooden door as her daughter refuses to let her go.

Inside, there is one large room made entirely of wood. It is empty aside from a few chairs and a table. The room is dominated by a large empty fireplace.

Standing in the corner staring at us is a man sporting a puzzled frown with his hands on his hips. Faith calls him 'Daddy' and they share the same eyes. All three of them are short but where Faith is lithe, both of her parents are thick-set, especially her father. His arms are bulky and he has greying hair that stretches to his broad, bare shoulders. His eyes are narrow and disbelieving. As his daughter approaches him, he places an arm around her but instantly begins patting her on the back as if he feels uncomfortable.

The cabin is warm and I take my hat off, allowing my hair to fall loose. As I look up, I see both of her parents staring at me, their mouths hanging open. There is an uncomfortable silence before Faith breaks it. 'Mum, Dad, this is Silver and Jela. Without them, I wouldn't be here.'

They are momentarily like statues until they both lunge forward at the same time, trying to shake our hands. Her mother tells us she is called Marion and that her husband is Burn. She then begins to fuss, asking if we are hungry or thirsty and trying to make us sit down. I want to say that we should be going but Faith won't catch my eye and I don't want to be the person who tells her she has to say goodbye.

Eventually, I give in, sitting against the edge of the fireplace next to Jela as we stretch our legs out. Marion insists on making us something to eat as Burn stands around awkwardly.

'What would you like?' Marion asks expectantly.

'Anything at all,' I say.

She glances to her husband. 'Do you want to go to our store and get some meat?'

'We don't want to be any trouble,' I interrupt.

'Nonsense,' Marion says. 'If he sets off now, he'll be back soon enough. Look at your arms.'

I feel uncomfortably self-conscious as I peer at the jumper covering the sticks connected to my shoulders. Burn nods an understanding and then stops to kiss Faith on the head before sending one more puzzled glance in my direction and heading outside. Marion bolts the door behind him and then sits in a chair in front of us with Faith next to her. I feel uncomfortable as her eyes keep darting towards my hair. In the end I put my hat back on, making the excuse that I am feeling cold.

Marion turns to her daughter and asks how she's feeling.

Faith glances quickly towards Jela and me, not wanting us to know about this part of her life. She rotates the broken thinkwatch on her wrist, hiding the yellow colour and sickle imprint that has branded her a Trog. 'I'm fine.'

Marion turns to us. 'Faith was such an active young girl

– running, climbing, all sorts. Even when she was a child, she was far stronger than she looked. Then, a few months before the Reckoning, she started to feel . . .' Marion peers at her daughter, shrugging and struggling for the correct word. '. . . *weak*, I suppose. The doctors are expensive and, well . . .'

'I'm not ashamed of being a Trog, Mum.'

Marion casts a scolding glare towards her daughter before catching herself and softening again. This is not really a conversation to be had in front of others.

'How did you end up coming this way?' Marion asks.

Before Faith can answer, I cut in, saying that we are just passing through and giving a hazy response, making sure I say nothing about our journey towards Middle England. Knave and Vez were right about one thing – there is no point in telling people more than they need to know.

'You've been on the news every night,' she adds. 'I was so worried. They're saying you tried to kill the King but you're my little Faith and I knew you wouldn't be involved in anything like that.'

'It's not true, Mum,' Faith says, before telling her how we were kept prisoner and badly treated. I rest my hand on the top of Jela's as she shakes next to me. As Faith speaks, I watch Marion and with each revelation, her eyes widen further.

'I didn't know,' she whispers at the end of the tale.

'How did you know you had to get away from your house?' I ask.

Marion glances at her wrist. 'Burn and I got messages on our thinkwatches. It hasn't really been working since, but I'll show you what it said.'

Adults' thinkwatches are all the same colour, a grey-white, because they have not taken the Reckoning. She flicks through a few screens and then begins to read: '"The child taken from you as an Offering is in trouble. Kingsmen will come. Take food, water and clothing. Go now and hide. Do not go back".' She peers back up to me and adds: 'We didn't know if it was serious but didn't want to risk it. We packed our things and then, when the screens turned on and showed us the King, we realised something wasn't right. We came here that night.'

I don't remember the exact words I sent out but it sounded like the message I wrote. It is fair to assume that if Faith's parents got the message, then all our relatives did.

'Are you all right, dear?' Marion asks as I break into a smile. I am thinking of my mum and Colt and the increased possibility they are safe.

'I'm fine,' I say but suddenly, with the burden lifted, the idea of food consumes me. My stomach gurgles greedily at the thought we will soon be eating.

'How much longer will Dad be?' Faith asks.

'Not long. We left so quickly that we couldn't manage

everything. We hid some food in an old coal store. It's around a half-mile to town and it helps us keep an eye on things too, in case there's anything going on.'

'Is there?' I ask.

'Not that he's said. I wait here.'

I wonder if that is because Kingsmen haven't come here yet – or because they were never coming at all. 'Has anyone bothered you here?'

Marion shakes her head and rests a hand on her daughter's head. 'Not at all. We've not seen anyone since we left.'

I peer at my watch and realise it has been two hours since we left the others. I glance towards Faith who looks away quickly but she knows what I am going to say. 'We really have to be going . . .'

Marion protectively moves her hand onto Faith's shoulder. 'Do you have somewhere to go?'

'We really shouldn't say. It might not be safe for you to know.'

She nods. 'I understand, but Burn will be back any minute. I'll make sure you're well fed before you go on your way.'

This time it is me who won't meet Faith's stare. I can feel her imploring me to allow her a few more minutes. I make a point of looking at my watch again. 'Okay, but we really have to go soon.'

Faith wants to keep us occupied and is quickly on her feet. 'I can show you my room if you like?'

She beckons us to follow, heading towards the back of the cabin into a bedroom. As she closes the door behind us, she grins sheepishly. From the contents of the room, it is no surprise. The bedding is a faded pink with a selection of soft toys on top, all a similar colour.

'I liked pink a lot when I was younger,' she says, although, from the way she picks up one of the toys and smells it, I'm not convinced it was that long ago. Her eyes are twinkling with happiness and she is a different person. Her bed is a little wider than mine in Martindale and although it is a tight fit, the three of us lie together enjoying the softness of the mattress.

'We really do have to go,' I say.

Faith's voice is gentler than usual. 'I know . . . it's just nice to see them again.'

'At least we know the message got through,' Jela adds.

'My mum and dad are both Elites,' Faith says, un-prompted. 'They do pretty well around the town and we always have a good share of rations. A few months before the Reckoning, I started having these pains in my chest. I felt really weak all the time. I couldn't go to school because I wasn't strong enough to get through more than an hour or two.'

Although she once told me she had been ill, this is the first time she has mentioned any details.

'How come you're okay now?' I ask.

'I'm not sure. Our doctor couldn't figure it out. I barely got out of bed for a month and then one day I woke up and felt almost normal again. No one seemed to be able to explain it but it happened not long before the Reckoning. When I took it, the Reckoning hurt me: I could feel it in my mind, burrowing and scraping. I didn't have the strength to stop it, let alone answer the questions. I threw up afterwards and knew I'd be a Trog before the results came out.'

In everything we have gone through, the Reckoning is still the biggest mystery. We are each connected to modified thinkpads and yet everyone's experience is different. Mine felt like a two-way conversation in which I refused to give ground. Faith's sounds like she was bullied.

She sighs in shame and I take her hand. 'Out of everyone that came with us, you're the one I trust the most.'

I move myself into a sitting position and see that Jela is holding Faith's other hand. Jela nods at me to say that she understands why it isn't her I singled out. She is resourceful in other ways.

Faith doesn't reply but she grips my hand so hard that I can feel the bones of her fingers. We stay silent for a few minutes more until Jela sits up as well. 'We really have to go,' I say.

As she raises herself up, Faith nods. 'I know. Just give me a minute to say goodbye.'

Jela stands first but, as she does, there is a loud bang on the front door. Faith reaches towards the bedroom door handle but I know something isn't right and grab her arm. 'If it was your dad, he'd knock gently,' I whisper.

Faith's eyes widen in fear as I creep towards the back window and nudge the corner of the curtain to one side, revealing half-a-dozen Kingsmen lined up on the edge of the woods, their swords drawn.

9

The front door bangs open and we hear a man shouting, 'Where are they?'

Burn's reply follows urgently: 'They were here, honestly they were. Three of them.'

Faith's entire body trembles as her father betrays us. Her bottom lip bobs up and down, silent tears rolling down her cheeks. I cannot begin to imagine what she is feeling but I am boiling with a mixture of rage at what they have done and sadness I can barely start to understand. Neither of those emotions even approaches the fear rippling through me – we are surrounded by Kingsmen.

'They're in her bedroom,' Marion says. 'I tried to find out if there were others but they wouldn't say. Do we have the deal?'

'Our Faith gets to go free, doesn't she?' Burn adds, voice wavering.

There is a shuffling of feet along with at least two other men talking over each other until Marion screams: 'You won't hurt her, will you?'

The bedroom door clatters open and there is a roar of fury from the Kingsmen. 'Where are they?'

Marion stumbles over her reply. 'They were there, all three of them, I watched them go in.'

There is more banging and the sound of glass breaking before we hear Burn's voice. 'That window has been sealed for years.'

As we crouch in the flood cellar underneath the cabin, I hold my breath. Faith showed us the hatch hidden under her bed which she found during a thunder storm when she was a kid. For whatever reason, she never mentioned it to her parents but if they are aware of it, then the game is up.

'Is there another way out?' one of the men demands.

'No,' Burn replies.

It feels as if the whole cabin is shaking as a Kingsman explodes with rage. We hear boots stomping and wood shattering.

'Was your Trog-scum daughter ever here?' the voice shouts, before the crunch of fist on flesh blares.

I cradle Faith to my chest, silently imploring her to be quiet. She is shattered, not only from the betrayal but now from hearing her parents being beaten above us.

'We just wanted our daughter back!' Marion's voice cries, but there is another vicious crack followed by a whimper.

'Were they ever here?' the Kingsman demands.

'Yes!' Burn replies, although there is a liquid sound to his voice that I recognise all too well, having tried to talk through a mouthful of blood when I was a prisoner at the castle. The crunch of a boot connecting with bone is eclipsed by the shattering of ribs as he cries out in pain.

'Send the men into the woods and get around the other side of the lake,' the Kingsman orders someone above us. 'They can't have gone far. Take these two back to the town – the Minister Prime wants someone for tonight's broadcast, so it may as well be them.'

As footsteps boom on the creaking floor above, Jela and I sandwich Faith between us, whispering in her ear that we are there for her. She is shaking uncontrollably, unable to speak. There are silent tears on Jela's face and I know I have to be the strong one.

By the time the noises above us dissipate, it is over five hours since we left Imrin, Hart and Pietra on the far side of the town. With the Kingsmen searching the area, I hope Imrin has been organised enough to have one person keeping watch.

As her sobs slow to a stop, Faith sits between us, her legs wrapped around me, arms clinging to my back, as if she is a child I am cradling.

'Is there another way out, Faith?' I whisper gently in her ear, but she doesn't respond. Slowly, I disentangle us but her red puffy eyes stare right through me.

'Faith?'

No response.

I turn to Jela and tell her to wait as I lift the hatch a sliver, peering at the carnage that was once Faith's bedroom. The bed is no longer above us; instead it is on its side propped against the wall. Every piece of furniture has been smashed. As quietly as I can, I slide the cover to one side and pull myself into the room. Both the bedroom and front door are open, allowing me to see all the way through the cabin to the lake outside. I risk a look out of the back window and the Kingsmen seem to have gone, so I creep through the empty cabin to the front door.

The sun is as high in the sky as it is going to get but offers little warmth and any degree of mist or dimming cloud cover that would have been helpful has long gone. The only benefit to the clear conditions is that it allows me to see there are no dark figures skulking around the edge of the water.

As I make my way back to the bedroom, I notice a large drying pool of blood in the centre of the room. Faith's state of mind is perilous enough as it is, so I grab one of the blankets and throw it over the puddle, before returning to the cellar.

Faith's gaze is still vacant but she does at least respond to my voice when I say we have to go. Jela tries to help her up but Faith shrugs her off and bursts past me, running through the door to the outside. She looks both ways and then begins sprinting along the dirt trail. We chase but struggle to catch up and for a moment, I think she is going to continue along the track towards the town. Apparently on instinct, she sidesteps through a gap between trees and bounds effortlessly up a slope to the side of the wooded area, sending a flurry of small stones and dirt tumbling down the hill behind her.

The air is so cold it hurts my lungs and as Jela and I support each other climbing the muddy bank, Faith streaks further ahead and disappears over the top of the hill. I cling to a tree trunk and haul Jela the final few steps, before we stop for a few moments to catch our breath. I am about to ask if Jela can see anyone when something hisses overhead.

Faith is sitting above us in the tree pointing towards the field we crossed to get here.

'There are Kingsmen all around the field and more surrounding the town,' she says. 'I can't see any on the far side where we left Imrin and the others.'

She sounds completely normal, as she did before the assault on the cabin.

'How can we get back?' I whisper loudly.

'There's a huge hedge that runs along the side of the field next to the one we crossed to get here. We'll be really close to the Kingsmen but, if we're quiet, they shouldn't notice us. We'll pass right under their noses. We'll have to go under the bridge and through the water, but then we'll have a clear run back to the others.' She tails off, before adding: 'You can swim, can't you?'

Jela says she can but I have never learned – the gully outside Martindale is a dry lake, filled with rubbish. Faith replies, 'I'll get you over' – and then jumps down, landing perfectly on her feet, before running off towards the field.

Instead of attracting attention by going over the stile, we slide under it, and run the length of the hedge in exactly the way Faith described. We can hear the Kingsmen's voices from the other side of the bushes but instead of cursing us, as I would have expected, they are complaining about the mud and being called out on another false errand.

At the bridge, there are no guards but because of the way the stone structure curves upwards over the water, we could be easily seen by any of the Kingsmen we just passed if we tried to walk over it. Jela swims across the river first, gasping in shock at how cold the water is, but quickly making her way over to the far bank. I wade in as far as I can until my tiptoes are scraping the gravelly bottom, unable to speak as the ravaging temperature chills my body. Faith wraps an arm around my chest and drags me across the flowing water until she says I can put my feet down. Her voice is crisp, as if the chill has not affected her at all.

My teeth are chattering, my body shaking, as we run towards the woods, hurtling past a set of bushes close to the edge until, finally, we reach the spot where Imrin and Hart are sitting on the ground, hidden by the trees. They are pleased to see us but curious as to why we are drenched. I ask where Pietra is and Imrin points upwards to reveal her hanging in a tree, staring in the direction from which we came. I want to find out how she got up there but there are so many other questions to ask first.

Imrin throws blankets around the three of us as I tell him and Hart that we were almost discovered by Kingsmen. I quickly add that everyone's families should have received the warning message, because Faith's parents got theirs. I don't mention what actually happened with her mother and father. I will talk to Imrin when it is quiet but I don't think Faith would want me to tell the rest of the group that her parents tried to sell us out.

Faith tells Pietra she can come down and, without waiting for a reply, climbs the tree until she is close to the top, many branches above where Pietra was.

'It's all clear,' she whispers loudly.

She is high enough to give us warning if any guards come close, making this as safe as anywhere for the moment. If we were to leave now, we could end up stumbling into a group of Kingsmen. I want us to take turns watching through the day but Faith refuses to come down. While the others snatch a few more hours of sleep, I sit at the bottom of the tree waiting for the relative safety of darkness with my eyes closed, listening to the sounds of the woods and wishing I was home in Martindale.

As soon as dusk begins to settle, Faith clambers through the branches before landing next to me. I want to ask how she is, but her eyes are focused as she talks me through the locations of the patrols. Most of the town is surrounded and it is clear the Kingsmen think we are hiding somewhere within the boundaries. The easiest way to get to Middle England would be by passing close to the town but that is out of the question.

Using the map on my thinkwatch, Faith points me towards another village a few miles out of our way that will add another hour to the journey. Allowing her to guide us, we walk back the way we originally came, keeping tight to the hedgerows and staying close together but stopping every fifteen minutes to allow Faith to shin up a tree and check for any Kingsmen patrols nearby. Because it is dark, we are hoping the Kingsmen will be using something to light their path and give their position away.

As we emerge from the woods, we dip into a valley that contains the village Faith told us about. Even from a distance, we can see two different patches of light around the streets, with five or six distinct torches in each group. I don't know if they are Kingsmen, or the capture squads that Knave told me about, but we can't risk going anywhere nearby. What should have been a short walk turns into a trek that lasts most of the night as we continue heading out of our way for a few more miles until we finally begin moving north again.

At first I think we might have problems judging our position as we have moved so far away from where we were, but then as we trudge over the top of a hill, the wonder of Middle England stops us all where we are standing.

Although we are still a few miles away, there are four beaming glass pillars of light towering into the air and turning night into day. Nobody speaks; our collective gasps of amazement say enough about the majesty of what is in front of us.

Each tower sits in the corner of one of the Realms, North, South, East and West, with a spot in the centre that means a person can simultaneously be in all four areas at the same time. The towers are our main trade hubs with each other.

On the train journey from Martindale to Windsor, I saw them from the ground, soaring so high that I couldn't see the top. Even from a distance, the way the towers are lit makes it look as if they are touching the sky; a true testament to what we can achieve as a people if we really want to. As it is, their magnificence overshadows in all ways the towns and villages which have been burned to the ground on our journey to get here. Many people around the country starve on meagre rations, away from their homes and packed into city centres, even though we still have the capability to produce something like the towers.

They are both hideous and beautiful – a perfect tribute to our King's regime.

The light spreads for miles in all directions, meaning there is little point in us moving much closer. Our chances of finding Rom during the night seem minimal too, but Imrin spots some buildings at the bottom of the hill we are standing on. They are partially caved in – four piles of bricks and tiles in a row that would once have been small houses. A path runs along in front, connecting the derelict properties, but there are rough overgrown patches of grass on the other side, cutting them off from the edge of the inhabited areas that lead to the towers. At first I am wary of straying too close to where other people might be, but the surroundings seem quiet and everyone could do with a night under a roof – even one that isn't completely intact.

Most of our tinned food has gone but Faith sets a line of snare traps on the edge of the field in the hope that something may stumble into them overnight. The way she ties her knots is so much more advanced than anything I managed in Martindale and I find myself trying to memorise the movements of her hands as she zigzags and crosses the ropes intricately before expertly concealing the tripwires and triggers.

Of the four homes, we pick the one that seems to be the

most upright. I am convinced we are wasting our time and that there will not be enough space for us, but Imrin points to the corners of the house which are still in place. We move a few pieces of wood aside and slide through a gap in the rubble until there is enough room for everyone, including Hart, to fit through. Inside, Imrin is proven correct. Although the edges of the rooms are filled with dust, tiny stones and broken furniture, the centre of what would once have been a living room provides a large enough area for us to rest in relative safety and comfort.

I want to find a moment alone with Imrin to talk through everything that has happened but it is so cold that we all huddle together under the blankets, using our body heat for warmth. Faith is the only exception; she curls up silently in a corner away from the rest of us.

As I snuggle close to Imrin, so much of my body aches that it is difficult to know if it is solely from the walking or because my injuries haven't yet healed. At the other end of the line, I can hear Hart coughing gently but he is so adept at stifling it, no one but him notices how bad it is.

I close my eyes, wanting to drift off to sleep, but the memory of what Faith's parents did and the way she wrapped herself around me in despair is so fresh that it feels as if her pain is my own.

Imrin's breathing quickly changes into the long gulps of

sleep as I slowly feel my mind drifting back to the familiarity of the woods outside Martindale.

As I lie on the banks of the gully staring at the sky, I can hear Opie's lumbering footsteps snapping twigs and scuffing across leaves. It is the day before the Reckoning and he is going to ask me if I can help him cheat because he doesn't want to risk being a Trog. He thinks he is sneaking up on me but has never had a gentle way of moving around.

Suddenly, I realise I am half-awake, aware of the room and Imrin's arm across me and yet Opie's footsteps still clump in my ears.

I open my eyes, staring towards the hole we created to enter the house, and it is only when I hear a man's voice that I realise the footsteps aren't Opie's. Instead there are two Kingsmen standing directly outside.

10

'Cold tonight, innit?'

The strong, thick voice echoes around our space, waking everyone instantly. It is dark but I see five sets of eyes flash towards the men and then me as the others realise what is happening. After we entered the dilapidated building, we wedged a piece of wood across the hole, but I thought it would be too much work to completely cover the entrance with stones from the inside, especially as we seemed to be so far away from the rest of the inhabitants and were only going to be here for a matter of hours. Now I wish we had spent five more minutes concealing our location.

Although the piece of wood covers most of the entrance hole, we can see the outlines of both Kingsmen leaning against the front of the house, their swords hanging limply from their waists.

'Did they even give a reason why we all have to be out here?' the other replies. 'I can't be bothered going into the woods. We'll just say we did.'

The second voice is slightly higher-pitched than the first but the casualness of their conversation is something none of us would ever have associated with Kingsmen. To us, they are authority figures in black but as they lean and chat, they seem more like men simply doing a job.

'Just something about being more vigilant,' the first man replies. 'It's been chaos all week since that castle stuff.'

'I heard the girl was spotted a few miles away this morning.'

'Silver Blackthorn?'

I feel a tingle slide along my back as everyone's eyes again turn to me.

'Aye. They spent hours looking for her but she either got away or wasn't there to start with. Some of the lads got to tear a few houses down looking for her, mind.'

They both laugh but I cannot stop watching Faith through the dim light as the knowledge sinks in that the actions of her parents have torn apart more lives than we knew. She is still in the corner of the room, cradling her knees to her chest, staring at the floor in shame.

We watch as the outline of the first man reaches down to scratch his thigh. 'What do you reckon?'

'Of the girl? Who knows? I don't know what all the fuss is about – some kid with fancy hair. What do they think she's going to do?'

'There must be something in it. Have you heard the people in the towers talking about the Offering? They're wondering what happens to all these kids after they get chosen.'

The second guard doesn't sound overly bothered. 'Not much you can do if one of them goes crazy and tries to kill the King though, is there?'

'Did you see what happened? It was really confusing. There was no sound and these kids were on the screen and then the King was choking and coughing. They said she tried to kill him but she was nowhere near him.'

Even without being able to see them from the waist up, it is obvious the second Kingsman feels uneasy. 'I try to keep out of it,' he says, trying to end the conversation.

'Someone said they've taken a handful of us down to Windsor.'

'Okay . . .'

'Think about it. We only get new people in when one of us is killed. If they've got that many people being sent down there, what do you think happened?'

The second Kingsman suddenly sounds interested. 'What are you saying?'

The first guard lowers his voice. 'People are saying the King's lost it . . .'

'Which people?'

'Just . . . *people*.' There is a definite edge of tension between the guards. 'They're saying that, if some girl can take out six or seven of us and try to kill the King, then something strange must be going on down there. Have you ever seen so much coverage? It's been on the screen every night and they've been giving out weapons so those capture squads can hunt her as well – not to mention the reward.'

There is a snigger. 'I wouldn't mind a bit of that myself. Have you seen what they're offering? A year's worth of rations and promotion to Elite.'

Imrin gasps at the revelation, which is enough to make everyone else uneasy. It is perhaps no wonder that Faith's parents betrayed us given what is on offer. In a warped display of parenting, they might even have been hoping their daughter would be made an Elite. The other thing that occurs to me is that Knave and Vez's plan is already in action whether I want to be a part of it or not. People are already seeing me as something I'm not. I certainly didn't kill six guards and the tan fruit that paralysed the King was unlikely to kill him. The myth is already eclipsing the truth.

'I'm sure we'll get something if we bring her in,' the first Kingsman says. 'Those capture squads are just getting in the way. Did you hear what happened out West?'

'I've been on crackdown – tell me anyway.'

'After the reward was bumped up the night before last, the streets were packed. It was hard work around here because there were all these people out after dark. We sent most of them home because everyone was tripping over each other – but it was worse in other areas.'

'What's the point of hanging around the towns and cities? She's not going to be hiding here, is she?'

I suppress a smile at how close they actually are.

'You're probably right but it doesn't stop everyone trying to find her,' the first Kingsman says. 'Someone spotted some girl with dark hair out after sundown. One guy shouted "there she is" and then all these groups set off chasing her. By the time our lot arrived, they'd strung her up from some pillar outside the town hall. Some bloke was saying he was the one who killed her, so he deserved the reward.'

'Idiot.'

'The girl's mother came out on the streets and was all over the place. She was grabbing onto the girl's feet, crying and saying they'd got the wrong person but this guy was still going on about how he deserved the reward.'

'That's what happens when you have these fools trying to do our jobs.'

'We hung him next to her as a message to tell them all to calm down in future. She didn't even have that silver streak.'

There is no sympathy in either of their voices for the girl or her mother; instead it is derision that someone has done a job badly. I can barely breathe and feel overwhelmed at the fact a girl was murdered because she was mistaken for me.

'Makes you think, doesn't it?' the first man says, moving his weight from one foot to the other. 'We've got all these people out on the streets looking for her and the Minister Prime was up here yesterday too. I saw him going into the North Tower but apparently he spent time in all four. What was he doing? I've never seen him here before.'

'Who knows? It's been a strange week.'

If what he says is right, it means Middle England is all the more important – although it doesn't help us to find Rom. Faith crosses the room silently and sits closest to the door. I'm not sure if she's trying to hear better, or if something else is going on. She is looking in the opposite direction to where the Kingsmen are standing and I don't want to risk making a noise by trying to attract her attention.

'How was crackdown then?'

The second Kingsman laughs. 'I was out yesterday in a town just across the border in the East. There were a few problems with food last week so we went in big style to put a few of them in their places.'

'I've not been on crackdown for weeks,' the first one replies. 'You begin to get a bit itchy for it when you're left on patrol.'

More laughing. 'You're right about that. It's been a quiet month but we made up for it yesterday. We set fire to this house in the centre. As soon as the men came running out, we were on them. That's all it takes: make an example or two and the rest fall in line. By the time we were done, there wasn't anyone complaining about their rations. It was fun while it lasted.'

The first guard chuckles again but the atmosphere feels different among us. The Kingsmen at the castle rarely spoke but the brutality of these men is clear.

'Do you think we've been away for long enough?'

There is a shuffling as the first Kingsman raises his wrist to check his thinkwatch. 'Probably. We'll head back slowly and say it was all quiet. I don't know why they think she'd be out here anyway. If she's got any sense, she'll be getting as far away as possible, not heading into trouble.'

I cannot meet anyone's eyes; the Kingsman's words make me feel selfish for doing exactly as he suggests – leading everyone into trouble. Imrin shakes his head slightly, reading my mind, but it does nothing to reconcile my guilt.

The Kingsmen begin to walk away and I realise I must have been holding my breath because I let out a large gasp, instantly feeling better. The guards' loud, leathery footsteps sound like thunder retreating into the distance as a sense of calm flitters through us.

I am just about to ask Imrin what he thinks when a deep rasping cough roars uncontrollably out of Hart's mouth, echoing around the room and escaping into the night.

11

Hart's hand is in front of his mouth but it doesn't stop the speckles of blood from splattering through his fingers onto the floor. There is only one way in and out of the house and it feels as if everything has stopped for a moment – including the Kingsmen's footsteps.

The pair of them had been walking away but now a silence envelops us until, terrifyingly, their footsteps begin to edge closer again.

I have often thought how strange it is that time seems to slow when I feel under the most pressure. I wonder if Imrin is seeing the room in the same way I am. Pietra and Jela both look to me, panicked. Hart is doubled over, trying to stop himself coughing again, eyes bulging in fear and shame. Imrin is reaching for his knife, knees bent, ready for action as I see a vein in his neck pulsing with adrenalin. Faith is crouching, coiled and ready for action. I reach for my own knife, determined to make sure that, if I am going to be captured, I am going to cause these two creatures as much harm as I can in retribution for all the people they have bullied and butchered. The rage is boiling through me and yet, strangely, I feel perfectly calm. Each footstep is like a call to action until the outlines of the Kingsmen are visible again. They stand still, silently plotting what to do, until one of them finally reaches down and takes hold of the wood that separates us from them.

As it is ripped away, it is like there is a whooshing as time speeds up again. Faith springs forward with a cry of fury, pouncing through the small gap. She elbows the first Kingsman and punches the second in the stomach before tearing off away from the house, her silhouette lit up by the moon and the bright white of the towers. We are so stunned that nobody moves and then, miraculously, both Kingsmen turn and run after her. I want to shout after them, to draw them away from the chase, but to do so would bring them back towards more vulnerable people.

By the time I have reached the exit, the Kingsmen are already following Faith along the pathway back the way we came. I edge into the garden, looking both ways to see if there are any other Kingsmen but the only sign of movement is the blur of the black figures lagging behind Faith. She continues to pull away from them, racing expertly up the bank towards the woods, before veering sideways, leaping over a metal gate, and heading back towards us on the field side of the hedge.

The Kingsmen follow and after a short time they are out of view. I keep watching the path until they come into sight again, having turned to start moving back towards the house. I duck out of view, watching their dark helmets bob behind the row of greenery. The others are tumbling out of the building behind me. Hart is apologising repeatedly but the only response I offer is to tell everyone to go back inside. Faith is my sole concern as I leave the building and race towards the path, pulling off my hat and pocketing it, grasping my knife in the other hand. As soon as the Kingsmen see my hair, they should switch to chasing me, which will keep the others safe and allow Faith to escape.

As I reach the road, there is a scraping sound and Faith emerges through a gap in the hedge. Her blonde hair is caked with mud and there is a smear of blood across her top lip. She is breathing heavily, using both hands to carry a pair of swords. I watch disbelievingly as she walks towards me, weighed down by the physical burden of the weapons, before she drops them at my feet, along with two knives that she unclips from her belt.

'What happened?' I ask.

She shrugs. 'I dealt with them.'

'Are you all right?' Jela asks from behind me. Although I wanted everyone else to stay hidden, no one has had a chance to return inside.

I look at the blades on the ground, expecting blood, but they are clean.

'Come,' Faith says with a nod of her head, turning and heading towards the hedge.

In the field, both Kingsmen have been caught in Faith's snares. Their legs are entwined with ropes and she has tied their hands behind their backs, stuffed one of their own gloves into each of their mouths, and wrapped more string around their faces to keep them there.

It would have been impressive for anyone to have taken down two fully armed Kingsmen in such a way, but for a girl half their size, it is astonishing.

I unclip each of their thinkwatches as they stare at me in disbelief, now aware of how close they were to claiming the bounty. The metal is a greyish-black, perhaps borodron but it is hard to know for sure.

'What are we going to do with them?' Jela asks.

'Just kill them,' Faith says dismissively.

The lack of emotion in her voice breaks my heart as I remember the girl hugging her mother yesterday. She is staring at the ground, refusing to look at anyone, least of all the two people she wants dead. Imrin and Hart are carrying the men's swords and look at each other awkwardly, wondering if they are the ones who should do the deed. The Kingsmen themselves are unmoving. They know this will be the fate that awaits them in any case, should anyone find out they had been so close to me and let me get away.

'We'll vote,' I say, not wanting to make the decision.

'Who's with Faith?' My anger from a few minutes ago seems so misplaced that I cannot bring myself to use the word *kill*.

Faith and Imrin put their hands in the air straight away, Jela following suit almost reluctantly, her arm bent at the elbow and barely reaching above her head.

'Who wants to keep them alive?'

We seem unable to look each other in the eye as, for a moment, I don't think anyone is going to vote. Hart, whose chin and hands are still a mottled mess of blood, slowly raises his arm and shakes his head. 'It will make us like them.'

'We're already like them,' Faith says harshly.

'Not yet. We've only killed when we've had to. They do it for fun.'

Pietra peers up from the floor until she is staring directly at me and then raises her arm high above her head. 'It's up to you,' she says.

I think of the Kingsman whose throat I slit; the way the blood dripped and his eyes bulged. I know that if I vote to kill them, I'm going to be the one who does it. I don't want two more people's deaths to be on anyone else's conscience but mine. Imrin is gripping the sword tightly, ready to do whatever I say, but Faith hasn't moved.

'I'm sorry, Faith,' I say. 'We'll tie them up but that's it.'

I want her to be angry with me, to call me names and

say that I'm soft and wrong. Instead, she shrugs uncaringly, pulling a knife from her boot and cutting the Kingsmen free from her traps. Hart and Imrin use the swords to direct them to the house we slept in. They are emotionless, doing what they're told and not trying to fight.

Inside, we strip their armour, cover them each in a blanket and let Faith tie them as securely as she sees fit. The biggest surprise is how small the men are. From the curves and shape of the armour, I would have expected them to be built like Opie: tall, with broad shoulders and a thick chest. Instead, the borodron armour is designed cleverly, giving the illusion the men are far more imposing than they actually are.

With the two Kingsmen secure, I remove the cord from around their faces and take the gloves from their mouths, nodding towards Imrin and Hart, who are nearby with the swords. 'Regardless of how we voted, if either of you try to escape or create any noise, then we won't hesitate a second time.'

Neither of them acknowledges me but I take a container of water out of my bag and they accept the drink.

'Who's Rom?' I ask.

No reply.

'How many more Kingsmen are there around this area?' The one with the higher-pitched voice, who revelled so blissfully in telling the story of the crackdown, has not taken his eyes from me.

'You're wasting your time,' he says firmly. 'If you're not going to kill us, then what else are you going to do? We both know you haven't got the guts to torture us until we talk.'

He's right and the mocking tone of his voice slices through me.

The Kingsman's eyes flicker towards Faith: 'She'd do it. Why don't you ask her?'

I reach forward and grab his chin, twisting it until he is facing me again. 'Don't look at her.'

His lips curl upwards slightly in a sneer of defiance. 'Whatever you say, *Silver Blackthorn*.'

Somehow he makes my name sound like an insult.

'Who's Rom?' I ask again.

'No idea.'

'How many more Kingsmen are there here?'

'Lots – more than there are of you.'

'How do I get into the towers?'

I'm not sure what I expected but the laughter takes me by surprise. 'You want to get *into* the towers?'

'Yes.'

He shakes his head. 'They've been saying you're crazy and out of control but I didn't expect them to be right.

Do you know what they're going to do to you when they catch you?'

'How do I get in?'

'They won't kill you, not at first; they'll start with your friends. They'll make you watch as they hurt them. You'll see them bleed, hear them scream.'

Spittle flies from his mouth viciously, his eyes glinting in relish.

'How do I get in?'

'Then they'll find your family. They'll burn them alive right in front of you and pin your eyes open so you can't stop watching.'

I want to stop him speaking but my arms feel limp and useless.

'After all of that, they'll start on you. They'll strip the skin from your hands and feet but they've got enough doctors to stop you bleeding to death. They'll do it slowly and they'll broadcast it to let everyone know what happens when you go against the King. They'll . . .'

Before he can say any more, Hart steps forward and cuffs him fiercely across the face. Once, twice, three times he hits him until the Kingsman slumps to the side, blood dripping from his nose and lip, a cruel grin still etched on his face.

'You'll see,' he taunts, before Hart stuffs the glove back into his mouth.

The other Kingsman has not spoken, but Faith secures both of their gags. I am fixed to the spot until I feel Imrin's hand on my back, guiding me to the far side of the room.

'It's all right,' he coos, but I can't think of anything other than the images of those I care about being killed in the way the Kingsman described. I refuse to look backwards, even though I can feel his eyes burning through me.

'What's the plan?' Jela asks quietly as the six of us huddle together.

I realise she is looking at me, expecting I have something in mind.

'We have their uniforms,' Imrin points out. 'They're not that much bigger than we are, so let's wait until the sun starts to come up, then Silver and I can head towards the centre. If we stay away from larger groups of people or Kingsmen, no one should pay us much attention.'

'I want to go.' The voice takes us by surprise and everyone turns to face Hart. 'I can do it,' he insists.

Faith would be too short, with the other girls the wrong shape. Aside from Imrin and myself, Hart would be the only one who could comfortably get into the uniform.

'You're not well,' I start to say, but he interrupts.

'I'm tired of being left behind. I'm fine – look at me.'

Unfortunately, his suggestion is exactly what rules him out. Although he has washed his face and hands, there are still spots of blood around his shirt and I can tell from the tickle in his voice that another cough could erupt at any moment.

'You should stay here and guard them,' I say. 'You're the strongest of us all and it's important someone keeps an eye on them.'

He is not fooled by my clumsy attempt to placate him and knows he's not coming with me because I don't want him to.

'Imrin and I will head towards the towers in the Kingsmen uniforms,' I say, even though it was his idea. 'We'll try to stay away from trouble and if there's anything that doesn't feel right, we can return here and have a rethink.' I nod backwards towards the guards. 'Two of you need to stay here at all times. Give them water every couple of hours but only when Faith is here to retie their mouths. All right?'

I look towards Faith, who nods gently, although I'm not sure she is listening.

'We're short on food but if it's quiet, there are squirrels and rats around,' I add. 'We'll be as quick as we can.'

I am trying to think if I have missed anything and it is Jela who states the obvious. 'What do we do if they try to escape?'

'I'll deal with it,' Hart says firmly, clutching one of their swords.

This time there are no objections.

I take off my thinkwatch and give it to Pietra, then slide one of the Kingsmen's onto my wrist. If we get caught, I want to make sure the others still have the maps to help them get away. Although the Kingsman's is made of a harder material, the screen seems identical to my own, though without the orange colour. I flick through to find routes and instructions and then try to see if there is any other information that could be useful. The search function throws up nothing about 'Rom' and there are no other codes, passwords or anything I think we could use.

Although I have held borodron before, the weightlessness of the armour is amazing. The sleek curves and the way the light almost bends around it makes it look as if it should be heavy but I am able to pick up the upper part one-handed with no effort. The inside of the armour feels as if it has been individually shaped to fit the person to whom it belongs and although it is tight around my chest, the body fits well. Pietra helps to secure me into the armour as Faith replaces the Kingsmen's gags with thicker twine so we can use the gloves. The boots are a couple of sizes too big but, aside from that, I am able to move easily.

The biggest problem is the helmet. Without it, we may as well not be wearing a disguise, but it is completely the wrong shape. It isn't that it is too big or small, just that each one has been moulded to the circumference of the guards' heads. Imrin's is a little snug and the remaining one pinches the top of my scalp but is loose around my chin. If I turn too quickly, it feels as if it is going to slide forwards, but when I tilt it backwards it exposes too much of my face.

After the drama of the last few days, I find myself laughing when Pietra suggests I should wrap a sock around my head to make it fit. I even try it, just to make the others laugh and suddenly some of the stress seems to lift, even if it is only for a moment.

It is a much tighter squeeze to get out of the makeshift entrance to the house with the uniform on and although I can just about walk in the boots, I realise how hard it is to do anything other than move in a straight line. I hold the helmet onto my head and then gaze up to see Imrin looking entirely different decked out in the uniform. If it wasn't for the colour of his skin, I wouldn't know it was him under the helmet. The early morning sunlight slides around him elegantly as he smiles.

'You look ridiculous,' he says.

I can't help but laugh. 'Thanks a lot.' The humour quickly fades as we stare at each other. The way he holds himself makes him look like a natural in the uniform. 'Do you think we can do this?' I ask seriously.

'I know you can.'

RENEGADE

Hart slides the sword into the sheath on my belt and then, with a thud of boot on concrete that doesn't feel as if it should be coming from me, we begin the walk towards Middle England.

12

As we near the towers, the number of people on the streets increases dramatically. At first there is a handful scurrying across the pathways from small shacks on the edge of the city, but when we enter the shadows of the towering steeples, the streets become a hub of activity.

I didn't expect the central area to be like Martindale but things are so different we may as well be on another planet. At home, we dress for the seasons – thick rugged materials to shield us from the winter cold; lighter, shorter clothes for the summer. Here, all of the men seem to be wearing suits, crisp shirts and shiny shoes. Some of the women are wearing suits of their own but with skirts above their knees and heels I don't think I could even walk in, let alone hurry from place to place at the speed they are. There are hundreds, thousands, of people: an army in a rush to get somewhere.

No one pays any attention to Imrin or me as we move into the central plaza. Unlike at home, Kingsmen are a regular sight around Middle England. In between the four towers is a large paved area interrupted only by a railway line that connects the North Realm to the South, with bridges that let people cross from one side to the other. As we watch, a train stops in the middle, giving me an almost overwhelming feeling of déjà vu, as I remember our journey through here to Windsor Castle. Another crowd of suited men and women emerges from the carriages, joining the rest and pouring through the main doors of each of the four buildings until, almost in an instant, the steady but deafening clatter of footsteps is over.

With the sound of people gone, I notice a low but audible hum that seems to be coming from all around us. The scale of the area is almost beyond comprehension, the sun bouncing brightly around the four buildings in a light show that is as impressive as it is disorientating. At first I move to shield my eyes but then remember it is not something a Kingsman would do. I stare up, trying to figure out where the noise is coming from but the helmet slips backwards, landing on the ground with a clatter. Imrin has drifted away and turns back sharply, although he doesn't say anything as I pick the helmet up and put it back on my head.

The dazzling combination of the sun and the glass is hurting my eyes, so I close them for a few moments, trying to adjust, before opening them to examine the front of each building. There are rows of rotating doors and above them a digital clock, flashing red curved numbers. I cannot stop watching as they hypnotically tick away each second.

It is one minute past nine in the morning.

As I watch the numbers climb, they swirl into a message, 'WELCOME TO EAST TOWER', before giving the date and completing the cycle by fading back to the time.

'Silver?' At the sound of Imrin's voice, I realise I have been watching the messages for over a minute. 'That's the North Tower,' Imrin adds, turning to one side.

If it wasn't for the way the letters and numbers blended into one another telling us which tower was which, it would be almost impossible to distinguish one from the other.

Only a smattering of people now remain in the plaza, making us stand out far more than is probably advisable. There are no other Kingsmen around that we can see. Feeling self-conscious, we hurry over the bridge that crosses the train track until we are directly under the North Tower's clock. In the full shadow of the titanic glass behemoth that soars over us, I feel a chill ripple through me; a sudden sense that I am a small, utterly insignificant sixteen-year-old.

'Silver?'

Imrin brings me back to the present again. He is pointing at a small box next to the tower's doors identical to the ones that operate the doors at Windsor Castle. There, we swiped a strip of borodron to make the doors open.

Now I press the stolen thinkwatch to the pad and am relieved as the door begins to rotate with a steady buzz.

Inside, the air is crisp and cool, breezing across my face artificially, even though we are surrounded by glass. The floor is a hard bright white marble, stretching into the distance as each step we take echoes ominously, announcing our location.

We know we have to look confident and authoritative, so I stride purposefully across the ground-floor concourse of the North Tower. On the far side, there are a few men and women in suits sitting behind a desk, with another clock etched into the glass above them, ticking away. Despite the hundreds of people we saw pouring into the building minutes ago, there are barely a dozen on this floor.

Lining the wall on the other side of the concourse is a row of stalls, with a small group of men in brighter clothes standing close by talking to each other. It reminds me of the market we have once a month in Martindale, where traders come to the village to sell their products and villagers gather to barter. When I was younger, my mother would sell clothing she had made to try to get us a little more food. I once made a bracelet out of dried grass which she took for me, saying she would do her best to sell it. She gave me extra food in the evening, saying it had been sold instantly to one of the traders who thought it was 'beautiful'. A few years later, I found it in a drawer, pressed carefully between the pages of an old book I didn't know she had. She had kept it herself and given me her own rations.

Although it seems like a market, the products are completely different to anything that would reach Martindale. One of the signs says 'Stay young, trust the green pill'; another stall has rows of creams and powders promising everything from smoother skin to the ability to stay awake for up to a week.

Despite the noise of our boots, no one is paying attention to us.

As we head in the direction of the desk, I spot a digital board made of glass on the wall next to a row of lifts. Imrin follows me and as we cross the floor, one of the lift doors fizzes open and a stream of people pours out, heading in unison towards the main entrance.

In Martindale, we are used to the power flickering on and off and have become accustomed to nights without warmth but there seems to be unlimited electricity here. I now realise the hum I could hear outside is from the power swarming around us. Inside there are bright overhead lights, conditioned air, doors and lifts that are all using energy. All of this could keep our villages warm for months.

After the group of people has passed, I turn my attention back to the board. As with the clocks, information is displayed within the glass itself, images and words fading into view. The first screen shows a map of the country before zooming in to show the North and then it fades to yellow. '76% RATION EFFICIENCY' slides across the screen, before being replaced by the words: 'DAILY TRADES: 41'. The total is climbing one number at a time, as the ration figure moves up to 77%.

I'm not sure what everything means but the essence is clear – that the people packed into the floors above us are busy controlling the lives of everyone dotted around the Realm.

I remember the weeks when the ration train would arrive with less food than we expected, Kingsmen standing imposingly around the carriages, daring anyone to complain.

Is this why?

Can it really be true that huge numbers of people are going hungry because of the way relatively small numbers of people conduct business in this building?

As the statistics fade, they are replaced by names and positions. At the top is 'FLOOR 90: CHIEF MINISTER PELL', with a photo of a grey-haired man staring wistfully into the distance.

The list skips floor 89 and goes straight to 88, which belongs to Deputy Minister Reith. He has a similarly posed picture, facing purposefully out of frame. He is younger than Chief Minister Pell but wearing the same borodron uniform that we are and has a purple scar that curves around his mouth.

After four more ministers are named, their apparent ages matching their diminishing ranks, the rest of the building's departments take over the screen and begin scrolling upwards. I look for anything that could indicate where Rom might be, but the closest thing I spot is 'ROYAL OPINION COMPLIANCE' on floor 30. Of all the places listed, this is perhaps the worst place to start.

Even if we did have the time to try all ninety floors, there is no way large numbers of people are going to be deceived by our disguises for anything other than a cursory glance, and I turn to Imrin to see if he has any inspiration.

He seems blank and my eyes are drawn to the screen above the entrance, inadvertently gasping at the enormous picture of my face stretching across it.

Above my image are the words 'WANTED' and 'DANGER' in gigantic letters and underneath is my name: 'SILVER BLACKTHORN'. I step to the side and see that the other buildings all have the same photograph. It is the one from the security camera outside Kingsman Porter's office but it seems as if they have done something to the picture. The silver parts of my hair are brighter and more defined but my skin is paler, my eyes almost red. They are trying to turn me into some sort of demon, wild and out of control. Not to be approached, not to be trusted.

I pull the helmet down further until the brim is completely covering my eyebrows. It stops me being able to look up properly, hiding the image from view, but in doing so I end up loosening it around my ears.

Another lift opens, allowing an additional sprawl of people to cascade towards the doors, a few of them glancing towards us as they hurry away. We have been standing still for too long.

'Where are we going?' Imrin whispers.

'Have you seen anything that could point us to Rom?'

'We could ask.'

'Ask who?' I realise I have raised my voice too loud, as the syllable echoes around the concourse.

'Look at us,' Imrin says. 'Do you think all those people in suits are going to ignore a direct question from a Kingsman?'

He has a point, although I tell him he should do the talking. Neither of us has ever seen a female Kingsman and although the uniform gives me a degree of anonymity, it is not worth pushing our luck.

I struggle to keep up as Imrin strides towards the stallholders, who are grouped in a gap between two of the central market stands. They are talking quietly to each other but as Imrin nears, one of them nods towards him and everyone stops. I stay a little behind just in case.

'Where's Rom?' Imrin asks. He has completely changed

his voice, putting on a firm, harsh tone that almost convinces me that he *is* a Kingsman.

At first nobody replies, the men looking at each other in confusion.

The one in the middle replies: 'Who?'

'We're here for Rom. Where is he?'

The men are looking nervous; the one who spoke is shifting his weight awkwardly, his eyes darting from side to side.

'None of us are called Rom.'

Imrin leans in, one hand on his sword. 'Don't play games. You guys are here every day – you know where all the departments are and probably most of the people too. Now tell us: where's Rom?'

He is controlled yet fierce at the same time, the force of his demand sending a shiver down my spine. I have never seen or heard him act like this but he is playing the role perfectly.

The men exchange looks again, muttering questions and speculating as to whether Rom could be a nickname for someone they know.

It is clear they don't have a clue but Imrin still warns them that they had better not be lying before marching away. 'If any of them knew, they would have told us,' he whispers as we walk side by side.

'We could start on the communications floor,' I suggest. 'It was on the list of departments and Knave is having a problem with communications. There could be something there?'

With no other plan, we head to the lifts, pressing the Kingsmen's thinkwatches to the sensor and stepping inside. I have never been in an elevator before but Imrin takes control, typing '43' for the communications department into a keypad on the wall and then winking at me.

Nothing happens for a second or two and then, in an instant, it feels as if we have been thrown into the air. My knees wobble at the sensation of zooming upwards and there is pressure around my temples as my vision becomes fuzzy. After a couple of seconds, the doors fizz open but my first few steps are more of a stagger as I try to get used to being on steady ground again.

'Come on,' Imrin whispers unhelpfully, stepping outside.

I try not to stumble as I pass three suited workers waiting to enter the lift. Their eyes are on me but I edge out of their way until Imrin grips me by the arm, pulling me towards the wall.

'Are you all right?'

'Just dizzy. I've never been in a lift before.'

'Me neither.'

As I begin to get my bearings, I see that we are in a white corridor that stretches as far as I can see in both directions. At regular intervals, there are either more corridors branching off on each side, or grey metallic doors.

Both ways look the same, so I start walking in the direction I am facing, feeling stronger with each step.

'When was the last time you ate?' Imrin whispers.

I ignore him, stopping to look at the first door. There is no handle but a small grey scanner fixed to the wall. The name 'Ulises Noon' is printed in the centre of the metal, in the same way the writing on the screens downstairs blends into the glass.

As we walk around the floor, I expect to be interrupted at any moment but there doesn't seem to be anyone around. There are hundreds of doors, all sporting different names, but we can't see anything that gives us a clue where Rom is. As we reach the far end, there is a corridor that encircles the edge of the floor. I stop to stare out over the plaza. My image has disappeared from the front of the buildings, replaced by the time and, for a moment at least, I forget where I am. Through the gap between the towers, I can see a mix of houses beyond the plaza and then miles and miles of green beyond that.

'Amazing, isn't it?' Imrin says.

'We can't stay here for much longer.'

'Did Knave tell you anything else about Rom?'

'Just that they thought he or she was in the North Tower. They didn't even know if Rom was a man or a woman. I don't know why I thought I'd be able to find them.'

Below us, there is a small group of people rushing from the North Tower in a straight line across the central plaza towards the South Tower. They are like ants, tiny dark dots against a bright white background.

'I think I've taken on too much,' I say. Hearing the words out loud makes it more real. It is something I have been thinking for a little while, ever since Vez held a knife to my throat. Perhaps before that.

There is a new-found enthusiasm to Imrin's reply: 'We can go and do everything we spoke about when we were at the castle. Think of all the houses we've already seen abandoned – there are all sorts of places we can live for years uninterrupted.'

'What about the others?'

'It's up to them. They can do their own thing or they could come with us. We've already shown we can get by without official rations. We can live freely.'

In the distance, the endless fields seem so welcoming; the bright winter sun makes them glow a wondrous shade of green. There could be much worse places to wake up but my mother and Colt flit into my mind. Throughout our escape and what we have gone through since, I have always had it in the back of my head that I would get back to them some day.

'We're getting nowhere,' I say, ignoring his suggestion. 'We'll head downstairs and check the department listings one last time. If we're at a complete loss, we can always head back to Knave and see if he has any other plans.'

Imrin doesn't reply but I can sense his disappointment.

We return to the lifts via the same route, passing a few larger rooms that are unmarked. For all I know, there could be a simple switch on the inside of any of them that could solve all the communication problems. As we reach the lifts, I see a glass information panel on the wall like the one on the ground floor. I don't remember it being there before but because of my earlier dizziness and eagerness to get away from the people waiting to get into the lift, it is no surprise.

It lists every person working on the floor and as I press the name 'Ruth May', directions appear, pointing us towards her office. Somehow we walked straight past it.

'What do you think?' I ask. 'Ruth something-beginning-with-O May? Rom?'

Before Imrin can reply, the lift doors hum open. A face I recognise steps out of the lift, the purple scar brighter in real life than in the photo I saw on the ground floor. Deputy Minister Reith glances both ways before settling on us. He is flanked by two Kingsmen who are standing to attention.

He takes a step forward and I think he is going to continue walking past us but then, in a snipped, efficient voice, he tells us to follow him.

13

Deputy Minister Reith spins on the spot and heads back into the lift, trailed by the other two Kingsmen. Imrin and I have no choice but to follow, the elevator door swishing shut behind us.

Although there is plenty of room for the five of us, my head aches as the lift glides upwards. There is the rushing feeling I had from before but I also have an almost over-whelming sense of being cramped. I try to focus on the space between us but that only makes it worse. Imrin is right that I haven't been eating enough but it feels like more than that, as if someone is squeezing my head.

Reith is facing away from me, the other two Kingsmen sandwiched in between us. Imrin is next to me but staring fixedly ahead and standing rigidly straight. My knees wobble and I almost reach forward to steady myself. Imrin glances sideways but doesn't move.

Just as I feel I cannot take the pressure any longer, the door slides open. I want a second or two to compose myself but don't get it as Reith bounds forward with the Kings-men in single file behind him. Imrin follows and I somehow force my legs to move. If any of the others were to glance backwards, they would surely see my uncertainty but they remain in line as the Deputy Minister marches away.

Floor 88 is a complete contrast to the communications level. Instead of long white corridors, there is an enormous open space. With no walls to impede the view through the window, we can see through a gap in the towers towards a horizon that is so far away it may as well be the edge of the earth. The small areas of houses I could see are now specks, the green of the fields interrupted constantly by grey flattened areas of destruction. Although my head is clearing, the view is so stunning that I have to remind myself to walk, skipping a few steps until I am behind Imrin.

Aside from the view, it is striking how empty the floor is. We are heading towards a wide desk that has a bank of screens and a clock integrated into the window behind it. We have been in the building for over an hour.

The first Kingsman stops as Reith walks around the desk and sits in a huge throne-like chair on the other side. On the table in front of him are six thinkpads and a few black and grey metal boxes. The monitors behind him are showing live images from cameras surrounding the plaza.

'Leave us,' he says crisply.

I am confused at what he means but the Kingsman in front spins and begins marching towards the lift from which we just came. The second follows and, as Imrin half-turns, Reith speaks again. 'Not you.'

Imrin meets my eyes but I don't know what to do. We are almost at the top of a skyscraper with one lift to get us in and out.

The other Kingsmen stride away, their heavy footsteps echoing rhythmically around the sparse room until they reach the lift. They step inside and the door slides shut behind them.

I turn to face the Deputy Minister but he is already staring at me, gaze darting up and down my uniform before settling on my face.

'Sit,' he says.

Imrin moves first, pressing into the hard metal chair in front of us. I follow his lead, feeling the pressure of the Minister's stare burdening me. The borodron slides against the hard seat and I do all I can not to look back up. I know he is still watching as an uncomfortable silence develops.

'Take your helmets off.'

I feel that familiar sinking sensation in my stomach. He must know who I am as there is no other reason he would ask. Imrin doesn't move but there is little point in resisting.

As I remove the helmet, there is a popping sensation in my ears and the dizziness takes hold again. I feel freer without it but there is now no hiding who I am. With the helmet on my lap, I defiantly pull my hair back, before flicking the silver strand forward, allowing it to fall across my face. There are stars in my eyes but I blink them away before finally meeting Reith's gaze.

'Ms Blackthorn, I believe.'

'Surely you don't need the reward rations?'

He smiles thinly. 'One can never have too many rations.'

I struggle to focus on his face, still blinking, this time in annoyance.

'I take it this is your first visit to Middle England,' he adds.

'Obviously.'

'You shouldn't worry about your eyes and your head. Most people get that the first time they use the lifts. It is a type of motion sickness. My people downstairs tell me it isn't uncommon.' I wonder why he is telling me this but then the tone of his voice changes. 'Oh . . .'

I cannot focus on him but then Imrin cuts in, stretching an arm across to me. 'You're bleeding.'

I raise my hand to my face, forgetting I am wearing gloves but then I feel a dribble of blood slide across my top lip and drip into my lap.

Surprisingly, it is Reith who reacts. He presses a button on the desk and a drawer slides out underneath him. He reaches in and passes me across a patch of cloth.

'Keep it,' he says.

My head feels so muddled that I take it and press the

material to my nose. It smells musky and masculine and when I pull it away, there is a wide red spot of blood.

'You're not the first,' he says. 'It's the vertigo from being this high as well. It's an amazing view but it takes some getting used to.'

'Who are you?' Imrin asks, removing his hand from my shoulder.

I see the shape of Reith's head shake. 'No matter. First, tell me about Windsor. We heard there was a commotion but real information is impossible to come by – even through *alternative* channels.'

Imrin starts to stumble over a reply but I close my eyes and take over. 'We escaped,' I say. 'We would have died there.'

Reith hums but it is hard to tell if it is in approval or surprise. 'Yes, Victor . . .' he says knowingly. 'It sounds as if he is getting more and more erratic. I suppose Bathix does not help either.'

Bathix is the name of the Minister Prime, the King's right-hand man. It is no particular surprise that Reith knows this, although he is the first person I have heard use his first name instead of the title.

Gradually I open my eyes, finding that the haze has cleared. Now I can see him clearly, Reith is tracing a finger along his scar, deep in thought.

'How did you know it was us?' I ask.

My question jolts him slightly, as if he had forgotten we were there.

'Oh, right, yes.' He spins in his chair, widening his arms to show the bank of screens. 'It is my job to monitor security in the building. We get Kingsmen in and out all the time but not many of them spend time walking around the communications floor.'

He presses a button on one of the monitors and the screen changes to show footage of Imrin and me doing just that, eyeing the name plaques on the doors. The camera zooms in at a point where I raise the helmet slightly to scratch my head, revealing a small flash of silver hair.

'Not clever,' Reith concludes, his hands flashing across the control panel. The images disappear, leaving a blank screen. 'It's standard that nothing from the past two hours is allowed to be deleted in our system,' he adds. 'It's for security reasons – but I'm the only person who has seen this. After two hours, anyone can manually remove footage, so I'll delete it later. Now, why would you come here?'

I have so many questions but, as the clock above him swirls and fades into his name, at least one of them is answered. 'You're Rom?' I say. His eyes narrow, focusing sharply on me. 'Reith Owen Moore,' I add, nodding to the letters in the glass behind him.

'How do you know that name?'

I almost tell him about Knave but then remember him

saying how none of them know each other's names. 'We found a resistance movement not far from Windsor,' I say. 'They said their communications had been down and that their contact was someone named Rom in the North Tower.'

Reith drums his fingers on the desk, peering from Imrin to me. 'What were their names?'

I shake my head. 'No names.'

He nods. 'Right answer. What did they tell you about me?'

'Not much – they said you helped the resistance groups communicate with each other. I got the feeling they thought you were in charge.'

Reith bursts out laughing unexpectedly. 'I can assure you I'm not.'

'I never said you were.'

He nods again. 'Lots happened after the war. King Victor took the crown and everyone was happy to rally around him. Within a year or so, Middle England had been built. It was intended to serve as a central location from where we could organise the rest of the country. The aim was to ensure that every individual got what they needed.'

'With rations?'

'I suppose. I wasn't in this job then, of course, but there was a different spirit. At the time we didn't think we would need rations. We hoped there would be more than enough for everyone.'

'What happened?'

Reith squirms in his seat and turns away from me, staring over my shoulder towards the lift. I spin to see if there is anyone there but the floor is clear. 'Let's just say some people are more equal than others.'

I don't know exactly what he means but it is obvious from the food I have seen heading into the castle – and the amount of electricity it takes to run the towers of Middle England – that we are not all treated the same.

'Who are you?'

The Deputy Minister focuses on me again, waiting until I meet his eyes. 'Just someone who thinks there has to be a better way. If I had been a year older, I would have been fighting in the war. Instead, it ended just before I was called up. My brother was eighteen months older than me and never came back. At first, I thought he had at least died for something but after a year or two, it became obvious things hadn't really improved. I somehow stumbled into working here and over the years I moved up.' He stretches his arms out to indicate the floor we are on. 'Literally, I suppose.'

'But you're part of the resistance?'

He breathes out heavily. 'There *is* no resistance, not really. Just small groups talking to each other without anything ever happening.'

'Isn't that better than nothing?'

He rubs his eyes wearily. 'I know it seems that I'm up here above everyone else and that I've got it easy. I suppose I can't deny that – I've got food, my wife and children are looked after but you . . .'

I'm not sure what he means and suddenly feel self-conscious, pushing my loose hair behind my ear.

'When we heard something had happened at the castle, it brought my brother's sacrifice back to me. I suppose I thought something might actually be changing.' He opens his arms to indicate the room. 'None of this really matters to me but I've always told myself it is easier to work from within to make a difference than it is to alter things from outside. After your *incident*, it was a day until we heard any more news. All anyone was talking about here was whether the King had been killed and who the girl with the strange hair was . . .'

'Thanks.'

He smiles. 'I didn't mean it like that. Anyway, Victor was on the screen again, still alive, and since then – aside from the fact your face is everywhere – it is as if none of it happened.'

There it is again, the same sense I felt from Knave and Vez – plus the two Kingsmen outside our hideout: change. Somehow, accidentally, the King and Minister Prime have set me up as a figurehead. Anyone who is hungry, anyone who has been abused by the Kingsmen, the mistreated Trogs and so many others are now somehow seeing me as more than just the girl I am.

It is terrifying.

'How did you come to work with the rebel groups?' Imrin asks.

He looks away from me and I can tell he feels embarrassed. 'I've worked in security most of my time here. This is the easy bit, with a few monitors to watch. I used to work in enforcement which is more . . . hands on.'

I get the implication: he was more of a traditional Kingsman than he is now.

'There was a bit of a disturbance on the edge of the city,' he continues. 'Some of my men and I went in to investigate and it was a group of male citizens. They were angry because rations were short that week. One of their wives had just had a child and he said he needed more for her.'

'What did you do?'

He pauses, breathing deeply through his nose. 'Rebellion is not tolerated.'

I want to push him, feeling the hairs prickling on the back of my neck but the way his voice tails away makes it clear this isn't something of which he is proud.

'My men weren't known for being particularly gentle,' he adds. 'There are cells under the ground floor of this tower and the Kingsmen were bringing the prisoners back.

I stayed on the fringes of the city to oversee things but we made a mistake by underestimating them. The disturbance wasn't what we thought – they wanted to draw us out. As soon as I was alone, four men came out of nowhere. Each of them had knives and I didn't even have time to get my sword out of my belt before one of them had a blade up against my throat.'

He breathes out heavily and scratches underneath his chin, remembering. 'I thought I was dead. It's not as if I could have blamed them, not after what my men had just done. They took me out to a building in the middle of nowhere and all I could think was that no one would ever find me.'

'How did you get away?'

'They let me go the next morning. They didn't even touch me. The man in charge said he wanted to show me that he was better than I was and then he sent me on my way.'

I feel another chill as the image of the two Kingsmen we captured drifts through my mind.

'When I came here the next day, we were going to release the prisoners anyway – sometimes that's the best message to send because they have stories to tell about what happens if you get caught. I don't know what came over me but, for some reason, I told one of them he should return if he ever needed anything and to tell his boss that he was right. Nothing happened for ages, maybe a year or so, and then I got this job. There was a big deal about it on the news, so I suppose one of them saw it. The next day, the man who let me go was waiting outside the doors of the North Tower. He told me his address and I went to see him that night. He asked if I knew about any cells of resistance around the country. I didn't but I managed to set up a secure channel for him to communicate on. The rest has grown from there.'

'But the communications aren't working any longer?'

He shakes his head. 'I'm not sure what happened. It was easier a few years ago and technology has begun to get away from me. The higher you get, the less you have to do. The authorities did some sort of software upgrade to our thinkwatches around a month ago and whatever they did took the system I'd set up offline. The problem is that, because it isn't working, I've not been able to tell anyone what the issue is. I thought someone might come looking for me – but I didn't think it would be you.'

It seems clear that 'Rom' isn't the person Knave and Vez thought he was. They set him up as some sort of leader but all he does is allow groups to talk to each other. He doesn't even understand the technology.

'I might be able to fix it,' I say.

Reith tilts his head and looks at me quizzically but doesn't query what I have said. He stands and leads us towards the lift. I assume he is going to take us to a different floor but instead he crouches, wedging his fingers into a thin gap between the door and the frame. With a hiss, the door slides open revealing a space that is dark and empty except for some thick cables hanging vertically.

'If you get vertigo, this is not the place to be,' he says with a thin smile before lying flat on his front and reaching down into the shaft. He scrabbles around for a few seconds before pulling himself up with a grunt. In his hand is a grey metal box, which he hands to me.

I am expecting it to be heavy but the container must be made of borodron or something similar as it weighs next to nothing. Inside, there is a mishmash of wires, sensors and various parts that are very similar to the bits and pieces I am used to tinkering with at the back of my thinkwatch and inside various thinkpads, not to mention the time I spent working with Head Kingsman Porter in Windsor.

'Did you make this?' I ask.

Reith shakes his head. 'It came from the man I told you about. He said it needed to be somewhere in the tower for it to work. I looked inside, obviously, but the technology comes from before the war and doesn't mean much to me.'

'What's in the lift shaft?'

Reith looks behind him. 'All of the cables – power, communications – run the full height of the various lift shafts. We have antennas on top of the building and huge generators underneath. There is only one lift that will get you up to this height, so that's why this particular shaft has everything packed into it. When I first moved up here, there were all sorts of technical issues and one time the doors of the lift popped open on their own. There are little cubby holes in there and when the man who spared my life told me the box needed to be somewhere close to the communication cables, I figured this would be as good a place as any to conceal it.'

I return to his desk, pulling the various pieces out of the grey box and placing them in front of me. 'I'll need your thinkwatch,' I say.

He sits behind his desk and looks to Imrin, as if wanting reassurance that I know what I'm doing. When Imrin nods gently, he unclips it from his wrist and hands it over.

The box has a keypad on the front and a sliding button on the side. I check a few obvious things and then begin to dig properly into the underside of the box. Within a couple of minutes, I know what the problem is.

'It's to do with frequencies,' I say. 'Let's say this building is number one. All communications go in and out of here by using that number. Your thinkwatch is also set to number one, allowing you to get in. For whatever reason, when the authorities upgraded the software, they put you onto number five – except this box is still trying to connect to number one. All I need to do is get the new code for number five from your watch and it will start working again.'

I only know this because I encountered a similar issue when I was working with Head Kingsman Porter at Windsor. He tutted but then showed me what the problem was. Much of the technology used throughout the Kingdom seems to be very similar, an odd mishmash of bits and pieces from before the war combined with brand-new inventions. It's a wonder anything works.

Reith sounds unconvinced. 'It's that simple?'

I can't help but laugh. 'No – I made it sound that easy just for you.'

It is simpler to work on the box without the Kingsman gloves, although Reith gasps when I use the tip of my knife to pop off the back of his watch. It is a huge crime to tamper with a thinkwatch.

'Is there anyone trying to organise the rebel groups?' I ask, not looking up, continuing to work.

Reith lowers his voice, even though it is still just us. 'Not as such but a lot of the chatter comes from further north.'

I catch his eye but he is nervous all of a sudden. 'Where from?'

He doesn't look like he wants to answer but glances towards the parts of his watch which are in my hand. I would never do anything to deliberately make his life more difficult but the thought clearly goes through his mind as he anxiously licks his lips.

'I really don't know. I can . . .'

Before he finishes his sentence, the bank of screens behind him all change until they are showing a fluttering St George's cross flag. The national anthem signals the beginning of a royal announcement. They happen intermittently through the year – the last one I saw was on the night of the Offering lottery.

'What's going on?' I ask.

Reith shakes his head. 'I'm not sure. We usually get a preview of any announcements but not this one.'

It is hard not to shudder as the flag fades, revealing King Victor sitting on his throne. His ginger hair and beard is tidy and his clothes have been recently pressed. He looks like a King should. Next to him is Minister Prime Bathix, dressed entirely in black and eyeballing the camera, as if he can see everyone watching and he is daring them to say or do anything untoward.

A voice tells us they are going to recap the events of the week and then the screen changes until there is an image of the King, coughing and choking. I was in the great hall when the effects of the tan fruit took hold on King Victor, but the memory of the event seems so different from what the camera angles are now showing on screen. Slow, sad music plays over the footage, before the picture switches to an image of me. Again, I appear different, paler and far more intense. I want to ask Imrin if that's how I really look but he is transfixed by the screen. The voice says that I am a traitor as they run through the images they have of me and then list the names of the people with whom I escaped.

The King rarely speaks, usually letting the Minister Prime do it for him, but as the camera shifts back to him, he licks his thin lips and begins to talk slowly. 'Our Offerings are chosen each year so this Kingdom can utilise their skills to best serve you. Because of the shocking nature of Silver Blackthorn's actions, this year we are left short of the talents this country needs to help us all thrive.'

The camera zooms out as he breaks into a wider smile, his voice joyous. 'As a result, this year – for the first time ever – there will be a second Offering.'

14

It feels as if every hair on my body is standing rigid. There is going to be a second Offering – thirty more teenagers sent to be tortured, killed and abused by our madman ruler.

I can barely take it all in but he hasn't finished. 'Because the previous Reckoning did not produce candidates of the required ability, I have changed the criteria for this Offering.'

I look sideways towards Imrin, whose eyes are wide with shock.

'There will be no additional Reckoning. Instead, everyone over the age of ten will be automatically entered, with eight names from each of the four Realms being chosen.'

It takes a few seconds to sink in. Colt started school at eight, like everyone else, and would have turned ten in the last few weeks – he is as eligible as anyone else. Has this all been done on purpose as a way of getting to me?

The only comfort I can find is that although two of Opie's brothers will be in the draw, his youngest, Imp, is still too young.

The King tells us that rewards for any family whose child is chosen will be doubled, before announcing that this year's second 'historic' Offering will take place in a week's time. The fluttering flag starts to fly again as the national anthem blares loudly and the King offers his best regal wave. The Minister Prime has not moved the entire time, fixed and frightening, before the screens flicker back to the images they were previously showing.

'My eldest son is eleven,' Reith says slowly. 'I thought it would be another five years . . .'

'It's to get to me,' I say firmly, returning my attention to the communications box on the table. 'My brother has just turned ten. They're going to make him as much a criminal as I am. If he is chosen and doesn't present himself – which he won't – the punishment is death.'

Neither Reith or Imrin tries to tell me I am wrong or paranoid as I work in silence. After a few more minutes, I clip the back of Reith's thinkwatch back on and return it. He glances at the underside, before sliding it around his wrist.

I slot the rest of the pieces back into the box and then push it across the table. 'That will work now,' I say.

'You fixed it just like that?'

I shrug: 'Just like that. Now what were you going to say you could do for me about the contact up north?'

Reith has either already forgotten telling me about the

'chatter' from the north, or he is trying to forget. He picks up the box and passes it from one hand to the other. 'I was going to say I could put you in contact if you get the box working again. I really don't know where he is and the only name he has is "X".'

'Do you know if it's definitely a he?'

'The voice is a man's.'

Reith puts the device back on the table and then takes a flat black box out of the drawer under his desk. 'What you just fixed lets everyone else talk to each other – but this is how I talk to them. It's supposed to be untraceable, so whatever I say can't be heard by anyone other than who I'm talking to. You'll have to check that it still works.'

I shake my head. 'I've already fixed it. If the frequency ever changes again, it will automatically send the new one to all the devices that were previously connected, including yours. It means the only way you can get cut off in future is if the box itself is destroyed – or the communication cable, I suppose. Any security that was built into it is still there. I had to do something similar when I was working at the castle.'

He shrugs, either not understanding or not caring about the details. I suppose all he needs to know is that it works. He slides a button on the side of the box and types in a code that will hook him up to the person he is trying to contact. After that, he presses the connect switch, a solid grey slider on the side.

'Where do you keep all the contact numbers?' I ask.

Reith taps the side of his head. 'It's the only safe place.'

The only thing that happens is that a flashing blue light appears above the keypad. The technology is older than I am and, despite what Reith believes, I suspect the biggest reason it is secure is because the machine is so dated that it doesn't hold any of the information needed to successfully trace whoever used it.

The clock above Reith's head ticks through an entire minute where nothing happens before the light on the box stops flashing.

A man's voice echoes hollowly out of the box. 'Who is this?'

'This is Rom calling for X.'

Neither of the men seem comfortable talking to each other but Reith quickly explains that there was an issue with the communications hub which has now been fixed.

'There is someone here who wants to talk to you,' he adds. 'She has been on the news a lot recently.'

Reith doesn't want to say my name but there is a satisfied-sounding hum of approval from the other end. The reply purrs through the speaker. 'Is it who I think it is?'

'Yes.'

'Can she hear me now?'

'Yes.'

I hear him clearing his throat. 'I've seen and heard so much about you.'

'It's not all true,' I reply.

X laughs theatrically. 'Oh, my dear, it never is. *Some* of it must be true though?'

'I suppose.'

'What is it you wanted?'

I realise that, although I had pushed for making contact with someone in the North, I actually have no idea what to ask. I came here to fix the communications for Knave and hadn't thought beyond that.

'I'm not sure . . .'

X laughs again. 'Well, you're only young, I suppose. Why don't we meet?'

'Where are you?'

'Quite a way away, I'm afraid. Do you have transport?'

'We can walk.'

'*We?* So there are more than just you?'

I grit my teeth in annoyance. Everyone knows that a dozen of us escaped but I shouldn't be revealing that I am not alone now. Even Reith seems surprised at my slip-up.

'*I* can walk,' I say, although it is a little late.

'Have you ever heard of Lancaster?'

I take a moment to think. 'Yes, but I don't know where it is.'

'How have you been finding your way around?'

The question could be perfectly innocent but, for some reason, it feels personal. Anyone in authority would assume my thinkwatch had been deactivated in the way the rest of our group's have. 'I stole a map on the way out of the castle,' I say. It isn't actually a lie – I just don't say what format it was in.

'And you are from Martindale, yes?'

That is more public knowledge but I don't like the fact that he knows this, or the way he says it.

'Yes.'

'Lancaster is south of Martindale. If you were on your way home, this wouldn't exactly be on your way – but it wouldn't be far off.'

True or not, I find myself prickling at the implication I should do what I'm told.

'Why should I visit you?'

'You contacted me, remember?'

I think of Imrin's suggestion downstairs – that we should hide somewhere and not look back. If that is what we are going to do then now is the time to stop all of this. I can walk out of the building knowing I have done what I told Knave I would. The rebels can take things from here, even if they are apparently disorganised at the moment. I know I should walk – I'm sixteen and there are groups of people hunting for me each night. I've escaped the King, taking my friends with me. I should be dead. Surely I've done enough?

'Are you still there?' X's voice reverberates awkwardly from the tinny-sounding speaker.

'I'm here.'

'So will you visit me?'

'You could come to me.'

He pauses, perhaps thinking it over. 'Are you sure it's best for you to be staying in one place?'

It wasn't a serious suggestion in any case, I was just curious as to what his reply would be.

'How do I know I'm not walking into a trap? No one can vouch for you because no one knows who you are.'

For a moment, I think the line has dropped. Eventually he asks the question I've been asking myself: 'What exactly is it you want?'

I remember my bravado with Knave but it has only ever been about one thing. Removing the King could make life better for a lot of people, or it could make things worse. I have no way of knowing but it's far more personal than that. It's about what he did to Jela and the way she isn't the type who would have been able to fight back on her own. It's about the girl I'll never meet who was killed because she looked a little like me and there is a bounty upon my head. Most importantly, it's about our very first night and the way the King killed Wray in front of me, as if he was an ant that needed stomping on. The way Wray stared at me as he realised what was about to happen and the terror and lack of understanding in his face.

'Revenge,' I say quietly. 'I want revenge.'

The admission feels wrong and yet it has taken until now for me to allow myself to understand the truth.

'Well, my dear,' the voice says. 'If it's revenge you want, let's just say I've got something you might want.'

'How will I find you?'

'Lancaster, my dear. If you're as smart as I think you are, you'll work it out.'

This time I don't hesitate. 'I'll see you soon.'

The light on the box begins to blink again but it takes a short while for Reith to react. I can feel Imrin staring at me but don't acknowledge him. Instead, I reach forward and turn the box off myself before standing.

'Let's go,' I say, feeling ashamed of myself. Have I really put my friends' lives in danger for revenge?

'Is there anything else I can do?' Reith asks, sounding slightly shocked.

'When you speak to the group near Windsor, tell them we're safe.'

'Okay.'

'I hope your son isn't picked as an Offering.'

'Thank you.'

I don't know what else to say, so I put the over-sized

gloves back on and try to make the helmet fit my head as best it can. It seems to be getting looser each time I take it off. Reith comes with us to the lift but we are halfway across the floor when the screens behind us spurt to life with a loud siren-like alert. The three of us turn at once but it barely takes a second to realise what is happening. On the screen is a picture of the four towers and my face with the word 'SPOTTED' in large letters across the top.

15

I stare at my own image on the screen; my cheekbones are jutting out of my thinning face and the flash of silver hair that has come to define me is on display for all to see. I struggle to place where this footage has come from and then remember my helmet bouncing onto the concrete plaza before we entered the North Tower. In the second or two between me staring up into the dizzying heights above and my helmet tumbling off, one of the security cameras captured a moving image.

They are playing the moment on a loop – me crouching, picking the helmet up, flicking my hair back, and then placing the helmet back onto my head. They know I'm disguised as a Kingsman.

'All citizens alert' scrolls along the top of the screen as a man's voice tells anyone watching that I have been seen in the plaza at Middle England.

I cross to the window but we are too high up to be able to see directly down, where I expect crowds of people to be swarming in case I am there.

'I don't monitor footage from outside the tower,' Reith

offers as an explanation. 'You've got to go. I'm head of security for the North Tower – I'll be missed if I'm not downstairs. That's if they're not already on their way here now.'

'We can't go in these uniforms,' I say, thinking I am stating the obvious but Reith shakes his head, indicating Imrin.

'You can't – he can. He wasn't on the footage.'

I try to remember the moment. Imrin had drifted away from me, getting his bearings. If the camera is automated, there is every chance he wasn't spotted.

'Do you have any spare clothes around here?'

Reith shakes his head. 'Only a Kingsman's uniform. There's a gym on floor nine. That's about the only place you'll be able to find women's clothes easily.'

'What's a gym?'

He stumbles over a reply. 'Somewhere you exercise.'

The concept seems strange to me but then I suppose that if people live somewhere like here, they wouldn't be able to run and climb through the woods in the way I do outside Martindale. I pace from side to side, trying to think. '*Go*,' I hiss towards Imrin. 'Get to the others and wait for me there.'

'I'm not going without you.'

I sigh and roll my eyes. 'Don't be stupid. Just go. You need to go back to the others. I can look after myself – *I* got us this far.' I am deliberately over-aggressive, knowing he won't react otherwise. He looks stung but it works and he heads for the lift with Reith.

As their feet echo across the floor, I have an idea and sprint after them. 'Everyone's got shiny shoes,' I say.

Reith swipes his thinkwatch at the lift. 'What?'

'You've all got shoes that look new – even you and you wear a Kingsman's uniform.'

'What about it?'

'You must have some polish around here.'

The lift slides into place and the doors hum open. 'There's some in the drawer under my desk.'

Without waiting for him, I sprint across the large open-plan room, sliding to a halt in front of the desk and pressing the button to make the drawer swish out. Inside there is another thinkpad and various bits and pieces I don't recognise. I pull the drawer out further until it is hanging loosely on its runners and then spy a small tub at the back.

After my father died, there was an almost identical pot which stayed on the windowsill over our sink for years. I don't even remember when it was finally thrown away, it was one of those things that became a part of the furniture and then one day I noticed it had gone.

Imrin waits by the lift as Reith hurries across the floor towards me, asking what I'm doing. I have already put the helmet on the table and scooped the dark goo onto my fingers. With one hand I pull my silver streak of hair forward, closing my fist around the sludge and running it the full length of my hair.

'Can you still see it?' I ask.

Reith is watching me, seeming both impressed and repelled at the same time. 'You missed a bit,' he replies, stepping closer and guiding my hand.

'How's that?'

'I wouldn't know it was you from a distance but you're still going to have to change your clothes.'

'I know.'

I smear what's left along the back of my hair until my hands are as clean as they're going to get. 'Did you delete the footage you had of us on the communications floor?'

'No, there's that two-hour window. It's to stop anyone tampering.'

'Where are the images kept?'

'The floor below here is archives.'

'That's not on the listing.'

Reith seems surprised by my knowledge, even though I only read it off the board downstairs, but he continues, 'We're not going to list such an important floor, are we?'

I slide the thinkwatch from my wrist and prise the back panel off, using a thin blade from Reith's desk. 'Will the floor be empty?' I ask.

'Yes, we're on a full evacuation. I shouldn't be here.'

'Are there cameras on this floor?'

'No.'

'Go then.'

'What about you?'

'I'll sort myself out . . . but when the moment comes, point and gawp like everyone else.'

'What at?'

'You'll see.'

He doesn't know how to reply, so again I tell him to go before clipping the back of my watch into place, grabbing the Kingsman's helmet, and following him to the elevator, where Imrin is still waiting.

'There are cameras in the lift,' Reith says nervously.

'We've been in there together already.'

'That was different – I was with four guards, no one's going to suspect that. By the time anyone gets around to thinking about checking that footage, two hours will be up and I will have deleted it.'

'I don't need to go with you now anyway.'

'Oh . . . right . . .' He sounds surprised, as if he expected me to argue.

As the lift doors slide open, Imrin and Reith step in and I move to one side. As soon as the lift doors slip shut, I crouch, wedging my fingers into the same spot Reith did when he was collecting the communication device. I have to stretch my fingers and use all of my strength but the doors spring open just as the lift compartment containing Reith moves slowly down and out of view, exposing the gaping space.

It is a leap of faith but I have no other option, jumping forward and landing heavily but safely on top of the lift compartment as it slides downwards. I know I have to be quick and as I pass the door directly below us, I leap sideways, clawing desperately at the row of holes in the wall. Gravity tugs me, willing me to plunge, until my fingers lock around a ridge. Small flecks of dust and earth slip through my fingers and, although my momentum sends me into the wall itself, I manage to hold on.

I take a few seconds to compose myself, breathing in and out slowly as I hear the thick lift cable sizzling with menace.

With my left foot, I can touch the door that leads onto floor 87 but it takes a few attempts to twist my body enough so that I can reach one of the gaps in the wall directly above where I need to be. A moment of panic jolts through me as I stretch across and, for a fraction of a second, there is only one hand supporting my weight. My shoulder stings as it bends in a direction it shouldn't but with an unplanned shriek of satisfaction, I arch my body down and drop, comfortably grabbing the ledge at the bottom of the door.

After another few seconds to compose myself, I press the small emergency button in the bottom corner of the doorframe, identical to the one on Reith's floor, and it slides open invitingly. It is only when I have fully pulled myself up and flop on the ground that I realise how exhausted I am. My fingers are stiff and every centimetre of my arms aches from supporting my body weight.

More deep breaths and then I force myself to stand. Floor 87 is a complete contrast to the one above it: dark and full of equipment. The constant hum of electricity that vibrates through Middle England is particularly loud here and I squash the helmet on my head in an effort to drown it out.

It doesn't take me long to find the central server where the security footage is kept and although there is a scanner next to it, I have used the frequency settings from Reith's thinkwatch to give myself the same level of clearance he has. The system is the same as the one from Windsor Castle and within seconds, I have found the footage from floor 43 with the correct day and time. I isolate a section where I was walking ahead of Imrin on my own and clear any parts in which he is visible. Reith is right: I cannot delete the entire footage but I am able to create a new file and save my edited version.

Finding the controls for the screen on the front of North Tower is simple enough and I also set up the screen above reception for good measure and set the timer for ten minutes. I can feel it: my plan is going to work.

I press the button for the elevator, waiting anxiously for it, before typing '9' into the keypad inside the door to head to the gym.

After the dizziness I had going up, I am braced for the same disorientation going down but all I can feel is my heart beating excitedly as the lift zips through the floors before sliding open to reveal another corridor. At the end I can see various pieces of strange equipment but rather than walk towards these, I head through the nearest door into a room lined with benches.

I check my watch to see I have a little over six minutes.

Over the tops of the benches are rows of locked cabinets. All are sealed shut but I use my knife to jab the nearest key holes aggressively until they pop open. In the third, my salvation is hanging neatly. I struggle with the catch at the back of the armour but the rest of it comes off easily. In under a minute, I am dressed the same as most of the other women – a clean white shirt, short dark skirt and black heels which feel far more alien than the boots that were too big for me. I tuck the knife into the back of the skirt, smooth my hair down and head back to the lift, pressing the button for the ground floor.

I emerge into the front hall with thirty seconds to spare. The reception desk and market stalls have all been abandoned, creating an eerie silence as I clip-clop towards the only way in and out.

The final ten seconds take an age until the giant screen above me changes from the images it has been showing on a loop into the footage I have just edited of me walking around the communications floor. To emphasise the point, the words 'Security alert: Floor 43' flash in red letters underneath. It takes a few seconds for everyone to notice but there is quickly a hum of excitement outside. Through the glass, I can see a black horde descending until the first Kingsman rushes through the doors into the North Tower.

'Floor 43!' I shout. 'She kept me up there, I only just got away. She's got a knife.'

The first Kingsman pulls me awkwardly towards him, swiping his thinkwatch against the sensor on the door and then angrily shunting me into the revolving door. 'If she's up there, why didn't you do something about it?'

His voice drifts away as the door rotates.

In less than a minute, I have moved through the crowd over the rail bridge until I am on the far side of the plaza. Everyone is watching the giant screen, muttering under their breaths about how I got in and what I might be after. 'I've heard she's building an army,' one of them says to another as I squeeze past, while I almost laugh as another speculates that I have a twin who has silver hair with a black streak.

As soon as I am out of sight, I kick the cumbersome shoes off and run as quickly as I can bare-footed through the empty streets until I reach the outskirts. Imrin got out before me and I can see him from a distance, sitting on a wall in his Kingsman's uniform close to the house in which we were hiding.

'Are they okay?' I ask, slightly out of breath as I draw level with him and continue towards the house.

'I'm not sure, I was waiting for you.' I can tell he wants to have a serious conversation but he can't stop himself from smiling. 'You look different,' he says.

'At least my old clothes are still in the house. I can't wait to get out of this.'

'You actually look like a girl.'

'That's what I'm worried about.' He smiles but it's obvious something isn't right. 'I don't think it was just me that got us all to this point,' I add. 'But sometimes, you've got to trust me. You don't have to be the one to say, "I'll save you". Sometimes, you can just run for it.'

Imrin puts an arm around me. 'What I was going to say is that you don't always have to be the one to put yourself in the middle of trouble. At the castle, you set the diversion on your own. You went with Faith to see her parents. You sent me away again here. I *do* trust you – the problem is that I'm not sure you trust me.'

He pulls me closer, not wanting a reply, which is good because I don't have one.

'We're not going to Lancaster first,' I say. 'I'm going to

see what X has to say but, if we're going that far north,
I want to go home to see if I can find my mum and Colt
and tell them about the second Offering. Colt could be in
bigger danger than he already is – we've got a week to get
there.'

'Okay.'

'If any of the others want to go to their families, they
can, but I've got to do this first. Hart's parents are in
Martindale too.'

'I know.'

'You don't mind coming?'

'No.'

It is good to hear he will support me but there was a
part of me, perhaps a large part, hoping he would say he
didn't want to go.

At some point, I am going to have to tell him about
Opie.

My feet are beginning to hurt from the hard ground as
we tread around the hedge onto the front part of the dilapidated house where we left the rest of our group. I stop
where I am standing and Imrin pulls me close.

'Are your feet all right?' he asks, but all I can do is point
to the ground where a trail of blood leads directly to the
crooked piece of wood sealing the entrance of the house.

16

I feel a stabbing pain shoot through my foot as I dash forward and tread on a sharp, loose stone. Imrin catches me and together we rush to the wooden board, throwing it aside. I head through the gap first, expecting a bloodbath – Jela, Faith, Pietra and Hart, any or all of them, tortured and dead as the two Kingsmen I voted to spare stand and sneer.

Instead, the drips of blood get thicker and larger, leading to a corner that is veiled in darkness. I smell the bodies before I see them. Both Kingsmen are dead, one with a gash that seems to go the entire way through his stomach; the other has had his throat slit. I turn away, not wanting to see any more.

Imrin peers around me at the bodies but says nothing.

'Is there anything to say where they've gone?' I ask.

'I didn't see anything.'

Together we search the other three corners of the crumbling room but there is nothing except the trail of blood. Outside, I check the walls for anything that may lead us in the direction of the others but the four of them have vanished. In the distance, the faint sound of the siren still chirps from the plaza. By now the Kingsmen must have realised I'm not on the communications floor. They will probably be checking the rest of the footage but I have set anything incriminating Reith to be deleted within the next few minutes.

I use the wood to re-block our improvised doorway and then follow the trail of blood towards the main path, looking from side to side to see if there is anything I've missed. Imrin is checking the underside of the hedges as the panic within me begins to build. There is no way they would have left without giving us some clue where they were going – not unless they had no choice. Could they have been captured? Have they had to run away? Is anyone hurt?

I know we don't have long before we have to get completely away from the city as well but that only adds to my unease as I pace quickly along the path. Eventually I return to the house, slowly walking along the trail of blood until, finally, I see the crumpled, drenched remnants of a daisy in the centre of the largest puddle.

Crouching, I pluck the tiny flower from the ground and wipe as much of the blood away as I can. The petals are now a dyed pink, the centre a bristling shade of orange.

That is all it takes for me to know they are all right. For whatever reason, they had to leave quickly, and I can imagine Jela's cool head taking control as they thought about how to safely let us know where they were going.

The second daisy is close to the wall at the edge of the path. I have already walked past it a few times but now I am looking for it, the bright white of the petals are practically glowing in the late-morning sun.

The trail leads on and on, at first towards the towers and then looping around the field where Faith captured the Kingsmen, until we are on the side furthest from the house in which we hid. Initially the daisies are dropped on the ground but then their placement becomes more creative. On the porch of a ramshackle house, four flowers have been fixed together and tied around a broken banister. A little further, a filthy broken bottle is lying in the gutter, where it has been for years. Inside is a single fresh daisy.

Eventually, we reach another battered row of houses similar to the one we left. Sitting on a broken window ledge is my soft tortoise, a crown of daisies on its head.

The house behind is a pile of rubble but there is a wooden board towards the centre that a person wouldn't look at twice if passing. It is only on closer examination that it seems out of place. The rest of the debris is brick, concrete and tile and, as we pull the cover away, it reveals a concrete staircase sloping downwards.

My bare feet hardly make a sound as I pad towards the bottom step where there is another door. Imrin waits at the top, leaving the cover off to give us some light as I knock.

There is no answer, so I thump a second time and hiss: 'It's Silver.'

This time, there is a small scrabbling until the door opens a fraction. I am about to say something, when the tip of a sword presses into my hip through the gap.

'It's me,' I add, before realising how different I look. The light is dim, my silver hair is still covered by the polish and I'm dressed like everyone else in the city. 'Imrin's here,' I add, pointing towards the hatch above.

Momentarily, I think that I've got it wrong – that I've walked into a trap – but then the door creaks open and I feel a pair of arms around me.

'Are you all right?' I ask Jela, hugging her into me.

'We didn't know if you'd be back,' she replies quietly, before letting me go and leading me into the room.

Imrin re-covers the stairs with the board and then joins us in what looks like a basement. Overhead, a dim light bulb illuminates an area that isn't quite as unkempt as the house in which we were previously hidden. Someone has been here relatively recently. In the corner is a bed, where Hart is rolled on his side, apparently sleeping. The mattress is bare but he has a blanket over him and I can see the slow rise and fall of his chest. Around the rest of the room, there is also a sink, small stove and three cupboards along the walls. Except for the furnishings, the room is empty. Who-ever was here before has cleared out.

'What happened?' I ask.

Faith closes the door behind us and sits with her back pressed against it. The floor is the only place to sit and, even though it is cold and hard, it still feels good not to be walking in bare feet.

'Everything was fine after you left,' Jela says quietly as she sits next to me on the ground. There is no need to whisper but I assume she is trying to let Hart sleep. 'Faith went out and picked a few berries that hadn't gone off and one of her traps had caught a squirrel.' She nods behind at the stove, which has a pan of water on top and I can smell the meat boiling inside. 'We were waiting for you but then we heard this siren from the centre. We thought you had been caught and we all went outside to see if there was anything obvious going on. We were on the main path but you can only just see the four towers from there. It was confusing, so we thought the best thing was to wait inside.'

Pietra is next to Jela, hugging a blanket around herself. 'It's my fault,' she says.

'It's not,' Jela replies, resting a hand on the other girl's knee.

I spot my bag in the corner and tell Jela to wait for a moment as I find the clothes I had been wearing originally and cross back to where everyone else is sitting.

'This stuff is really uncomfortable,' I explain, unzipping the skirt stolen from the gym.

Jela smiles thinly as I drop the alien clothes to the floor and begin to change. 'When we went back into the house, they were waiting for us,' she says.

'The two Kingsmen? How did they get free?'

Pietra sniffles. 'When Faith went to check her traps, I gave them some water. The quieter one said he had lost all feeling in his arm. He was really apologetic, saying he knew I had no reason to trust him but that if I could loosen his ties, it would make a big difference. He looked as if he was in a lot of pain and I thought it couldn't do any harm. I undid the knots and then tied them again – but I guess I didn't do a very good job.'

There are tears streaming down her cheeks in a flurry of silent sobs and nothing we can tell her will make it any better. The truth is that the Kingsmen saw her as the weak link – voting to keep them alive was something they saw as a flaw in her personality, not the act of humanity it actually was. They couldn't target Hart as he was the biggest person left – and holding the sword – while Jela had voted to kill them. Faith would have probably made the knots tighter, so they picked on Pietra, using her compassion against her.

'What happened?' I ask.

'Hart went in first,' Jela replies. 'By the time the rest of us had gone back through the gap, one of the Kingsmen had Hart around the neck. They didn't have any weapons but the one holding Hart said he would snap Hart's neck if we didn't throw our knives on the ground.'

'But you got away?' My question has an obvious answer but it's still surprising how resourceful we have become as a group.

Jela glances towards Faith, who still has her back to the door. She is watching us, listening, her face unmoving. 'The three of us dropped our knives and started to move towards the wall like they said but he pointed at Faith and told her to stop. He made her walk to him and then . . .'

The bulb above is a murky yellow colour and only really offers light in the centre of the room. The edges are still largely in shade and as I squint through the gloom, I can see the mark on Faith's face, a gash under her cheekbone and swelling around her eye socket.

'Did he . . . ?'

Jela nods and I find it hard not to contain my rage. The Kingsmen were fully grown men and, although Faith is sixteen, she is only the height and build of a twelve- or thirteen-year-old.

'I'm not sure I even remember it clearly,' Jela says, her voice dropping away until it is almost nothing. 'At first he punched her across the face. He didn't hold back, it was all of his weight and there was this wet slapping sound. I can still hear it.'

'And then?'

'He had Faith on the ground. We were trying to be quiet because we knew it would only get worse if we were screaming and could attract more attention.' She shuffles closer to Pietra, perhaps subconsciously. 'He had a knee on her chest so she couldn't move and then he looked at us and smiled, asking if we were going to have fun watching. I looked at Hart and his face was purple and red. He was trying to fight the other one off, but the Kingsman's grip was really tight. It looked like he was going to choke. Then I glanced back to Faith and the Kingsman had flopped on top of her. At first I didn't know what was going on, but then I saw the blood squirting from his neck. I didn't see what happened.'

I sneak a look towards Faith, who is still watching and listening, but she says nothing.

'I saw it,' Pietra says. 'It was just a flash. The Kingsman was looking at us but Faith must have had a second knife. The moment he looked back at her, he was dead.'

Jela nods. 'The other Kingsman must have loosened his grip because Hart made this roaring-type sound and threw him off. Hart still had the sword in his belt and the Kingsman didn't even have time to move.'

I nod, playing the scene in my mind and remembering the state of the bodies. They got what they deserved.

'Did you like the trail?' Jela adds with a weak smile, twirling a daisy between her fingers.

I pull myself up, ignoring the aches shooting through my back and legs and enjoying the protection of my normal shoes. 'It was beautiful,' I say, leaning over and pushing a leftover daisy into her hair.

'Are you going to be all right for a few minutes?' I ask, looking at Imrin.

He nods, so I walk across to Faith. 'Fancy a walk?' I ask. She shakes her head but I reach down and offer her my hand anyway. 'Come on.'

She doesn't reply, nor look at me, but she does take my hand and let me pull her up. Outside, I know there will be Kingsmen piling onto the streets, wondering how I escaped, but we should be safe for a while as we are on the very outskirts of the city.

I lead Faith back onto the main path and then head for the woods we first came through to get here. It is where we both feel more at ease. We are only a short distance in when I spot the perfect tree which has a thick, sturdy branch that is also low enough for me to reach. My arms still ache from swinging around the lift shaft in the North Tower but I haul myself up and begin climbing. Faith follows without a word, balancing, jumping and taking risks.

Soon, I am as high as I know I can get and sit with my legs either side of a strong-looking branch. Faith sits astride a bough on the opposite side of me. We both have our backs to the trunk, facing opposite directions.

'Did you enjoy that?' I ask.

'You're a pretty good climber,' she replies softly.

'I've had a lot of practice. How's the eye?'

'It works.'

It is the brave response I would have expected from her. 'Your parents were trying to do the best they could for you. The reward on my head is so big that they wanted to use it to give you a better life. You can't blame yourself for that.'

The only noise is the gentle call of a bird somewhere in the distance. I let the silence sit and then add: 'Do you remember what I told you just before the Kingsmen arrived at your house?'

There is no reply.

'Faith?'

'I remember.'

'I told you that I trusted you more than anyone and that's still true. Utterly, completely, brilliantly true. The others may look to me and ask what to do, but I look to you. I look at the way killing the person in the castle stayed with you all this time. I look at the way that just after everything happened with your parents, you were leading us back to safety – up trees, across rivers, doing whatever you could to get us away. Even today, there are three people in that basement alive because of you.'

When she replies, Faith's voice is so quiet that the breeze lifts the words away, leaving me to replay the sounds over in my mind until I can understand what she said. 'I'm not sorry I killed him.'

'You don't have to be,' I say after a while. 'All I need is for you to be with me. I know you're hurting but if we're going to get everyone to safety, it has to be us: me and you. Imrin's amazing at certain things but he doesn't have the mental strength or the planning ability you do. They need me and I need you.'

At first I'm not sure I have heard her properly but her reply reverberates around the trees, floating on the wind in and out of my ears. 'You're the only family I have.'

She speaks so sadly that I want to cry for her. She is as much a part of my family as Colt – the sister I never wanted but now I cannot do without.

'We should go back,' I say, loosening my grip on the branch and allowing myself to drop to the one below. Faith falls effortlessly, gently brushing herself against the branch below to steady the descent, before landing perfectly on her feet and standing hands on hips while I gradually make my way down.

'Are you okay?' I ask.

'Yes. Where are we going now?'

'I'll tell you all inside. We should probably stay here until it's dark. I've got lots of news.'

Faith giggles slightly, a wondrous sound that makes me smile too. 'You looked ridiculous in those clothes.'

'I thought so too.'

We are careful as we walk but the streets on the edge of the city are as empty as they were when we arrived. The train tracks run in the opposite direction and with the number of people who arrive at the plaza, it is likely that most of the population of Middle England live outside the city itself.

'It was a nice idea of Jela's with the daisies,' I say.

'We were going to wait there at first but it didn't feel right. We'd been noisy, plus there were the bodies. We wanted to go but didn't know how to get a message to you. That's when she said she had talked to you about the flowers and that you would understand.'

It is nice to know that the moments I have spent individually with everyone have been as rewarding for them as for me. I remember Jela telling me she wanted to see the fields of daisies in Martindale. Perhaps that will be possible one day. As the thought of the flowers slides into my head, it dawns on me that I've missed something.

'The first daisy was in a pool of blood outside,' I say.

'Was it? She did that.'

'But they said everything happened inside with the two Kingsmen.'

'It did.'

'So why is there a trail of blood outside?'

We have been walking carefully but, as Faith replies, I break into a desperate run. 'Didn't they tell you about Hart?'

17

When we first entered the basement, I thought he had been sleeping but as I hurry through the door a second time, panicked at what I missed, the first person I see is Hart sitting on the bed sipping water from one of our containers.

I am out of breath and frantic. 'You're okay?' I pant.

I can tell from his pained 'I'm fine' that he isn't.

'Let's see it,' I demand, striding across the room.

He huffs and puffs and generally acts like a boy about things, before finally rolling up his sleeve. Across his forearm are strips from some of the clothing salvaged from Beaconsfield that have been pressed together and bound tightly.

'It was the best I could do,' Pietra says, joining me by the bed.

'It was only a nick,' Hart says with an infuriating half-grin.

'You've been injured since we left the castle,' I say. 'You don't have to keep pretending it doesn't hurt.'

He looks away, annoyed. 'You're one to talk.'

'How did it happen?'

Hart stares at the ground, this time in embarrassment. 'I did it myself. The sword's heavier than it looks. After everything with the Kingsman, I overcompensated when I was trying to pull away.'

I have held the swords myself and know that it isn't so much the weight that is awkward, more the way they are balanced. Once you start to swing one, it is as if the weapon has a mind of its own, yanking you forward. For a group as unskilled and untrained as we are, it was only a matter of time until we ended up hurting ourselves.

'Knave's people gave me a little ointment and some painkillers just in case,' Pietra says. 'We're not going to be able to do any better than that. It will need cleaning a couple of times a day but I can do that. There was a lot of blood but it is longer than it is deep. It looks worse than it is.'

'How's the cough?' I say, looking at Hart again.

'Still there.'

'Are you still bringing up blood?'

'Not as much as I was.' I wait for him to meet my gaze, eyebrows raised suspiciously. 'Honestly,' he adds.

Pietra shrugs to indicate she doesn't know enough to say differently.

It's nice that the sink has running water and the first thing I do is wash the dye from my hair to feel more like myself. By the time I am finished, I have to scrub my hands until the blackened filthy liquid finally runs clear. Under the sink is a small circular mirror cracked in three separate places, though it is enough for me to check myself over and see that I look more or less like I did before.

We only have a few cans of food left but the squirrel Faith caught is plump and has been boiling for long enough to be wonderfully tender. We pull off the meat and share it out equally and then sit in a circle as I tell them about my escape. Everyone oohs and aahs in the right places as I find myself playing up the story ever so slightly and actually enjoying myself. There is even a gentle round of applause and laughter as I finish by telling them the rumour about my twin who has the opposite colour hair.

The last thing I tell them is about the second Offering. There is a general sense of outrage, especially when I reveal that ten-year-olds will be judged too. I hope a similar type of anger is spreading around the country.

'My brother turned ten a few weeks ago,' I say. 'I'm pretty sure this is going to be their way of making him as wanted as I am.'

The nods of agreement are reassuring in that it doesn't make me feel paranoid but at the same time, it would have been nice if someone told me I was imagining everything.

In a rush, I continue: 'There is a contact called X in Lancaster in the North Realm who says he has something that can help me take the fight to the King but first I want to go home to Martindale. My family are more or less in the same direction as X and my mum and brother will be hiding somewhere. I need to find them and tell them about the Offering in case they think they're safe. You don't all have to come if you would rather go to your own families.'

Jela and Pietra both insist they are coming as they have no brothers or sisters. Going further north takes them closer to home if they change their minds.

'I've got six sisters,' Imrin says. 'They all know what they're doing. I'd only get in the way.'

Hart is blinking back tears, which he says is because his arm is stinging – but his one other word gives him away: 'Home.'

I am looking forward to seeing the dusty streets, frosted meadows and damp trees of winter in Martindale. I only left a few months ago but Hart hasn't been home in over two years, since he became our village's first Offering.

Not everyone knows what happened with Faith's family but if they were unsure of where her allegiance lies, she leaves them in no doubt. 'Where you go, I go,' she says firmly.

We spend the remainder of daylight resting as best we can, with two people on watch, one inside the hatch, one outside. This time we wait until it is completely dark, not just dusk, before heading out. Directly north would take us through Middle England, so we spend half the night edging around the city to the west before the smattering of houses turns into the green fields that looked so appealing when Imrin and I gazed at the view from the top of the North Tower.

As we rest during the day, the sun shines consistently but offers little heat and the clear skies make each night colder than the one before. It would be more comfortable if we could find derelict houses in which to stay during the days but we see many more pockets of light around the towns and villages than we have before. We assume they are either Kingsmen or the vigilante squads. It is likely the reward for capturing me has increased since we left Middle England. The way I escaped from two of the most secure buildings in the country – Windsor Castle and the North Tower – is an embarrassment to everyone involved.

The more the King offers, the more people will venture onto the streets desperate to find me. More girls will be harmed for looking like me – collateral damage in a conflict I don't want and didn't start.

I can't help but think Knave and Vez will be delighted at how the myth surrounding me is growing greater than ever.

With the lack of any roof other than the forests, any inhibitions we may have had are long gone as we huddle together under blankets, leaves, bushes and anything else we can find to stay warm. Pietra is spending more time with

Hart, while I'm still drifting towards Imrin for comfort in the dark.

After our third night of walking, just as the sky is turning blue, it begins to snow. It is hard to tell where the flakes are coming from as the morning is bright, almost cloudless. Somehow, the gentle flurry continues, drifting softly to the ground and settling as we huddle in a hollow surrounded by small saplings. We drape the blankets across some of the lower branches and sit underneath, packed together, watching as the green and brown around us slowly turns white.

'Do you guys have Christmas?' Imrin asks, his breath drifting into the centre of our circle.

'Doesn't everyone have Christmas?' Jela replies.

There is a general nod of agreement. It sounds ridiculous but, until recently, none of us had any contact with people in the other Realms. Jela, Pietra, Hart and myself all come from the North but Faith is from the South, Imrin the West.

'When it was Christmas a few years ago, it snowed like this,' Imrin says. 'There's this big hill near where I live and we trekked to the top and slid down on a bag. Me and my sisters did it over and over until it was dark and our dad had to come looking for us. At first he was shouting about how we'd missed our presents and that we weren't going to get anything. Then he went up and tried it himself. Half an hour later and Mum was out, hands on her hips, bellowing at us for being late. Poor Dad was halfway down the hill on a bag when she arrived. He was giggling like one of my sisters but when he reached the bottom, Mum started shouting at him, saying he was setting a bad example. He took all the flak for us and then we went inside and had this big meal. Mum had been keeping a bit of our rations back each week for months. We ate and ate.'

'Did you get your presents?' I ask.

Imrin laughs. 'A pair of woollen gloves. Mum had knitted them herself. They were brilliant – but would have probably been more use before I spent six hours sliding down a hill in the snow.'

Because of the temperature, nobody seems tired, so we spend hours sitting and talking. We share our memories of various Christmases. Somehow, it is a tradition that hasn't been lost and we talk about gifts and food, until we move on to our ideal meal. Imrin's is chicken, which has everyone telling him that the squirrels we eat taste just like chicken anyway.

'Not like my mum makes it,' he says. 'She does this thing where she soaks the chicken in leaves and spices for days at a time. Then she'll leave it cooking slowly for another day. By the time we have it, the whole thing is falling apart.'

We are all feeling hungry as he finishes but it doesn't stop everyone else from explaining their favourites. Faith comes to life as she tells us about a scone she once had from the bakery in the centre of her town. Jela talks of a stew her mother makes while Pietra, who has lived in a city her entire life, tells us about a bar of chocolate she was given as a child which she says she can still taste if she closes her eyes.

None of us talks about the vast banquet we went to once a week at Windsor. At the start, I remember enjoying the food but when I try to think of it now, everything seems stale and grey.

'What's your favourite?' Faith asks, just as I think I have escaped the conversation.

'This is going to sound silly,' I say. 'But jam. My mother got me some before the Reckoning. It was this little pot and I made sure she and my brother had some but it was amazing.'

'Out of everything, you choose jam,' Imrin says disbelievingly.

'At least I didn't go for glorified squirrel.'

Everyone laughs, but slowly the tiredness is beginning to filter through us. Faith is the first to doze off, her head resting on my chest as the rest of her body curls around me, as if I am her comfort blanket. I cradle her with Pietra pushing into her other side so she is sandwiched between us. Imrin is behind me, his breath making my ear itch.

'I've got a present for you,' he whispers.

'What is it?'

'We'll call it an early Christmas present seeing as it's snowing. You can have it later.'

'Can I have it now?'

'No.'

Hart and Jela stay up on lookout as the four of us drift to sleep. Imrin and Faith take the next shift and by the time he wakes me up, the snow has stopped and the beautiful white frosting has turned to a slushy mix of mud and grass.

'Can I have my present now?' I ask sleepily.

'After I've slept.'

'Now – or I'll keep you awake by constantly asking you for it while you're trying to sleep.'

Imrin stifles a yawn. 'I wonder if everyone around the country would be so impressed by you if they heard this?'

I hold out my hand. 'Who cares? Present.'

Imrin reaches into his bag and takes out a square object wrapped in leaves with thin tree branches tied around it holding everything in place. 'It can get boring on lookout,' he offers as an explanation.

The object is heavy and I have to use my teeth to break through the vines before the leaves fall away. Inside is a strange-looking black and grey metal box.

'What is it?' I ask.

'I don't know. It seemed electrical and I thought you'd like it.'

As I twist it around in my hands, I realise that it seems familiar. 'Where did you get it?'

Imrin rubs his eyes. 'I stole it.'

'Where from?'

'It was on Reith's desk. When everything was happening, I spotted it and thought we might be able to use it more than him. Well, if we can figure out what it does.'

There is a grate of small holes across the top but no apparent buttons. 'You're very thoughtful,' I say sarcastically, pushing it into my own bag and kissing him on the forehead. 'And a thief.'

He laughs. 'Can I go to sleep now?'

'I'll wake you when it's dark.'

Imrin is still smiling, even with his eyes, so I ask him what he's so happy about. 'Two more days and I get to meet your family,' he says.

He's right – but it is also two more days until he meets Opie.

18

Overlooking Martindale on the opposite side from the gully is a vast field that slopes upwards before levelling out and stretching far into the distance. At the start of last summer, Opie and I decided we were going to get up early and see what was on the far side. Our legs – well, mine – were aching after barely an hour and a half, and the only things we saw were more fields, trees and hills in the distance. No matter how far we walked, they never seemed to get any closer.

As the sun reached the top of the sky, I decided that my legs could take no more. Because we had already walked for half a day, we still had half a day's walk to get back. We hadn't seen a single person the entire time; our only company had been pheasants, pigeons and squirrels. I sat on the ground complaining that I couldn't walk any further. Opie looked down at me, scratching the back of his neck and tilting his head to the side, grinning in the way he always does.

As Imrin, Pietra, Jela, Hart, Faith and myself settle ourselves at the top of the slope that overlooks Martindale, I remember the conversation as if it happened this morning.

'I could just leave you here,' Opie says, half-turning away as if heading to the village.

'Go on then,' I dare, knowing he won't.

He takes two steps away but I don't budge. 'Are you coming?'

'No.'

'You can't stay here forever.'

'I can.'

Opie sighs. 'What about your mum?'

'She'll blame you for leaving me.'

He snorts at the suggestion. 'Don't you want to see Colt again?'

'He'll blame you too. He'll say, "Why, Opie? Why? Why would you leave my only sister out in the open?" His little face will be all upset and it will be your fault.'

Opie shakes his head. 'You can't blackmail me.'

'Want to bet?'

'What do you want?'

'A piggyback. You're all big and strong and male. I'm a little girl. Look at me.'

'I'm not carrying you all the way home.'

I smile, knowing I am winning. 'You don't have to take me *all* the way back – we've already come some of it.'

'I'm not taking you the rest of the way. It's too far.'

'Think of poor Imp. He might be your brother but he

looks at me like a sister. Who's he going to fight with if you leave me here?'

Opie shakes his head and starts walking away. I run the grass between my fingers, plucking individual blades and counting under my breath. I get to eight before he turns and screams my name. It echoes around the vast open space as he runs back towards me, throwing himself onto the ground as we roll around, giggling uncontrollably. His big arms are wrapped around me as I cradle my head into his neck.

'You're a menace, Silver Blackthorn,' he says.

'I'm *your* menace,' I correct.

I twist and flail around until I am on top of him and then lean in.

It is a day I will never forget – we are fifteen and he is the boy I have always loved. The boy I teased, tormented and bullied. My first kiss.

The grass feels fresh and prickly between my fingers and the day smells of sun and summer. Everything is perfect until he eventually stands. He heaves me onto his shoulders and walks the entire way back to Martindale, putting me down only when we are outside my front door.

'Goodnight, Silver Blackthorn,' he says, leaning in to kiss me.

I slap him softly across the face and smile. 'Don't push your luck.'

As I lie on my front at the top of the bank overlooking the town, I remember his aggrieved face before he gave me that smirk of his. 'I'll see you tomorrow,' he said.

Now, Imrin is lying next to me, the six of us in a row. 'There's no way we can just walk in during the day,' he says.

Between us, we have counted six separate Kingsmen patrols, with two guards in each unit. The only time I have seen this many people in black was on the last Reckoning day but that was because people from other towns had been brought in to make the adulation of the King seem a lot more fervent in front of the cameras than it actually was.

These Kingsmen are here for me.

'It could be as bad at night,' Hart says. He is desperate to see his parents again and has twice pointed across to their house.

'If anything happens, it's easier to run and hide when it's dark,' Imrin says.

'Your parents might be hiding too,' I tell Hart.

He shakes his head. 'They're old. Even if they got your message, they wouldn't have been able to go anywhere quickly.'

'Other things could have happened . . .'

I don't want to say the words but Hart shakes his head again. 'The reason you're so sure your mum and brother are safe is because they would have appeared on screen if they had been caught. It's the same for mine – if they had been arrested, it would have been broadcast. My parents have grey hair, my dad walks with a stick, my mum has a stoop. It's not going to go down well if the Kingsmen hurt them and show what they have done. They'll be at home but someone will be watching in case either of us tries to make contact.'

His logic is relatively sound. For all the atrocities committed, the one thing of which the King and Minister Prime are careful is that everything is either blamed on somebody else, or that it happens to someone who looks like they deserve it.

'How are you going to see them then?' Pietra asks.

Nobody speaks for a few moments until I push myself up and peer across to Jela and Pietra. 'I need a volunteer,' I say.

'I'll do it,' Faith says.

'Sorry, it's got to be one of you two,' I add, indicating the other two girls. 'It's going to be dangerous.'

'It's my turn,' Pietra says with a confidence I can tell is forced, although it is admirable at the same time.

'Do you want to know what it is first?'

Pietra smiles knowingly. 'I'm not going to like it either way, am I?'

*   *   *

We wait until late in the evening, watching the lights of patrols skirting around the village. It is at least heartening that I can't see anyone other than Kingsmen on the streets – no one who knows me has formed a capture squad. Hart and I talk Imrin and Pietra through the layout of the streets as best we can, asking them questions over and over until their knowledge almost matches ours.

When it is time, Imrin and Pietra head to one end of the village as Hart and I go to the other. I expect one group of Kingsmen to be devoted to circling my old home but as we arrive on the street, we can see nothing other than the faint glimmer of candles through people's windows. Tonight is one of the many without electricity.

We edge towards the front window of my house and I peep quickly through, before ducking back out of sight. I can't see anyone, so we move to the back of the building. My bedroom faces a narrow cobbled alley that is often teeming with rubbish. It is as quiet as ever and I use a thin piece of wire from the ground to unlatch the window.

'You look like you've done that before,' Hart teases, helping me in.

With all my early-morning trips to the gully and the woods, I quickly learned how to get in and out of my room without having to go through the front door.

Hart clambers through the window and we pull it shut behind us. I am almost overcome by the smell of home: the aroma of my mother's cooking, the dried mud from the shoes under my bed, the soap my mum uses. I breathe it all in, before composing myself.

'I want to check for clues to where they might have gone.'

'Wouldn't the Kingsmen have already checked?'

'Probably, but they might not have known what to look for.'

We move into the main part of the house but everything seems as it was the day I left. The dining table is laid for two and the chairs arranged around the heater for the rare night it offered warmth. The sink and draining board are empty, with everything tidily packed away in the cupboard. If the Kingsmen have been in, it must only have been to look for people, not for clues.

I have a quick glance around Colt's room but it is so messy that a Kingsman may as well have thrown everything around. Typical of my younger brother.

'Anything?' Hart asks.

'No.'

I head back to my room, ready to leave, when I remember our conversation in the snow and move back into the kitchen. There, I open the cupboard above the cooker, reaching to the very back and pulling out my jar of jam, which is still half-filled. A dim moonlight glints through the kitchen window and as I unscrew the lid, my fingers tremble in anticipation, knowing that any clue would be here. I run my finger around the inside of the glass, expecting some sort of note hidden within the mixture.

There is nothing, but as I lick my finger clean and go to screw the lid on, I see three words written in clear letters – my mother's handwriting.

Out all day

I say the words out loud, hoping that hearing them will help me make sense of their meaning – but I cannot come up with anything. In the bedroom, I show the lid to Hart but he shakes his head slowly.

'What's out all day?' I ask.

He shrugs: 'The sun?'

'It depends on the day. Plus, what would that mean? Do you know anywhere called the sun?'

'Is it a saying?'

'Not that I've ever heard.'

Hart shakes his head again and takes a step towards the window. I know he is desperate to see his parents.

'Five more minutes,' I assure him, checking my watch.

Outside, we wait in the back alley for a small group of people to pass and then dart across the street, keeping to the shadows until we are close to Hart's parents' house.

I check my thinkwatch again as we wait in silence, sheltering in a gloomy corner in between two houses.

Pietra and Imrin each have one of the thinkwatches we took from the Kingsmen and, almost exactly on time, I hear the commotion in the distance. Hart takes a step forward, edging into the light, but I grab him until he is back in the shadow with me.

'Wait,' I say firmly.

He seems annoyed as the noise continues towards the town hall. Around a minute later, the door of the house opposite Hart's parents' house opens. Two Kingsmen bound onto the street before heading in the direction of the disturbance.

Hart now seems chastened but I give him a shove and follow him around the side of his house before he reaches the front door. He taps gently on the window three times before ducking down next to me. At first there is a scratching and then the front door opens a crack. Hart doesn't need to say anything before the door is pulled open. We both dive through but Hart can barely wait for the door to be closed before he has his arms around his father.

I close the door for them and turn to see the pair with tears rolling down their faces. The walking stick belonging to Hart's father has been abandoned on the ground as his son crouches and holds him. 'Son,' the older man whimpers.

Hart's mother is in a rickety old rocking chair. She has wild grey hair that shoots off in all directions and is holding two knitting needles, her fingers click-clacking back and forth seemingly without her realising as she stares at her husband and son with tears in her eyes before turning to look at me.

'You brought him back,' she says to me.

'It wasn't just me,' I reply, but she drops the needles and wool into her lap and waves me over.

'I can't stand very well,' she says, pulling me towards her. I kneel and allow her to hug me close. 'I knew you'd be back,' she adds. 'I just knew it.' She calls louder, so her husband can hear. 'I told you, didn't I, love? I told you she'd bring him back.'

She lets me go as Hart replaces me in his mother's arms.

'You're all anyone's talking about,' his father says after I hand him back his walking stick. He looks as if he has aged dramatically since I left; the wrinkles in his face have grown into one, his hair receding until it is barely there. 'All everyone out there wants to do is talk about what they're saying on the news.' He settles into a chair, rubbing his back as Hart lets his mother go and joins me on the floor between his two parents. 'You didn't try to kill the King, did you?' Hart's father adds.

Hart and I exchange a glance. 'Sort of,' I say. 'Although, in fairness, he tried to kill us first.'

We don't have long but Hart quickly tells them what it actually means to be an Offering: the abuse, the degradation, the way you think each day could be your last just because you cough at the wrong time or laugh at the wrong thing.

His mother keeps repeating, 'I knew it. Didn't I always tell you that King was no good?', while his father replies, 'I don't remember you saying that.' On and on they go, a double act they have no doubt been replaying over and over since the day they were married.

We leave most of the details out but tell them enough to let them know that we're not the people we've been made out to be.

'I knew it,' his mother says one more time.

'I've got to go, Mum,' Hart finally says.

Before we leave, I take the jam jar out of my pocket and unscrew the lid, showing it to both of Hart's parents.

'Do you have any idea what it means?' I ask.

'Out all day,' his father repeats, scratching his chin. 'Have you ever heard of that, dear?' he calls towards his wife.

'What?'

'Out all day?'

'Who's out all day?'

'No one, that's what I'm asking you. What does it mean?'

Hart offers me an apologetic grin and whispers in my ear: 'They're always like this.'

After everything we have seen and done over the past few months, it is nice to hear two people still together after all this time.

'Your mum might be right,' I say as a thought pops into my head.

'How?'

'We were asking, "What's out all day?", but it could be "Who"?'

Hart looks at me, puzzled. 'Well, who is out all day?'

'I know. Wait here – I'll be right back.'

I open the front door and slide through the gap before hurrying through the back streets until I reach the inn. There is no one outside but light flickers through the windows and there is a faint hum of activity. I sneak carefully around the side of the building until I reach the narrow rubbish-filled back alley that is similar to the one which runs along the rear of my own house. The inn blocks the moonlight, clouding the area in darkness. I hold my hands out, using them to feel my way around until my eyes gradually become acclimatised.

'Mayall,' I hiss. There is a faint rustling from what I assumed was a bag of rubbish close to the back door of the inn.

As I crouch next to him, the town drunk rolls over and growls at me. 'I ain't got no money.'

'Mayall, it's me, Silver Blackthorn.'

'Who?' His voice echoes around the alley and I shush him harshly.

'Mayall, do you remember me? It's Silver.'

He shunts himself up until he is resting against the wall. He is wearing a thick dark coat that comes down to his knees, with a pair of woollen socks covering his legs. On his feet is a pair of tatty mismatched shoes, each with holes in. His breath reeks of alcohol.

'Oh yeah, Silver. I remember – that weird girl?'

I snort involuntarily. 'I suppose.'

'With the stupid hair.'

'All right, all right,' I reply, a little put out.

'And the mud hands.'

'Um . . . With the what?' I'm not sure what he's talking about.

'You were always with that other one, the big one, what's his name?'

'Opie?'

'Yeah, that Dopey kid. It was raining and you had this dirt on your hands. You were looking for somewhere to wipe them but there was nothing in your pockets. So you went over to him and patted him on the back. You were all like, "Hi, good to see you, Dopey", and all the time you were wiping the mud on him.'

As Mayall finishes his story, I realise that he is telling me something I have long since forgotten. I had been out in the woods and tripped on my way back. I had dirt all the way up my arms but didn't want to let my mum know what I had been up to.

'That was about seven or eight years ago,' I say.

Mayall cackles before it turns into a cough. 'Yeah, that Dopey kid, he's really got a thing for you. Don't think I haven't seen you all those times, sneaking around late at night when you think there's no one around.'

Even though I was creeping around public places, I feel a little violated that someone else may have seen me. 'Mayall, do you know where my mum and brother went?'

'Oh, your mum . . .' Mayall's voice is a low hoarse whisper as he coughs again. 'Do you know, she says hello to me all the time? She gives me little bits of food. I'm all like, "Thank you, Mrs Blackthorn," and she's like, "Oh, that's no problem, Mayall," and then I'm like . . .'

'Mayall, has anyone except me come to see you in the last couple of weeks?'

I'm not convinced Mayall's version of events is an accurate description of any conversation he may or may not have had with my mum but it does seem likely she would say hello and offer him food on occasion. The reason I understood her clue is because she would always tell me that if I stayed 'out all day' then I'd end up like Mayall. It was meant as a warning, albeit an affectionate one.

Mayall doesn't seem too put out by my interruption,

scratching his chin thoughtfully. 'What's that little Dopey kid called?'

I run through the names of Opie's brothers: 'Samuel?'

'Nope.'

'Felix?'

'Nope, what sort of name is that?'

'Eli?'

'Nope.'

'Imp?'

'Yeah, that little one. He's a right little swine.' Mayall thrusts a bottle of something that smells strongly of alcohol into the air. 'I was sleeping this one time and he replaced my drink with a bottle of pop.'

I struggle not to laugh. 'If you were asleep, how do you know it was him?'

Mayall flaps his hand dramatically at me. 'Bah. Are you saying it's not?'

I shake my head. It does sound like something Imp would do. The alcohol probably ended up being sold back to the inn before, inevitably, being sold back to Mayall. Thieving it may have been, but Mayall could probably do with a few nights away from the bottle.

'What did Imp say when he came to see you?'

'Something about a lake.'

'Did he tell you they were going to the lake?'

Mayall coughs again and his glassy eyes suddenly shift

into focus as he turns to face me. 'You really are her, aren't you? The one they're all talking about.'

'Yes.'

'They're at the centre of the lake, my dear.'

I take the jam jar from my pocket and press it into Mayall's hands. 'Thank you.'

He looks at my gift and pushes it back towards me. 'Bah! Call that a drink?'

I put the jar back into my pocket. 'I didn't actually but thanks again. Goodnight, Mayall.'

'Goodnight yourself, weird one.'

I stick to the shadows, snaking my way back to Hart's house. This time I head towards the rear and tap gently three times on the back window. We could have done this when we arrived but neither of us knew what state his parents would be in. Hart has been listening for my signal and quickly tries to open the window. It sticks in the corner and I shunt it from the outside until it opens.

'It always does that,' he says.

'I know where they are,' I reply, adding: 'Let's go.'

He shakes his head and I can see in his face that something isn't right. 'You should come in,' he says. 'It's the Offering – it's happening now.'

19

Hart helps me through the window and secures it behind us. 'The screen switched itself on about two minutes after you left,' he says. 'They've already done the South – there was one thirteen-year-old and another girl who was fifteen.'

In the living room, Hart's parents both turn to face me. 'Did you get what you needed, love?' his mum asks.

'Yes, thank you.' I sit next to Hart on the floor and whisper in his ear. 'They're at the centre of the lake. All the junk is piled highest there but, if they know where they're going, they can find little caves carved out of smashed-up cars and old electrical items.'

'How would your mum know about somewhere like that?'

'It will be Opie. We used to go there all the time and call it the gully. On the train before we left for the Offering, he promised he'd keep them safe. It's a lot longer walk than you think to get to the middle. If you didn't know they were there, you'd never find them.'

Hart nods but then quickly leans back. It's doubtful he's ever been there. 'Why are you telling me?'

I make sure he is looking at me when I reply. 'Just in case.'

A fanfare sends our attention back to the screen where a presenter is standing in front of a map of Britain with a wide grin on his face. The authorities clearly want this Offering to have the same sense of scale and reverence as the usual one. 'That's the South and the West all sorted. Sixteen down, sixteen to go. Let's get some reaction.' He presses a hand to his ear. 'Jay, are you there? Jay?'

A man appears on the screen wearing a tight-fitting grey suit. He is clean-shaven and has his hair slicked back, a hand pressed to his ear. 'I'm in the West Realm in the city of Bristol,' he shouts, as a crowd of people largely shrouded in darkness cheers behind him.

He turns to a woman standing close, who is awkwardly hopping from one foot to the other. She looks freezing and jumps as he places a hand on her shoulder. I wonder if there is a Kingsman a little out of shot, weapon ready just in case. 'What do you think of the second Offering?' the man asks.

A quick glance off-camera and the woman smiles broadly. 'I think it's brilliant.'

'And what do you think about the fact anyone over the age of ten can be chosen?'

A gulp, another glance. She's not doing well. 'It's fantastic that all the little ones get a chance to serve their

King as well. My lot were dead keen. They were really hoping to be chosen.'

'We can't all be the lucky ones!' Jay's joke is weak to start with but the woman doesn't sell it. A fake laugh, a third glance at the person off-camera. This is not going to end well. 'And what about the person who caused all this?' the man adds. 'What do you think of Silver Blackthorn?'

The woman's eyes flicker both ways, as she licks her lips, trying to remember whatever the line was she was given. I can see the panic in her. 'She's bang out of order, isn't she?'

Whatever it was they wanted her to say, I doubt it was that. Jay takes the microphone away before she finally remembers. 'Oh,' she shrieks, grabbing his arm. 'And she's a traitor, isn't she? She's put us all in trouble and brought this all on herself.'

Jay scowls at her and yanks his arm back. He turns to another woman on his other side, trying to compose himself. 'Now, you actually know one of the Offerings, don't you?'

The woman grins broadly. 'Oh yes, little Georgie. She's fifteen.'

'And how do you know her?'

'She lives next door to me – I've known her all my life.'

This woman is far more natural on camera. Whether she's misguided, or if she believes everything that she has been told, she is genuinely pleased for the child.

'What about Georgie's parents?'

'Oh, they're thrilled.' She looks straight into the camera. 'It's a massive honour to serve your King, isn't it?'

'And do you have a message for Silver Blackthorn?'

Another mention of my name. The strangest thing is that they don't even realise what they're doing. This is one big show to try to convince everyone it's business as normal but by constantly talking about me as the enemy, they are making me just that.

The woman's face contorts in fury. 'I can't wait until they catch her,' she snarls. 'I'd string her up myself.'

Jay turns back to the screen and then there is a shout from over his shoulder. A man's voice, clear for everyone at home to hear: 'She's a hero!'

Jay's hand shoots back to his ear, eyes darting towards whoever is behind the camera as murmurs of support and panic bounce around the crowd. Before he can say anything, the screen turns black, before the original presenter reappears, looking flustered. 'Welcome back. A few technical errors there . . .'

Hart's father laughs. 'Did you hear that, dear? They called her a hero.'

His mum leans forward in her rocking chair, fingers flashing back and forth with the knitting needles. 'They called who a what?'

He nods towards me. 'They called her a hero.'

'I know, I'm not deaf.'

I suppress a smile, even as the presenter points towards the map on a screen behind, which zooms in automatically.

'And now to the North,' he says, 'which I should remind you is Silver Blackthorn's Realm.'

At first, I'm not sure why he has pointed that out but then the name of the first Offering has the words 'aged ten' written underneath. The second is eleven, the third twelve and the fourth ten.

And therein lies the message – if one of you steps out of line, we'll hit back hard. If a handful of sixteen-year-olds won't obey us, we'll take your ten-year-olds instead. If they can't make people hate me by setting me up as the central figure in a traitorous conspiracy, they will make people blame me for their children disappearing instead.

Every other Offering has been based upon the results of the Reckoning. The test is meant to determine which types of job we should be doing to best serve the nation and only from that are we chosen, apparently at random.

None of the presenters has explained what criteria are behind what is happening on the screen but there can be no doubt that these choices are targeted. Three more Offerings are chosen from our Realm – the eldest being thirteen.

As the names scroll across the bottom of the screen, with just one remaining to be picked, I know whose it will be. There is no surprise when it settles in the centre.

Colt Blackthorn, Martindale, North, ten

The presenter presses a hand to his ear. 'And I'm just hearing,' he says, eyes looking skywards, 'that Colt Blackthorn is indeed the younger brother of renegade Silver Blackthorn.'

A shocked look, a gasp of disbelief, another hand to the ear. As if it was ever going to be anyone else. A look off-camera.

'I should remind you, ladies and gentlemen, that the rules of the Offering are very clear. Anyone chosen must present themselves at the designated points tomorrow. If there are any non-attenders, the penalty is as it always has been.'

He speaks solemnly and authoritatively. I always knew it was coming but to hear it out loud makes it seem so final.

My brother will be given a death sentence.

I turn to Hart, having heard all I needed to. I am about to tell him we should go – but both our heads spin dramatically as the door is almost smashed off its hinges by the deafening thump of someone's fist.

20

Hart and I dash to the bedroom as his father calls: 'I'm coming.' I head to the window but Hart yanks me back just as I'm about to open it. 'I can't,' he says. 'They're my parents.'

I hear the scraping of the front door. 'They wouldn't want you to get caught,' I hiss, but by the time I stretch for the window, it is too late as we hear the front door bursting open.

I remember how awkward the window is. There is no way we're going to be able to open it without alerting the person I assume is a Kingsman in the other room. With no other option, we slide underneath the bed, allowing the sheets to flap around us.

'Where is he?' a voice bellows, making it feel as if the whole house is shaking.

'Who?' Hart's father replies.

'Your son. Where is he?'

'I told you the last time – I haven't seen him in two years.'

There is a heavy clomp of boots pacing around and the bedroom door swishes open before slamming again. Whoever is here made only the briefest of glances into the room we are in.

'You know we're going to find him, don't you?'

'You've said.'

'And you know what we're going to do to him, don't you?'

'You've said.'

A pause. 'Are you back-talking me?'

'No.'

'No, *Sir*.'

'No, Sir.'

More thudding boots as I expect a crack of fist or shoe on bone. Instead the door slams, sending a gust of air through the house that carries under the bedroom door and sets the sheets billowing. Neither of us moves, not knowing if it is safe.

Hart shuffles uncomfortably as we hear his father's voice from the other room. 'I tell him the same thing every time, don't I, dear? I don't know why they *keep watching our front door* but, if our son were here, it would be a good time to tell him how proud we are.'

*　*　*

Hart's father's final statement made it clear we shouldn't go through the front. Without a final chance to say goodbye, we head out of the back window, darting into the shadows and passing through the side streets that are so familiar until we arrive back at our spot at the top of the field where the others are waiting. They are snuggled under blankets in a semi-circle as Pietra washes chalk from her hair, a grin on her face.

'How did you get on?' I ask, taking the tub of water and sitting in front of her, wiping a smear of mud away from her face.

'It was fun,' she says, and I can tell she is telling the truth. She hasn't been central to much of what we have achieved so far and this has given Pietra her moment to shine. 'I just can't get this stuff out of my hair.'

I catch Hart's eye as he squeezes under a blanket next to Jela. 'That chalk is vicious,' he says.

I nod in agreement. 'When I was a kid, I was on that chalk path that circles the town. I was running back and forward but tripped and slid along on my hands and knees. There was blood all over but I was caked in the white as well. It was in my hair, up my nose, in my ears; everywhere. Mum spent an hour with me washing it all away.'

Pietra pretends to be annoyed but can't stop herself smiling. 'You could have told me that before I covered my hair in it!'

I dampen my fingers and then use them to gradually brush away a few more flecks of white. 'Would you have gone anyway?'

'Yes.'

'No harm done then. Anyway, what happened?'

Pietra is separating out a piece of hair: 'We did what you said. I went to the town hall and waited in the shadows. At the time you said, I moved into the middle of the square where the moon was brightest. Imrin shouts, "It's her, there's Silver Blackthorn", and I swish my head around to let everyone see the chalk streak. As soon as someone else started shouting, I ran for it.'

'Did you remember the route okay?'

'You made me go through it enough.'

I pull her hair apart and wipe away the remaining spots of chalk, before telling her she is clean again and climbing beneath the blankets.

'Were there any hiccups?'

Pietra shakes her head. 'No, it was all twists and turns for that first bit and I didn't stop running until I got past the trees. I heard a few people passing by but I had such a good head start that no one got anywhere near me.'

I squeeze her on the knee and then nod towards Imrin. 'Brilliant. What about you?'

'I didn't have to do much. As soon as that first guy saw

Pietra, there was a ripple around the town. After about a minute, there were Kingsmen everywhere.'

'Didn't you run for it straight away?'

He shakes his head, even though that was the plan. 'No one was looking at me anyway – but there was one thing. Apart from the Kingsmen, there weren't that many people out but the ones that were, well . . . they're crazy.'

'How do you mean?'

'This one guy, he was pointing towards the back of the town hall and telling the Kingsmen you'd gone that way. Then another woman was swearing blind you'd gone in the opposite direction. If it had been you, you'd have got away anyway. The Kingsmen didn't have a clue.'

I can't help but grin as an enormous feeling of satis- faction grips me. The people of Martindale have known me my entire life and haven't given up on me – just as Hart's father said. They don't know if I tried to kill the King but, if I did, they presume I had good reason. I love the idea of the Kingsmen being sent one way and then the other, not knowing I was standing behind them the whole time.

I shuffle into the middle of the semi-circle so that I have everyone's attention and point to the other end of the town. 'On the far side of those woods is a lake,' I explain. 'I call it the gully. At some point, all of the water was drained, making it one giant pit in the ground. After that, the authorities started bringing everyone's rubbish here. It is full of old electrical items that no longer work – mostly from before the war. It's massive, many times bigger than this field, but at the centre are most of the bigger objects, like old cars and scrap metal. My mother and brother are hiding there.'

'Shall we go?' Imrin asks, already removing the blanket.

I shake my head. 'There are all sorts of sharp edges and broken things in there. It's not worth any of us hurting ourselves in the dark.' As I glance towards Hart, wanting to make a joke, I see his eyes flicker sideways towards Pietra. 'What?' I ask.

Hart looks down at the ground, so Pietra replies. 'His arm might be infected. I've been doing my best but we're out of ointment. There's a thin line of pus just inside the wound. I've been cleaning it each day and squeezing the rest out but someone who knows what they're doing needs to look at it.'

'Why didn't you tell us?'

Hart doesn't reply but Pietra does. 'He wanted to see his family. There's nothing wrong with that.'

'There's a doctor in town,' I reply. 'We could have sneaked him in.'

Hart cuts across me. 'I didn't want to put anyone else in danger. It feels fine.'

'Are you sure?'

He lifts his arm and rotates it, as if to prove a point. 'Look.'

I'm not convinced but there is no point in arguing. 'Let's get a bit of sleep. We'll head out an hour before sunrise, so we should be at the edge of the lake just as it's getting light.'

* * *

My plan would have been perfect except for one thing. I am woken up by the gentle drumbeat of rain after barely two hours of sleep. When I think of Martindale, I think of the drizzle tinkling around me as I shelter in the woods. This isn't just a gentle shower though. Within minutes, the skies open in an apparent attempt to wash us all from the face of the planet.

There is little point in doing anything other than heading towards the gully, which Imrin jokes will be refilled if it continues to rain like this. If I could breathe anything other than rainwater, I might have laughed.

In single file, we traipse around the silent village, sheltering under blankets, clothes, bags and anything else we can find. The only comfort I have is that I cannot see any of the Kingsmen duos walking around the village hoping to find me. It seems they don't like the rain either.

As we reach the woods, I feel a phenomenal sense of

being home. I smooth my hands along the tree bark, pluck the leaves and listen for the snap of the twigs or the scurry of an animal trying to shelter from the conditions. Even the rain feels as if it is right here. I want to run, to climb, to cover myself in mud and then dash home and let my mother clean me up again.

My enthusiasm is tempered as everyone else is thoroughly miserable – not that I can blame them. The water is everywhere, rain running down my forehead into my eyes as I try to lead the way. I can feel it dripping from my nose, running down my back, squelching into my shoes.

At the edge of the forest, I look around for the others but can see nothing but vague silhouettes walking beside me through the gloom of the night and the storm.

The first part of the gully drops down steeply. I am used to each ridge and handhold but these have all been washed into one large hill of mud. Instead of heading along the route I know best, we continue to walk around the crater, looking for a place where we can descend without sliding perilously towards the mounds of rubbish. We are just over a quarter of the way around when I spot the chassis of a train carriage lying on its side. I have never seen it before, although this is the first time I have walked this far around the pit and really examined its contents. Usually I would head towards the centre, hunting for small parts I could salvage. The train carriage is so enormous that I cannot begin to guess how they managed to dump it here. I slide down the bank and land with a thump on the thick metal. There is no way I'm going to keep my footing, so I sit in a puddle and use my hands to pull myself along until I reach a door that is hanging inwards. After checking that everyone else is following, I lower myself through the gap and drop into the carriage, landing awkwardly on the broken remains of a cushioned chair.

Despite the difficult journey to get here and the endless rat-a-tat-tat of rain on metal, this is the most secure structure in which we have tried to sleep since leaving the castle.

We try our best to dry out but much of what we are wearing feels more liquid than solid. None of us sleep; instead we sit around talking as the monsoon finally slows to a stop just as the sun begins to signal the start of a new day.

We share out the dry clothes we have, making ourselves as comfortable as we can be, and then, through a combination of piggybacks and stretching, lift each other out of the compartment. Slowly, I lead the way across the sea of discarded junk. I tell the others to follow my footsteps, crunching across various pieces of electrical debris until the path begins to dip down and I find myself in a more familiar area.

As we get closer to the centre, the rubbish is more spread out but everything is larger, with cliffs of old fridges piled alongside the husks of vehicles. It looks rickety but the trail is surprisingly straightforward as we bound across the cars until we reach the bottom of the gully and find a route along the natural bowl. With soil under our feet again, the towering wreck of rubbish soaring above us is almost as impressive as the towers of Middle England. Under both structures I feel tiny as I skip my way around another pile of metal until I emerge into a clearing.

As soon as Mayall told me my family was in the gully, this is the spot where I knew they would be. I have been here once before and as I stride towards a pile of cars that have fallen into a pyramid-type structure, the first face I see walking towards us belongs to the person I was with when I first found this spot.

He runs towards me, calling my name, arms out-stretched as the rest of our families emerge from the improvised tepee behind him. As he reaches me, he wraps his arms around me, lifting me from the ground as if I am a rag doll.

'I knew I'd see you again,' he says, spinning me around.

'It's great to see you too,' I reply, as Opie places me on the ground next to Imrin.

21

Pietra, Jela, Faith and Hart stand and stare as Imrin looks quizzically at Opie, whose eyebrows are raised and nose is wrinkled as he stares down at me, wondering why I don't seem more pleased to see him.

'It's getting long,' I say, pointing towards the dark beard which has grown on his chin. When I left it was a few wiry spikes but it is as if he has changed from boy to man in the few months since I last saw him. As I have wasted away through hunger and non-stop exercise, he has grown bigger. I recognise the cream T-shirt he is wearing but it fits him in a way it never did before, bulging across his upper arms and chest.

Opie runs his finger along his chin, smiling. 'It's good for keeping you warm out here.'

Over his shoulder, I see my way out. My mother is standing in the gap at the front of the shelter, hair even greyer than when I last saw her, looking tired as she wipes her hands on her skirt and grinning as Colt stands next to her, staring open-mouthed.

'I've got to go,' I say, striding past Opie and leaving the

others. There are members of Opie's family but I only have eyes for mine as I bound forward and embrace my mum, wrapping my arms around her and bursting into tears. I feel Colt clinging to my leg but the only words I hear are hers, telling me how she thought she would never see me again.

I don't know how much time passes until she releases me but it's not long enough. She looks me up and down, licking her thumb and wiping something away from my cheek. 'You're so thin,' she says, stating the obvious. 'But you've got taller.'

'I haven't, Mum.'

'Don't argue with your mother. I say you have and you have.'

It's nice to be back.

I crouch and give Colt a proper hug, going through the motions of telling him how grown-up he seems and asking if he's been looking after Mum for me. He has got a bit taller and his hair has grown out more. He tugs at it, staring at me as if I'm a ghost. He seems happy that I'm back and then, sheepishly, asks if he can go and play. Just behind him, I see one of Opie's brothers, Eli, watching us. As soon as I look towards him he glances away.

'Hello, Eli,' I say and he reluctantly acknowledges me. I laugh and tell Colt he can go and have fun. I didn't find this place until I was older but this is a perfect playground for a ten-year-old.

As I am about to stand, I feel something clatter into my side. The force knocks me sideways, leaving me flat on my back staring up at the blue of the sky. Imp is suddenly on top of me, looking more like his eldest brother than ever, even if his eyes are green in contrast to the piercing blue of Opie's and the rest of his brothers'. Imp has let his hair grow out slightly too, as if there are no scissors in the entirety of this place, so it is the same flopping mass of blond that his brothers have. There is something about Opie's smile which never seems natural. If you tell a joke, you can't be sure he has got it because his eyes rarely match his lips, as if his face cannot work as one to convey what he is thinking. It's one of the things I find wonderful about him; that half-look of confusion before he starts to grin. Imp is completely different; with smiles and an expression of adventure permanent features on his face. Now, his cheekbones seem a little higher, his skin slightly darker and his eyes are perhaps more turquoise than green.

Like the other Cotton brothers he is becoming a mini-Opie.

He straddles my stomach and punches me in the shoulder. It only hurts a little but I'm still strong enough to teach him a lesson. I feign twisting one way and jolt back the other before he has time to adjust his knees. It sends him flying into the dirt and I leap onto him before he can react, using the biggest weapon I have in my armoury – the one that always wins a fight.

Basically, I cheat.

I stretch my fingers underneath his top and start tickling him just above his hips. He squirms and squeals, screeching and shouting with joy. I hear him saying 'stop' but he has no chance.

'Do you give up?' I ask.

A grin. He is enjoying it. 'No.'

More tickling. He writhes so much that he rolls onto his back, giving me more areas to target.

He is out of breath, panting and crying. 'Do you give up?'

'Yes!' he shouts. I can't stop laughing myself as I roll off and lie next to him on the floor. He twists over until we are next to each other, backs in the dirt, staring up at the sky.

I don't know what it is about him but even though he is only seven, there's no one I have more fun with than Imp. 'I've missed you, mate,' I say.

'I didn't miss you.'

'Oh, yes you did. I can tell. You missed my tickles, didn't you?'

'No.'

'I suppose you won't want your present if you didn't miss me.'

'What present?'

'I've been away all this time – you didn't think I'd come back empty-handed, did you?'

'What is it?'

I shift onto my front so I can see Imp properly. His curious eyes are staring into mine, trying to figure out if I'm lying. 'It doesn't matter now. If you didn't miss me, I'll probably give it to someone else. Felix might want it, or perhaps I'll keep it.'

'No, no . . . I missed you more than Felix.'

Felix, the middle brother, is chasing around the edge of the clearing with Eli and Colt. Samuel, the next eldest after Opie, is talking to his father, Evan, close to the shelter. There are Cotton family members everywhere.

'Samuel looks like he missed me,' I say, nodding towards the other boy.

Imp rolls onto his front. 'No way, he and our dad both said you were a traitor. I stole his shoes and hid them so he couldn't go out.'

'Did you give them back?'

A wicked grin. 'Eventually.'

I haul myself into a sitting position and put an arm around Imp. He doesn't even shake it off. 'Can you do me a favour, mate?'

'What?'

'Can you go and play with Colt, Eli and Felix for a while? I need to talk to a few people.'

His face falls. 'Talking's boring.'

I pull him towards me and point towards our parents. '*You* know it's boring – *I* know it's boring – but look at all these boring people. Boring people don't know that talking is boring, that's why they're boring.'

I see his eyes rolling slightly, trying to work it out, before he smiles and nods. 'So boring people are boring because they don't realise that talking is boring?'

'Right. And they talk a lot.'

He continues nodding slowly, as if I have explained the meaning of life to him. 'So you have to go and be boring for a bit?'

'Exactly.'

'But you'll come and play later?'

'Obviously.'

'And I'll get my present?'

'Of course. You'll just have to keep it quiet from your brothers so they don't get jealous.'

He nods, thinking it is a fair exchange, and then leaps to his feet. 'Okay, see you later.' In a blink, he is gone. His little legs whirl manically, seemingly unable to keep up with the rest of his body as he charges off towards the far end of the clearing where the others are playing.

For a few seconds, I fall back onto the ground and close my eyes. It is as if everything has been worth it just for the few minutes I've been able to spend with Imp.

At the same time I have learned something worrying. At the very least, Opie's father and one of his brothers don't just think I'm a traitor, they've been saying it out loud. Evan Cotton has always been a huge royalist and a massive supporter of the system we have. He lived through the civil war that brought the King to power and is certain this is a better way. I have never been that close to Samuel. He is two years younger than Opie and even though we have never fallen out, we've never had much of a connection. Eli and Colt are both ten and have grown up playing together, while Felix is a little older but still young enough to join in with their games. Opie, the eldest, and Imp, the youngest, have both been drawn to me – and that leaves Samuel as the only one who has never been much of a part of our two interconnected families. I can only suppose he is following his father's opinions.

I want to be able to rest here all day, listening to the sounds of the children running and playing – and perhaps even join in myself, jumping and climbing, fighting and arguing.

Then I remember why I am here. I haul myself to my feet and walk to where everyone else is congregating. As I get closer, I see there are two separate shelters. The first is the pyramid-shaped pile of cars with a large gap underneath, but behind it two more cars are resting against the structure, creating a lean-to and another wide space for people to sleep under.

Around the rest of the area are many more broken vehicles that look as if they were dropped from high above one after the other. There is no order or structure, which is exactly why it works. As I step across the ground, I see there are patches of green shoots in various spots. I cannot help but feel that, with so many places to rest and hide, we could make this a community of our own.

Mum is talking to Jela in front of the tepee but my eyes are drawn to the lean-to at the back. Opie is arguing with his father, their voices raised, although the breeze is sending their words in the opposite direction. Evan jabs a finger into Opie's chest which is slapped away angrily. Opie is a few inches taller than his father and, just for a second as his shoulders arch back, I think he is going to hit him. Instead, another finger shoots out, which Opie grabs, before pushing his dad away and storming off through a gap in the cars.

I stride towards my mother, who now has Pietra's attention, as well as Jela's. She is showing them around the campsite, the three of them talking as if they are old friends. I hear Jela say something about 'where I come from', before my mum tells her that it sounds very nice.

Realising it is awkward, I interrupt their conversation. 'Is it just our family and Opie's living here?' I ask.

My mum seems a little put out by my manners, her eyebrows drawing downwards in disapproval. She answers anyway. 'Yes.'

'We all need a talk, just the adults, plus me and my friends. I need to go and find Opie.'

She nods as the other two girls look at me, confused. 'Okay, I'll make sure everyone is here before you get back.'

'Thanks.'

I turn and head away from the shelter towards a spot where Imrin and Faith are standing and watching. 'Can you do something for me?' I ask the pair of them.

Both seem a little annoyed that I have ignored them until now, but neither refuses. I nod towards Opie's father. 'Imrin, I need you to go and talk to Evan and keep him occupied. We're having a meeting in a few minutes and I need him calm. Don't talk about me and don't talk about anything to do with our escape.'

'What am I supposed to talk about?'

'I don't know – what do men usually chat about? Make something up but, whatever you do, keep him calm.' I nod towards Opie's mother, who is now talking to her husband. 'That's his wife, Iris,' I say to Faith. 'Get her on her own and tell her everything you can think of about what we've been through.' I peer closely at the cut, which is almost healed on the side of Faith's face. 'Tell her about the Kingsman who did that – how much bigger than you he was and what bullies they are.'

Faith nods and doesn't ask the obvious question, although Imrin can't resist. 'Why?'

'I need you to trust me. I know these people.'

'Where are you going?'

'I've got to go and find someone.'

Imrin's pupils suddenly seem enormous, huge dark pools of endless black that let me see his innermost thoughts. From the moment Opie called my name, Imrin knew there was something there. I can see him asking me exactly what is going on. Is Opie just an old friend, or is he something else?

Before he can ask anything out loud, I repeat myself – 'I've got to go' – and then turn like the coward I am, dashing past the shelters in the direction in which Opie headed.

At first, the piles of metal are well-spaced, providing a maze easy enough to negotiate. I hurry along the pathways calling Opie's name but the passages quickly narrow until I realise that the labyrinth is so dense, he could have gone anywhere. I retrace my steps towards the centre when I spot Opie sitting in a corner between two washing machines, watching me with a hint of a smile on his face.

As I approach, I slap the machine with my hand and sit between his legs. 'My mum would love one of these,' I say.

'She was always going on about what it was like when she was a kid and everyone had something easy to wash their clothes with.'

'I saw you run past,' Opie admits.

'Why didn't you call after me?'

A tingle zigzags down my spine as his fingers close around my hips in a way they haven't done in ages. 'It was nice watching you.'

'We've got to go back so I can tell everyone why we're here.'

'Why *are* you here?'

'A few reasons – I'll tell everyone together.'

'Not for me then?'

He sounds aggrieved and I know I have brought this on myself. 'We'll talk later, just not now.'

'Who's the other kid?'

I feel another tingle but for different reasons. 'Who do you mean?'

'The lad with the brown skin.'

'His name is Imrin.'

'Who's he?'

I have rarely heard Opie's voice like this. Usually, I lead our conversations and get to say what happens. Now it feels as if I am being interrogated.

'He's someone I escaped with. I'll tell you about it if you come with me.'

I try to pull myself up but Opie grips my hips and pulls me towards him. In days gone by we would roll around and play-fight but I'm not strong enough any more. My arms feel like twigs to his tree trunks.

'Do you remember being kids?' Opie says.

He has always been about the present and the future. I cannot ever remember him speaking about our pasts before.

'What about it?'

'Have I ever told you how much I hated you?' He laughs gently but it is the first I know of it.

'You hated me?'

'You were always such a bully. When we were really young, we would do things together but then I became this big, lumbering kid and you did everything you could to make things worse. You'd hide my things and call me names. I was miserable.'

Everything he says is true but I've never heard him speak like this. When we started hanging around as friends and doing everything together, it was as if everything before had never happened. I remember it as jokes, he remembers me being mean.

'I was just a kid,' I say, not knowing how else to defend myself. Suddenly, it feels as if I am the big strong one and Opie has the spindly, tiny frame. I push myself onto his lap and turn so I can cradle his head. 'Why are you thinking about this now?'

He shakes his head. 'When I said I knew I'd see you again, that wasn't true. We both thought you'd be off doing something else after the Reckoning – but you were always going to be somewhere nearby. And then, with you being chosen for the Offering, I didn't know what to think. No one has ever come back. I thought you were gone. It took ages for it to sink in. I'd go out to the woods and sit under our tree by myself.'

I gulp. *Don't cry.*

'I'd walk to the edge of the gully and look at all that junk, thinking about those times where you'd send me out there looking for little bits and pieces that you needed to help mend some thing or another. This one time I was there on my own and it started to rain. Nothing serious, not like last night, just a little sprinkle. I thought of you and the way I'd head for cover but you'd walk slowly with your arms out, enjoying every drop.'

His voice cracks and his fingers tense around me. I am blinking so quickly that I give up and close my eyes instead. *Not now.*

'Just as I was coming to terms with it all, our screen switched on that night and it was you and something to do with the King. We couldn't tell what was going on but you were at the centre of it and it was so brilliant to see your face again. But your mum got that message telling her to get away. She came round with Colt but didn't know if it was serious. I knew it would be so we ran. They didn't know where to go but I remembered the time we came here. I sent Imp off to tell the drunk guy in case you came back and we never stopped. We all got the alerts on our thinkwatches saying you tried to kill the King and that we must hand ourselves in. My dad was ready to do it but we kept him here somehow. We don't have a screen so no one knows what's going on. I guess I just thought that after seeing the message about the King, they would catch you and that would be that. I always hoped you'd come back.'

'I'm here now.' My voice doesn't sound like my own. It is raw and croaky and my nose is blocked.

'The reason I was thinking about when we were young was because I never got to tell you that, even with all you did to me, there was still that bit of me deep down that just knew . . .'

I know I should stand and lead him back to the others. Whatever I do I shouldn't hold him tighter. I shouldn't breathe in the smell of his neck and I definitely shouldn't ask the question . . .

'Knew what?'

'That I've loved you since the day I saw you.'

And that's it. He was my first kiss. He's my first love. The first boy to tell me he loves me. As my arms tighten around his neck I know without doubt that I shouldn't have asked.

22

I can tell straight away that Faith and Imrin have done the job I needed them to. Opie's parents are next to each other as we sit in a circle around the edge of the tepee. There are a handful of makeshift chairs that have been created from various pieces of scrap metal, but most of us are on the ground. Opie's mother is angling away from her husband, with obvious tension between them.

I am next to my mum at the opposite end, with Jela by me and Hart on the other side of my mother. Hart seems pale and has been guzzling water all morning but insists he is fine. Pietra is by Imrin, with Opie on the other side of him. Imrin and Opie haven't said a word to each other, both looking awkwardly towards me. Faith is by Opie's mother, Iris, in a piece of perfect placement engineered entirely by her. Samuel has been sent outside to keep watch over the rest of the children, much to his annoyance.

'I know you haven't got a screen, so there has been a lot of confusion about what's happened since the Offering,' I say. 'It's true that I am wanted for attempting to kill the King and it's true that all of you are in huge danger, not only for hiding away from the authorities but because I'm here too.'

I pause to let it sink in. Evan Cotton says something under his breath but his wife instantly leaps to my defence. 'Will you just sit down and shut up,' Iris bellows, leaving him to look suitably chastened, exactly as I wanted. Faith catches my eye from across the room but neither of us needs to say anything.

After that, I run through everything that happened from the moment the train left Martindale to us walking into the camp that morning. Unlike with Hart's parents, I don't skip over details. Opie's mother's hand shoots down to rest on Faith's shoulders in sympathy at various points, as she sends dagger-like glares at her husband in between.

Evan is unconvinced. 'If all of that is true, then why wouldn't you hand yourself in? It's obviously a mistake that they think you tried to kill the King – you escaped because you were unhappy being away from home. Anyone could understand that.'

I don't even need to reply. 'Did you not listen to a word she said?' Iris thunders, turning to Faith. 'Look at her face. Where do you think she got those bruises from? Do you think she's lying that it was a Kingsman who did it?'

Faith touches the mark with expert timing and winces slightly, even though I'm pretty sure it no longer hurts.

Evan looks at her and shakes his head. 'I'm not saying

that . . . it's just, maybe there was some confusion?' He points towards me. 'If all the Kingsmen thought she was a traitor, perhaps they got a bit rough because of that?'

'Don't be so ridiculous.' His wife turns her back to him.

He looks clueless trying to defend a regime he doesn't understand, simultaneously turning the room against him. I feel slightly sorry about my manipulation. I needed him to look foolish because a person *should* look silly if they are attempting to defend the King. I realise Opie's father has lived through a war and thinks that the way we live now is better than what went before – but at this moment it is more important that he believes what we are telling him. For some, gentle reasoning would do it but I have known him for too long. This humiliation and slap down via his wife is the only way.

Opie's father stares towards me, his head shaking back and forth. 'So are you saying that every Offering that has ever been sent to the castle has either been killed or traded?'

'Yes.'

Hart speaks up. 'Of the thirty Offerings from my year, there were just two left by the time Silver arrived.'

Evan's reply is spluttered and confused. 'But why would the King do that? I mean . . . he's the King.'

He has asked one of the few questions we can't answer. Only the King knows why he does it all – but I doubt even he can explain his actions. I suspect it is partly madness and, ultimately, he does it because he can. If no one stops a person from behaving in a certain way, then who's to judge what is wrong?

I shake my head. 'There's something else.' I take my mum's hand. 'There's going to be a second Offering. They announced it last week and made the draw yesterday. They've changed the criteria so it isn't based on the Reckoning this time and they've lowered the age limit.'

I feel Mum's fingers tense around mine as she draws me to look at her. I give her a gentle nod to confirm her thoughts before saying it out loud. 'Colt has been chosen. He's supposed to be in Martindale this morning to be taken away.'

Mum grips my hand so tightly that I have to pull away.

Evan leaps to his feet. 'We should get going now then. We all know the penalty if you don't submit yourself.'

Nobody else moves until Iris stands and slaps her husband across the face. 'He's dead anyway,' she rages. 'If he stays here, he's got a death sentence; if he becomes an Offering then you've already heard what goes on.'

I feel my mother trembling at the phrasing, but she is right: Colt is marked to be killed regardless.

'We're not going back to Martindale,' I say firmly, taking charge. 'There's plenty of rainwater to gather here and as long as you store it sensibly, you'll have plenty. Food is more of an issue but I know you brought lots with you.

As soon as spring comes, there'll be berries and fruits on the trees and there are animals to hunt. Between you all, you'll get by.'

Everyone around the circle nods, even Opie's father – but it is Opie himself who actually notices what I've said. '*You'll* get by,' he repeats. 'Aren't you staying?'

I feel my mother's head swivel to face me. 'I've got somewhere else to go. If everything goes well, I'll either return here or, hopefully, we'll be free to go home.'

'Where are you going?' Opie asks.

I start to reply but then stop myself. 'It's better if I don't tell everyone. You never know what might happen. If you don't have information, you can't be forced to give it away.'

'I'm going with you.'

Opie states it as a fact, not a question. Imrin spins to look at him, although they still don't say a word to each other.

'You're *not* going,' his father says.

'You can't stop me,' Opie replies dismissively.

'I'm your father and you'll do what I say.'

Opie doesn't reply but he shakes his head.

'I've got a few things to sort out and then we're going when it gets dark,' I say. 'If any of you need to ask anything then I'll be around.'

I hope Imrin and Opie don't take that too literally as I

have no intention of discussing anything unrelated to where we are heading with either of them.

I look from Hart to Jela, Pietra and Faith, making sure I acknowledge each of them. 'I can't begin to thank you for everything you've done getting me here. You know where we're going next. If you want to come, you're welcome, but if you want to stay, there's no better or safer place. Just make sure you say goodbye before I go.'

I push myself up, nodding towards Opie's dad. 'Can I have a word?' He seems surprised but slowly gets to his feet and follows me out of the hut.

I peer around, making sure nobody else is in earshot. 'I need to know that you're going to stay here and look after everyone,' I say.

He stares at me harshly, probably wondering why a sixteen-year-old girl is telling him what to do. 'You've put my family in a lot of danger,' he replies.

I nod and stare at the ground, letting him see that I am sorry. 'I know, but there's nothing I can do about that now. I hope you believe what the reasons were. There were six of us in there who have lived through this. You can't think we're all lying.'

I can see he is weighing it up in his mind. 'I don't know what to think . . .'

'We're going tonight. If you don't want Opie to go then I'll tell him to stay. Whatever you think of me, he'll listen.

I'm not saying he should go or stay, but I do think he should be allowed to decide. He told me it was him who brought you all here and kept you safe, so I think you owe him something. Whether he stays or goes, you're the one everyone looks to here. My father died a long time ago and you've got all those wonderful sons who think you're the best thing around. Then there is my mum and my brother too. Everyone here needs you so much more than they need me.'

He begins to nod and it is almost scary how quickly I have manipulated him. Imrin calmed him down, Faith wound his wife up, Iris embarrassed him, making him feel like he was an outsider, and then I gave him the role he wanted all along. He gets to be a dad not only to his own sons – but to the entire campsite.

He lowers his voice. 'I won't stop Opie going with you if that's what he wants.'

'Thank you.'

'And I'll make sure everyone stays here safely.'

'If Opie comes, someone else will have to learn how to hunt. Samuel would be perfect. It's something you could do together – provide for everyone.'

He nods again, more enthusiastically this time. 'You're right,' he says, before stumbling over his next sentence. 'I, er, hope everything works out for you.'

'Thanks.'

He steps away from me, calling for Samuel, ready to tell him of his new role. With that taken care of, I send Opie out to gather me some spare parts, much like the old days, as I set myself up to work atop a car bonnet. I spread out the parts he brings and dismantle a selection of thinkpads, trying to salvage anything that could be useful. Through the afternoon, everyone comes to say their mixtures of hellos and goodbyes. Hart is the first, asking what time we are leaving and saying he'll be ready. Jela and Pietra follow shortly afterwards, holding hands and standing slightly away from me.

'Do you mind if we stay?' Jela asks. I turn and grin, stepping towards them and wrapping my arms around the pair. 'It's your mum,' Jela adds. 'She's brilliant. She's trying to turn this into a proper little society. It reminds me of the place I had to leave before we were moved to the city.'

'I'm really pleased you'll be able to help,' I say. 'Just keep an eye on Opie's youngest brother . . .'

Pietra interrupts. 'That Imp kid?'

I burst out laughing at the irritated look on her face. 'What did he do?'

'He had this bean that he said was magic. He was trying to sell it to me and when I told him I wasn't interested, he pinched me on the leg, called me a name that I shall not repeat, and ran off.'

I try to look sympathetic but can't manage it. 'I'll have a word,' I say. 'He's a bit of a handful.'

Jela is managing not to laugh much more successfully than I am but we hug again as I tell them I'll see them before I leave. I'm glad they are staying – I'll miss them but they deserve some normality in their lives.

Just as I am beginning to get somewhere with my work, I see Imrin hovering nearby. At first I ignore him but his presence is distracting. 'You can still talk to me,' I call over, not looking up.

He seems reluctant as he crosses towards me. I continue to focus on the inner workings of a thinkpad.

'Do you want me to come with you?' he asks.

'It's up to you.'

He sighs and rests both hands on the bonnet. 'That's not what I asked.'

I finish removing a tiny screw and turn to face him. 'I'd like you to come with me. We've done all of this together and it isn't just about me. If it wasn't for you, I wouldn't be here.'

He nods but doesn't seem overly pleased. 'What about you and me?'

I turn back to the pad, fixing my eyes on a connector switch and trying the connection to trace the power source. 'I don't know.'

'What about you and *him*?'

'I don't know.'

He stays next to me for a few seconds longer as I feel his eyes skimming my face. His voice is husky and low. 'It was clever what you did with Opie's father.'

'How do you mean?'

'You know.' I don't reply. I *do* know what I've done but I was naively hoping no one other than Faith really understood. 'He's already made a makeshift spear and has been showing Samuel how to throw it,' Imrin adds.

'Good.'

'Do you ever think about how all this started? Was the King a good man one day and then it went to his head over time? People never said "no" to him, so he kept on pushing? He had people doing whatever he ordered until it became so natural that nothing seemed off-limits?'

I feel an uncomfortable prickling around my ears and refuse to look away from the thinkpad. 'What are you saying?'

'You know what I'm saying.'

Before I can reply, he turns and walks away, telling me over his shoulder that he'll see me later. He has made his point and I realise that he knows me better than anyone, even Opie. I had been feeling proud of my manipulation but it can be a dangerous thing if you forget where that line is. Have I crossed it? Is this something Opie would ever be able to say to me – or would he even see it?

Imrin and Opie: my conscience and my temptation.

I am almost finished as my mother arrives. I don't hear her coming; instead I feel her fingers pulling my hair behind me. 'Silver Blackthorn,' she says wistfully, pronouncing our last name with a long 'O' in the middle in the way only she can.

'I'm sorry I have to go again.'

She rests her head on my back and hugs herself into me. 'You're the head of our family now. You do what you need to.'

I turn until I am holding her properly and realise she was right – I have grown slightly since I last saw her. 'I hope this will all be over soon.'

She sniffles away a sob. 'I'm really proud of you. Who would have thought my little girl would be the most famous person in the country?'

I laugh at the suggestion. 'I'm famous because they want me dead!'

She sniffs again, holding me tighter. 'I didn't mean it like that. It's because you're the one who has been brave enough to say things aren't right.'

That's not what was in my mind when I told X that I was after revenge – but the myth that surrounds me is big enough to take in my own mother.

'I've got something to show you,' I say, releasing her and turning towards the thinkpad on the car bonnet. 'I've had to take five of these things apart to find enough pieces to make one work and Opie has found all sorts of other odds and ends.'

I flick a switch at the back and push my thumb against the edge of the screen, showing her how to turn it on.

'This will work as a screen,' I say. 'You'll be able to watch all of the broadcasts from now on. You'll find that I'm on the news and, although it's almost entirely lies, you'll at least have some idea of what's going on away from here.'

She takes the device and tries turning it on herself. 'This is really clever.'

'I'm going to tell Colt it's a present for him so he doesn't get annoyed that he hasn't got anything. Most of what you'll want to see will be on after he's gone to bed anyway.'

She hands the screen back and brushes some loose hair away from my face. 'You're so grown-up,' she says, before hugging me one final time and saying she is going to round the children up.

As dusk slowly begins to settle, everyone gathers at the outside of the tepee. Imp clings to one of my legs, Colt clasping the other. They are arguing over who can get me to stay.

There was never any doubt that Faith would come with me and she has her bag on her back and is half-turned away from everyone, anxious to get moving. Opie has said good-bye to his family, apparently making peace with his father, and has taken Jela's pack, filling it with all the clothes he had with him, as well as a tarpaulin given to us by his father. He found it in the rubbish dump on their trek away from the village but it is in a good state and will serve us well. As for Opie, it will be good to have someone strong and fit with us.

Imrin is ready too, although there is clear tension between him and Opie as they look in opposite directions, refusing to acknowledge one another, even though they are next to each other. I'm still not sure if they have spoken yet.

Lastly, Hart is looking as healthy as he has done since we left the castle. His face still seems pale but he heaves his rucksack onto his back easily, showing strength he's not had in a long time.

'Where's my present?' Imp complains, slapping me in the back of the knees.

'If he gets a present, I get one!' says Colt.

I shake them both off and crouch, opening my bag and taking the thinkpad out. I hand it to Colt, who happily begins to jab at the screen. 'Mum will show you how this works,' I tell him. 'If she ever needs it, then you listen to her and let her have it. Understand?'

'Yes.'

I try to hug him but he pulls away, fascinated by his new toy.

Imp is yanking on my leg. 'Is there one for me too?'

'I've heard you've been playing tricks on my friends?'

Imp puts on his best innocent voice. 'No.'

'Something about magic beans . . .'

He looks at his feet. 'Do I still get my present?'

'Are you going to be nice to my friends?'

'Yes.'

'Promise?'

'Yes.'

'Okay, come here.' I pull him towards me and squeeze him to within an inch of his life. 'Here you are,' I say, reaching into my bag and giving him my soft toy. 'It's called a tortoise.'

He squishes it in the middle and turns it over. 'What does it do?'

'A tortoise is an animal that they have in other places around the world. They move really slowly and when they get scared, they hide their arms, legs and head inside their shell.'

'All the way in?'

'Yes. This is one of my favourite things and I'm giving it to you to look after for me. Can you do that?'

'Yes.'

He is poking the toy in the head, seeing if he can force it into the soft shell. 'Look at me,' I say, waiting for him to do so. 'If there is ever any trouble, if any men come, if there are any bangs or anything like that, I want you to think of the tortoise. Grab Colt, grab Eli and hide somewhere. Okay?'

His face screws up as he continues to poke the tortoise in the eye. 'All the way in?'

'Exactly. Don't get into trouble; don't think you're helping out, just hide. Make sure your arms, legs and head are all hidden somewhere safe.'

'Okay.'

'I'm relying on you to take Colt and Eli with you.'

'I will.'

'Thanks, mate.'

I push myself up until I am standing, heave my bag onto my back and walk across to the others.

'Ready?' I ask.

Nobody answers but the four of them turn to follow. We are heading south from our location, as we looped around Lancaster in the first place to get here. Having had a chance to rest, eat and drink over the past day, at a decent pace we should arrive as the sun is rising.

I lead the way, stepping onto an improvised ramp that heads towards a place we can easily clamber up the side of the gully.

Just as I hop from one car bonnet to another, I hear the crunching thud of flesh on metal. My shoes slide as I spin to see Hart lying flat on his back, eyes rolling back into his head, blood pouring from his nose.

23

Opie drops his pack and falls to his knees next to Hart. 'What do we do?' he says, looking at me.

I struggle to control the shock and concern in my voice as I stammer a reply. 'Get him to my mum and Pietra.'

With a grunt, Opie heaves Hart into his arms and hurries back the way we came. I don't know why he has collapsed but assume it is because his infected arm has never healed. Imrin and Faith stand waiting to see what I'm going to do but I feel lost too. Throughout everything, Hart has been there. As his body hangs limply in Opie's arms, I remember the look on his face as his father called through the house to say he and his mother were proud of him. There was a sense of self-worth I hadn't seen in him before.

I follow Opie, not knowing what else to do and by the time I arrive at the shelter, my mum has already cleared everyone out. Hart is on a pile of blankets, unmoving.

'You've got to go,' my mum says without looking at me.

'What's wrong with him?'

Pietra is on her knees on the other side of Hart, pulling away the sleeves of his top to reveal an ugly yellow gash. My mother peers at it and winces, then mutters something to Pietra that I don't catch.

'This cut is infected,' my mum says. 'He might have blood poisoning. We've got a few odds and ends here.'

'Is he going to be all right?'

For the first time, she looks up. 'I don't know. Now go.'

'Mum . . .'

'Silver, go and do what you have to do. We'll do what we can for him here.'

'How long will he survive if you don't have enough medicine?'

'Silver!'

It is the first time she has shouted at me in years.

'Just tell me and I'll go.'

She shakes her head in frustration and Pietra returns with a bowl of water. 'It depends on lots of things. Now go.'

I take one final look at the mess that is Hart's arm, wondering why he let it get that bad, and then turn and walk away.

* * *

Imrin, Opie, Faith and I walk in near silence for the entire night, only stopping once for a drink before ploughing on. Almost the whole journey is through fields or woodland

and we don't see a soul from the moment we climb out of the gully until we reach the outskirts. We have moved so quickly that there is at least an hour before the sun comes up. Imrin and Opie work together to fix the tarpaulin to a tree as I take Faith to the edge of the woods that overlook Lancaster.

'What happened to this place?' Faith asks.

We have passed many towns and cities, plenty that were deserted but there have always been at least some buildings almost unaffected and still standing. This place feels different – it is a sea of wreckage. The moon is fading as daylight prepares to take over but the dim light allows us to see for a couple of miles across to where there are more fields on the far side of what was once the city. In between, there is nothing but concrete and carnage.

I indicate a spot below us, pointing out the remains of a castle. We see the outline of what could be a moat but it is filled with rubble, circular patterns of interconnected bricks the only indication of what it once was.

'Is that where this "X" person is?' Faith asks.

'I have no idea. He said I'd be smart enough to find him but where could he be? Everything's flat. Can you see anything that looks even remotely liveable?'

'No.'

Neither can I, which means we are going to have to explore ourselves.

'At least there are no Kingsmen,' Faith adds.

She is right – there is nothing to patrol. We head back to where Imrin and Opie have done a good job of creating a shelter. They are sitting underneath the tarpaulin, each fiddling with his pack, not talking to one another.

When we are all under cover, I start to speak, aware that Opie doesn't know as much as the other two. 'All I have to go on is that we are supposed to be meeting someone called "X". He said we should visit him here but didn't say exactly where he was. I never asked because I didn't realise there would be so little here.'

'Do you have a way of communicating with him?' Opie asks.

I shake my head but it is something I should have thought of.

'What do you want to do?' Faith asks.

'Usually it wouldn't be safe to go out during the day but there's nothing here. If we wait on the edge of town and watch for a few hours, we can see if anything happens. With any luck, we'll spot some sign of where X is but if not, and it's quiet, we'll explore this afternoon.'

I don't know if it is worse to leave Imrin and Opie together, or to go off with one of them, leaving the other. Hoping that a miracle occurs and they become good friends when I am not around, I tell them to get some sleep as Faith and I head back to the spot we found earlier. In the time we sit together, the only thing we see is a pair of fighting seagulls. Faith names the smallest one after her, insisting the larger one is called Silver, and then tells me it isn't an omen when Silver gets pecked and scratched until she flies away.

After three hours, we awaken Imrin and Opie and try to sleep ourselves. Although Faith's breathing becomes heavy within minutes, my mind is clouded by Imrin and Opie. Once they were interchangeable in my dreams, now they are both in front of me giving me a straight choice. I know it is absurd that this is what's keeping me awake when there is so much else going on. Meanwhile, poor Hart has battled so hard to make his way back to see his parents and now he could end up dying just a short distance away from them, without them knowing what has happened.

Time crawls to a stop as I try to fall asleep, even though I am as warm and as comfortable as we are likely to get sleeping outdoors.

Opie and Imrin arrive back just as my eyes are about to give in to much-needed sleep. I yawn three times in a row, which would usually be a signal for either of them to ask me if I'm all right. In the world I have somehow created for myself, neither wants to pick a fight with the other, so they remain silent. In case we need to make a quick escape, we pack our bags and cover them and then head for the castle.

We trace around the outline of where the castle walls

once stood, before moving towards the centre. There is a constant crunch of rubble and glass as we cross the debris, stopping regularly to look at anything that appears out of place. There are signs which would once have hung over shops, twisted pieces of metal entwined with tattered items of clothing fluttering in the breeze, random shoes buried under piles of bricks. On and on we search but there is nothing other than destruction.

After hours of traipsing around, we head back towards the castle shortly before it is about to get dark again. We have wasted an entire day walking and hunting around, only to find nothing. I can feel myself getting angry at whoever X is for bringing us here. I try to replay the conversation with him in my mind, wondering if there was a clue he gave about his location, but also cursing myself for not pushing him on the simplest of questions: how do I find you? I was so consumed that he had made me admit to myself that I was motivated by revenge that everything else became irrelevant.

We start one final lap of the castle site. I focus on the moat as the others find their own way around the rubble. It is hard to tell the colour of the remaining water because the space is filled with rocks, moss covering almost every surface. I reach in, pulling out a fistful of the velvety green sludge, although I have no idea what I'm hoping to see.

'Silver.'

Opie is standing in the centre of the castle, looking towards the mass wreckage of the town through which we have spent the afternoon hunting. The remnants of the walls are low but I can just about make out the shape of the structure.

'What?'

'Come here.'

I throw the moss to the floor and pull myself up. I am so used to the long days and nights of walking that the twinge which shoots along my back is almost an afterthought.

'What am I looking at?'

Opie points towards a spot at the edge of the castle. 'What do you see there?'

I look along the line of his finger and squint. 'Bricks. What do you see?'

He places both hands on my hips and shunts me into the spot where he was standing. Underneath my feet is a metal grate. 'Look again.'

This time I see it: one of the pieces of metal I had walked past and ignored earlier has been bent and twisted into a very deliberate X-shape. A couple of steps in either direction and it looks as if it is at random but from this central point it stands out.

I start running towards it before remembering there is a moat in the way. Embarrassingly, I have to retrace my steps before I can catch up with Opie, who is already halfway towards the metal. He gives me a look as if to say I haven't changed, as I call for Faith and Imrin to join us.

When we reach the spot, I realise why it was so hard to see. The metal isn't twisted into an X at all; instead it is a Y-shape. What makes it look like an X is a separate piece of metal a short distance away. When they are lined up at the right angle, the illusion is formed.

Imrin nods approvingly as Opie talks him and Faith through it, although I'm not sure if he is impressed by the fact Opie spotted it, or that someone managed to create it.

At first, I think there might be something under the Y but both pieces of metal are sticking out of huge concrete slabs. We count the steps between the concrete until we have a solid idea of the central point between them – and then we start digging. Because of the way the hatch looked at Knave's hideout, I think I have a pretty good idea of what we are searching for. It takes less than a minute before I try to pick up what I think is a rock but find it attached to something far larger. The sensation surprises me so much that I overbalance, collapsing into a heap.

'You found it then?' Faith says with a grin, helping me up.

Between the four of us, we push away any loose stones until we find the edges. None of us can find anything to grab on to, as the stones that are stuck to the hatch are either too small or too smooth to pick up. Imrin finds the trick this time: by simultaneously pressing the stones in the four corners, the cover pops downwards and then clicks up. Unless they were particularly flexible, it would be impossible for one person to open this by themselves.

Imrin slides the hatch to one side and we stare into the darkness below us. The fading sunlight reveals a rusting metal ladder descending one of the walls. Opie stares at me asking silently what I want to do but this is nothing new for the rest of us.

'I don't suppose anyone thought to bring a light from Martindale, did they?' I ask.

Imrin and Faith look at me blankly.

'Me neither,' I add, before I notice Opie reaching into a pocket inside his top.

He hands me a box of matches. 'I took these from our house when we were leaving. I've never taken them out.'

I pocket them and begin climbing down slowly. The rust feels rough on my hands but the rungs are at least solid as I descend carefully. When I reach the bottom, I can hear the tip-tap of footsteps above and then Imrin's voice echoes downwards: 'Should I seal it?'

'Yes,' I call and, as the hatch is pulled into place, the final traces of daylight are blocked, leaving us in darkness. I try to remind myself that we were invited here, even though we haven't had much of a welcome.

When everyone is at the bottom and we have finished apologising for bumping into each other, I strike the first of the matches. The light it provides is minimal and I have only taken three steps when it is blown out.

'That was a stupid idea,' I say, nudging the person I think is Opie with my elbow.

'I'm Faith,' she says with a hint of annoyance at the fact I have hit the wrong person.

'Sorry.'

'This way,' says Imrin's voice. 'Follow the walls.'

I reach forward until I feel the crumbling bricks and then keep one hand moving along as I walk in the direction of his voice. We round a couple of corners until the walls turn into a curved shape. I am about to call out to Imrin to say I think we should stop when there is a gentle click which is instantly followed by a loud clang. Light pours from the ceiling above so unexpectedly that I yelp inadvertently and cover my eyes. Through my eyelids I can see the bright white seeping through and blinding me.

Slowly I remove my hands and open my eyes a fraction but the light is too startling to see clearly.

I sense the others shuffling nervously next to me and, as my vision begins to return, six men with guns pointing directly at us drift into focus.

24

As we are marched through the tunnels, I try to tell the dark-suited figures that I was invited here by X. They don't even acknowledge that they know who he is. The question I asked him floats into my mind, word for word: 'How do I know I'm not walking into a trap?'

He never answered.

Guns were part of our education growing up. We always knew they were used extensively in the war but, since then, they have become rare. With factories no longer producing ammunition, they are almost obsolete. Until I saw the weapons in the guards' hands, I hadn't even thought about facing an enemy with guns – even the Kingsmen only have swords. With no trade between countries, it means we have to create everything for ourselves. I don't know how guns are made but there must be a reason why bullets aren't being manufactured any longer. Whatever the reason, it doesn't seem to be affecting the people pointing the weapons at us and it is safest to assume the guns are loaded.

We are led through tunnels until we reach a sheet of metal stretching from the floor to the ceiling. The guard at the front swipes his thinkwatch against something I can't see on the wall and the barrier shoots up and out of sight. The next room is large and circular and the metal floor feels springy. The metal door slots back into place behind us but there are two other exits from the room. Around the other walls are long workbenches, a few solid grey cabinets and one long bank of old-fashioned computer equipment. I can see the types of keyboards and screens I have spent most of my life picking apart but have never been able to get working.

The guards stand in front of the exits, leaving Opie, Imrin, Faith and myself in the centre of the room.

'You don't seem massively worried by the men pointing guns at us,' Opie whispers.

'It's not the first time we've been dragged underground by people with weapons.'

Opie coughs in surprise, making one of the guards twitch. 'How often has it happened?'

'Just the once – last time we were blindfolded.'

'So this is a step up?'

'Not really, they only had knives last time.'

'Shouldn't we be concerned they have guns pointing at us?'

'Think of it this way: if they were going to shoot us, they would have done it already. Out there it's just bricks. In here, there's shiny stuff everywhere. It's much harder to clean.'

Opie is sounding increasingly confused. 'You think they're not going to shoot us because they'll have more to clean up?'

I'm about to reply when Imrin beats me to it. 'This is what it's been like for the past month. People like pointing weapons at her.'

Out of the corner of my eye, I see Opie nodding. I am both annoyed and a tiny bit relieved, seeing as it is the first thing I've heard either of them say directly to the other without talking to the group as a whole.

Before I can think about defending myself, the guards turn and walk through the doors, leaving us alone.

'Does that usually happen?' Opie asks, louder this time.

I start to reply but am distracted by the heavy clatter of someone approaching.

The first time I ever saw a Kingsman in person, as opposed to on screen, was in the centre of Martindale when I was six years old. My mum had held my hand and led me to the town hall, saying there was something I had to see. At the bottom of the steps, a small red and white booth had been set up that was completely sealed except for a rectangular gap at the top. One either side, Kingsmen were standing rigidly, their hands behind their backs. 'Ignore them,' Mum whispered when she saw me staring.

Crowds began to gather behind us, mainly of parents with their children, and just as my legs were beginning to tire, a man came out from behind the booth and shouted 'Hello' at everyone. Although I had been transfixed by the Kingsmen, I couldn't stop looking at the new figure. He was dressed all in purple and had a flowing dark cloak that rippled behind him in the wind. There was something about his tone and the way he spread his arms that has stuck in my mind ever since. He would come back once a year until I was about ten and there would be some sort of puppet show. By the time he stopped coming, I had forgotten everything about the act except for the fact there were Kingsmen there – and the way that man dressed and talked.

Despite the guns that were recently pointed at us, the metal, the electronics and the people around me, I am suddenly that six-year-old girl again as a man sweeps into the room through one of the doors the guards just left by. A breath of air breezes across us as if we have stepped outside. He is tall but thin with tight black hair pulled away from his face and the hint of a beard. His cloak is just like the travelling entertainer's and he pronounces his words in a way that demands attention.

Before he can introduce himself, I know exactly who he is.

'Ms Blackthorn,' he says.

'Minister Prime Xyalis,' I reply.

His eyes narrow in surprise as I feel Imrin, Opie and

Faith staring at me. 'I've not been called that in a while,' he says. 'You really are as impressive as they say.'

Head Kingsman Porter once told me about the first Minister Prime, who was the King's right-hand man at the end of the war. He disappeared after a few months when he realised the King wasn't quite the man everyone thought and was replaced by Bathix – the person responsible for so much of what we escaped from at the castle.

'Everyone thinks you're dead,' I say.

'They're meant to.'

'You're the person who invented the Reckoning.'

Xyalis' eyes flicker to the others as there is a collective gasp. Our entire lives have been spent building towards the test which defines everyone who takes it – and now the inventor is standing in front of us.

He doesn't reply instantly, taking his time to choose his words carefully. 'I wouldn't put it exactly like that. I came up with the technology and the concept but it was never meant to be used in the way it has been.'

'How was it meant to be used?' Whether he meant it to or not, Opie's question is brimming with aggression.

Xyalis' eyes scan Opie up and down, perhaps wondering who he is, or maybe trying to figure out if he is a threat. 'The war was a terrible thing. So many people died and the country needed rebuilding. Tell me something you're good at.'

His demand is so direct that Opie blurts out an answer immediately and then puts a hand to his mouth, surprised. 'Hunting.'

A thin smirk crosses Xyalis' mouth. 'Exactly, but let's say you're really good at sewing . . .'

'I'm not.'

The smirk turns into a full smile. 'Let's say you are. You could spend your whole life *thinking* you're good at hunting when you are really the best person in the whole land when it comes to sewing. You don't even know it. The idea was to find people's hidden talents. That way, if that's what they wanted, they would be able to use those skills to help put the country back together again. Does that make sense?'

Opie nods. 'I suppose . . . I still can't sew though.'

I can't stop myself from laughing because even though he is only in my peripheral vision, I know Opie has that look on his face to show that he understands even though he hasn't quite processed it yet.

'I should apologise for the guns,' Xyalis says, his initial expression of authority returning. 'It wasn't my choice but my guards are very protective.'

'You could have at least told us how to find you,' I reply.

'If people are deserving of my attention then they work it out.'

It is pure arrogance but then, seeing as we found him, I suppose it is also a compliment.

Xyalis turns theatrically, sending his cloak flowing behind him. 'Come – we'll find somewhere more comfortable than this to talk.'

He strides away so quickly that I have to run to catch up. The corridors are lined with sheets of metal; the floor is made of a similar material, bouncing slightly as we walk on it. Xyalis leads us into a circular room that isn't too dissimilar to the one we left, except that it is around twice the size and packed with so many pieces of technology, both ancient and new, that I find myself turning in a full circle trying to take it all in.

'Impressed?' Xyalis asks as I realise my wide-eyed expression has given too much of myself away, making it obvious I know what everything is.

'There's a lot here,' I reply.

In the only area that isn't filled with banks of equipment, there is a circular table. Xyalis invites us to sit and then skirts around the edge. 'You must be Imrin,' he says, offering his hand to shake, before doing the same to Faith. He will know them from the broadcasts but Opie perplexes him. 'And you are . . . ?' he asks, holding out his hand.

'I'm Opie . . .' he replies, but I interrupt before he can add anything else.

'He's someone I know.'

Xyalis clearly wants to hear more but I'm nowhere near the point of trusting him enough to give away anything more than I have to. He nods and sits across from us.

Before he can ask anything else, I get in first. 'If the Reckoning was meant to be used as you described, what happened?'

Xyalis turns to face me, staring intently before replying. 'It was Victor. It's hard to explain what it was like as the war was ending. It didn't finish because there was a winner, but because people didn't want to fight any longer. There used to be a King or Queen a long time ago but they were simply there and didn't do very much. While the fighting was still going on, there were secret meetings between people high up on both sides. Everyone wanted to find a way to make it all stop and they came across the idea of a figurehead everyone could unite behind. The problem was that neither side wanted to give ground – so it couldn't be the leader of either the rebels or the nationalists. They started researching the old royal bloodline and that's when they found Victor.'

'He wasn't anything to do with either side?'

Xyalis shakes his head. 'Not only that, he was hiding away in a town somewhere in the south east because he didn't want to fight. Apparently, when they went to find him, he thought they were there to arrest him for refusing to be a soldier.'

It's not exactly the story with which we have grown up.

'So he went from hiding to running the country?'

Xyalis nods. 'Essentially, but it was never meant to be like that. Everyone knew the leaders of each side had to step aside. I'd been part of the nationalists, mainly working with technology. They took people from each side to form a government. We were supposed to work together to rebuild the country with Victor there as someone the nation would unite behind. The problem was that he took things too literally. We thought he was this scared kid and that he'd listen to whatever we told him. After he first went on screen, everyone really got behind him and that's what made him realise he could do what he wanted. Instead of listening to us, he'd say, "I'm the King", and that would be the end of the conversation. His first big act was to take the leaders of both sides and execute them live in front of the nation. After that, he kept pushing it further and further. Suddenly, all of our ideas about things like the Reckoning were either ignored or twisted to suit him.'

'But didn't you put him in place?'

'Not me personally, but yes. We wanted someone who wasn't one of us that everyone could say ended the war. It was nothing to do with him – he just happened to be born to the right mother. Both sides got together to stop things but the public were so tired of both of us they would never have accepted any of us. That execution went down so well with the public that Victor started believing he was exactly what the country needed. If anyone was caught stealing or committing crimes in the towns and cities, he'd bring them to Windsor and have them killed live on screen. It made him more and more popular but quickly spiralled out of control. Before we knew it, it was too late. I knew almost straight away that we'd made a massive mistake but we couldn't do anything. The country loved him – but they didn't see what was happening around the castle. People would be killed for making too much noise or using a word he didn't understand.'

'Why didn't you do something to get rid of him?'

Xyalis laughs but there is no pleasure in it. 'If we had done anything, it would have started another war. He was the one person holding the country together and yet he was completely crazy whenever the cameras were off. Instead of the Reckoning working the way I designed it, he made it more or less what it is now. It pushes you much more than it was ever meant to and causes some people permanent harm if they're not up to it. The system of Elites, Members, Intermediates and Trogs was his idea. He wanted a way to know which people could be used in the way he deemed to be useful. I wanted something that would help everyone to contribute but he twisted it into a way of discarding huge numbers of people.'

'How much of it is your design?'

He glances away from me awkwardly. 'More than I'm proud of but you don't know what it was like in those first few months. We never knew if we were going to wake up with someone holding a knife to our throat in the castle . . .'

'We *do* know what that's like,' I shoot back quickly.

He nods an acknowledgement. 'When Victor started talking about how he wanted things to work, I said we would need four points to help centralise the results and be able to broadcast them.'

'The four towers in Middle England.'

'Exactly.'

'You're why they were built?'

Xyalis shrugs and looks away again. So much of his legacy is negative. 'Not the towers as such – they were Victor's idea. My idea could have used four pylons but he wanted to create something that made a statement. He demanded we build a testament to his new rule that would stand for years to come. That's where the towers themselves come from but, yes, you're right, it *is* my technology within them – the results of the Reckoning are processed there.'

'What about the Offering?'

'Victor's idea. Once he realised we could find everyone's strengths and weaknesses, he said he wanted a group of people around him that he could mould to create the country he wanted. That was the reason I left.'

'Why?'

He holds his hands out, indicating us. 'You should know. Anyone who spent any time around him could see that creating a country in his image was going to be a terrible idea. Not only that, but there was no way he would be able to tolerate so many new people with different ideas and personalities. It was always going to be a bloodbath.'

Suddenly I feel angry. 'If you knew this was going to happen, why didn't you do something to stop it?'

He doesn't react. 'What would you have had me do? At least half of us went along with everything he wanted because the alternative was to be executed as a traitor live on screen. I spoke to a few people about my concerns but as soon as I realised I didn't have great support, I knew I had to go. I packed what I could and left in the middle of the night. I know they told everyone I was dead because it didn't suit them to let others know there was anyone alive who disagreed with what was going on. I suppose I figured I could be more use trying to fight against everything from outside, rather than being killed in my bed.'

'But that was years ago, what have you done since?'

This time my words do sting. Xyalis glares back at me and I can tell he is suppressing his anger. 'I escaped with almost nothing. Since then, I have built up all of this and helped to stabilise the few rebel groups there are. Things take time.'

He continues to stare at me before Imrin tries to defuse the situation. 'Why Lancaster?' he asks.

Xyalis blinks and then turns to face Imrin. 'This was one of the rebel strongholds during the war. They used the castle as a base and a storage area. I was on the other side and we had been scouring the country for any leftover fuel supplies. We didn't have much but we had enough for a handful of bombing raids from the planes we still had. We thought that if we could destroy their main operations area, then the rest would fall. We threw everything we had here, using the last of the fuel and bombs to flatten the place. We thought it would be a big turning point but it had hardly any impact because the rebels were so spread out over the country. After I escaped Windsor, I knew this would be one of the few places there would be no patrols. What you see overground is more or less as it has been for the past twenty years or so.'

'Where are we then?' I ask.

'These were the catacombs under the castle. We've managed to expand slowly and fortify. I've salvaged all sorts of useful things from various places and gradually recruited people I thought could be useful.'

'Is that what we are?'

The hint of a smile returns. 'It's *you* who said you wanted revenge.'

I feel embarrassed, even though none of the others reacts.

'Why do your guards have guns?' I ask. 'Not even the Kingsmen have anything other than swords and knives.'

Xyalis laughs patronisingly and then apologises. 'We don't have much ammunition if that's what you're really asking. We have enough to defend ourselves but not enough to mount any sort of assault, especially not on Windsor. You're clever enough to have worked it out but it's not about the guns, it's about the ammunition. If you manufacture bullets, there's a good chance they will eventually find their way into the hands of your enemies. Victor could arm all of the Kingsmen if he wanted – but they have enough authority with the weapons they have. The bigger danger is if the guns and bullets found their way into the hands of rebels. He's very sensible with things like that because he doesn't need guns anyway – there are far bigger weapons out there.'

'Like what?'

He doesn't reply but his narrow smile is becoming infuriating. 'Let me ask you a question,' he says. 'Have you ever heard of Hadrian's Wall?'

'Who's Adrian?'

Xyalis grins and his entire face changes. I sense this is a story he is going to enjoy telling. 'When I was a little younger than you, I used to enjoy history. So much has happened in the last few years that history is all around us but it wasn't like that back then. A long, long time ago, a group of people called the Romans ruled this country. They controlled vast nations throughout the world but they were obsessed with defence. Every time they fought and won a battle, they would focus on making sure it was as secure as possible before moving on to the next place. When they invaded our country, they had a lot of problems with barbarians further north than this. Because they didn't want to lose the ground they had won, they built a wall the entire width of the country to stop the barbarians attacking them.'

'Why are you telling us this?'

'You've probably heard of "Scotland". That's the country north of here, beyond that old wall – Hadrian's Wall. When the war started, the Scots decided *we* were the barbarians and that they didn't want any part of it. They found a way to rebuild the wall with technology even I don't understand. They cut themselves off from the rest of us.'

'Is that why Scotland doesn't appear on any of the maps?'

'Exactly, which is probably the way they would have it as well. The thing is, they're still there beyond that wall.'

'Is that where you're going to ask us to go?'

Xyalis recoils, looking at me as if I am stupid. 'Of course not! If you went anywhere near the border you'd be killed on sight. I'm asking because it was one of the things Victor always talked about in those early days, saying we had to get them back on side. I think he actually wanted a bigger Kingdom to rule but I was wondering if you had heard anything while you were in the castle?'

I look across to Imrin and Faith, but their faces are blank. All of this is news to us. 'We didn't hear much at all about what was going on beyond the castle walls,' I say.

Xyalis seems disappointed. 'I always thought Scotland would be his weak point. If he attacked there, it would leave him unprotected elsewhere . . .'

He tails off but it makes me realise that he does at least have some ideas.

'One of our friends is sick,' I say. 'He has an infection but we don't have access to the medicine we need. Do you have anything?'

Xyalis shakes his head. 'Only to cure very minor ailments.'

I try to block the image of Hart from my mind and concentrate on where we are. I knew it was going to be unlikely that Xyalis would be able to help but I had to ask. Finally, I get to the point. 'When we spoke, you said you might have something I wanted?'

Xyalis stands and steps towards the nearest workbench. 'I may have been a little hasty . . .'

I can feel the mood change as Imrin stares at me across the table, his mouth wide open. I start to speak but he gets in ahead of me, shouting angrily. 'You told us to come here because you had something we could use!'

Xyalis remains calm. 'I still might. In theory, I had what I needed but, unfortunately, I am a part short.'

'What is it?' I ask.

'I wouldn't want to say until it is ready . . .'

'What do you need?'

Xyalis turns to face us and I realise that everything we have spoken about beforehand has been a prelude to this moment. I have played into his hands.

'I think the question you should be asking is "where". If it's any consolation, it's in the same place as the medicine you will need for your friend.'

In the same way that I played Opie's father, I know Xyalis is about to do the same to me. Not only that but I've given him more ammunition than he had already – he is going to use Hart's illness against me.

He licks his lips, scanning the others before focusing back on me. 'There's only one place in the country that has what you need – Windsor Castle.'

25

The air feels so heavy that I struggle to breathe and end up coughing loudly. Everyone is staring at me. 'You want us to go back?' I stammer.

'It's up to you. I'm not asking you to do anything.'

'But we spent so long trying to escape. Now you want us to walk back in, steal what you need and walk out again?'

'It's not what *I* need. You said you wanted revenge, this is for you. You said your friend needed a cure, this is for him.'

I manage to compose myself in order to reply. 'Tell me about the medicine.'

'Before the war we started to stockpile tiny samples of all the diseases we knew about. Most cures are based in some way on a minute amount of the disease it is healing. When Victor found out, he thought we would be able to create weapons from the viruses. In fairness, it was something we had discussed during the war but we never wanted to go that far.'

'So he has lots of diseases he can use against everyone?'

'Not exactly, although it isn't for the want of trying.

When this type of weapon couldn't be created quickly enough for him, he had the chief engineer killed and shut the whole thing down. What they created by accident was a formula which can cure most illnesses and diseases.'

It takes me a few moments to take in what he's saying. 'It can keep someone alive?'

Xyalis starts to say something but stops himself and flaps his hands about, trying to find the right words. 'It's not something that can give you everlasting life. It doesn't stop you ageing or dying. If you're stabbed in the heart, you still die. It's a combination of all the diseases and ailments that have ever been isolated. It cures every illness you've ever heard of – and many more. It's very powerful but Victor isn't interested in curing people.'

'And this formula is in the castle?'

'Yes.'

'How do you know?'

Xyalis points behind us towards the bank of computer equipment. 'I built most of the technology there. I still have my ways in.'

'What about *our* way in? We can't just knock on the front door.'

Xyalis crosses towards where he was pointing and beckons us over. 'If you choose to go, there is plenty I can help with.' He presses a string of buttons, bringing up a collage of small squares on the screen. 'I have access to the security cameras and can make sure you're not seen . . .'

Imrin catches my eye. This was something I managed to do by myself during our escape.

'I also have something that will get you out safely and quickly. The only real issue is, as you say, getting you in. I have an idea but won't be able to offer you much protection.'

'What is it?'

'There is a supply train which arrives once a week . . .'

'We know,' Imrin and I say together.

'One of the Kingsmen is loyal to me. He will be able to get you on it but if any of the others find you, he will act with them. You'll have to conceal yourselves and hope for the best.'

He speaks so matter-of-factly that he doesn't even try to conceal the fact that he had much of this planned out from the moment he invited me here. I try to ask him again what he might have that interests me but he waves me away, saying he won't reveal anything until he is certain it works. Perhaps he would have told me if I hadn't given away the information about needing a cure for Hart.

'There is something else I should show you,' he adds, flicking on another monitor. 'I recorded this earlier.'

On screen, the national anthem plays before the 'breaking news' strap scrolls across the bottom. The presenter excitedly tells us that Colt Blackthorn has failed to present himself for the Offering. The photo of me with reddened eyes and pale skin is shown again as they remind everyone of my crimes, before a large number one appears next to my face.

'Silver Blackthorn is, of course, number one on the nation's most-wanted list,' the voiceover says as a picture of my brother appears on screen with the number two flashing next to him. 'Number two is Colt Blackthorn, with – for the first time ever – three members of the same family comprising one, two and three in our most-wanted chart.' My mother's image scrolls into view, accused of harbouring known criminals.

The newsreader sounds overly cheery as the camera switches back to her. 'The punishment for their crimes is, as we all know, death.'

The reward for anyone who catches me has almost doubled since I last saw the figures, which probably explains the increased number of capture squads we saw on the streets on our journey away from Middle England.

Xyalis switches the screen off and says that he thought I would want to see it. It wasn't a surprise but it was still shocking to see my brother's face displayed so publicly and the promise that he is to be put to death.

'I have beds you can use for the night,' Xyalis says. 'I'd advise you to sleep on things. If you want to return to the castle, we can talk through the specifics tomorrow. If not, we can go our separate ways.'

I know he showed me the footage deliberately to let me know that I don't have too many options. Imrin's warning about manipulating people is as relevant to Xyalis here as it was when he was talking about me. I know nothing about the person I am allowing to lead me – but it is either that, or walk away with a death sentence hanging over me and my family and return to watch Hart die. I also want to know what it is that Xyalis claims to have for me.

My choice was already made the moment I decided to come here. 'I don't need to wait until the morning. I'm going.'

Xyalis claps his hands together. 'Excellent. There's a lot to discuss but it can wait until morning. Is there anything else you need to know before then?'

I am about to walk away when I feel the weight in my pocket. I take out the grey and black box Imrin stole from Reith's office and hand it to Xyalis. 'Do you know what this is?'

His grin tells me that he does as he flips it around and begins to stroke an area on the back. 'Oh, yes. I'm the one who invented it.'

26

As the train pulls into Middle England, the enormity of what we're doing begins to dawn on me. We are crouched in silence, the crates of food providing an easy enough space to hide behind. No one has checked on us since the Kingsman loyal to Xyalis waved us on not far from Lancaster as the train stopped for supplies and told us to sit down and shut up. He hissed at us to stay out of view and added it was unlikely any of his colleagues would leave the cabin at the front.

The journey is exactly the same route I took when I was chosen as an Offering, which was only a few months back but feels like a lifetime ago. Except this time Opie is with me. He sits in a position where he can watch out of the window, taking in the mass of destruction mixed with endless fields that we saw on the way down to Windsor, and trekked through on the way back. The last time the train came this way, we stopped frequently, zigzagging into various towns and cities to pick up all of the Offerings to huge ovations. This time, each place is a blur as we fly through without stopping.

I have to tell Opie to move away from the window as we pull into Middle England. The four towers are as magnificent as ever and I feel harsh telling him to stop looking when I know he has never seen them before. We lie flat behind the crates of food as the cargo doors open and the Kingsmen begin to drag more items on board. Through the open door, I can hear the familiar hum of electricity which makes me think about what Xyalis had to say. The Reckoning results are processed in the four towers above us, with all broadcasts going through them. I wonder if the bargaining prize Xyalis has for me might be able to help undo the amount of hurt he has caused.

When the Kingsmen have finished loading the train, the doors slam shut and we sit up again. The train slowly drifts away from the station.

'Do we all know what we're doing?' I ask, trying to reassure myself more than the other three.

'Are you sure Opie is best going with you?' Imrin asks. 'Wouldn't he be better paired with Faith?'

Faith doesn't say anything but her scowl is enough to convey she doesn't need looking after. I'm not convinced; I suspect the reason he is saying this is because he wants it to be him who comes with me instead of Opie.

I speak as firmly as I can, trying to make it clear I'm not simply trying to engineer time with Opie. 'You and I know the passages around the castle as well as anyone because we snuck out at night.' Opie turns to face me, wanting to query exactly what we were doing each evening but I don't have time to placate the pair of them. I turn back to Imrin. 'You stay with Faith and round up the new Offerings, Opie and I will go for the medicine and what Xyalis needs. How are the uniforms fitting?'

Imrin still has his Kingsman uniform from when we were in Middle England and Xyalis has been able to provide Opie and I with two more. Opie's fits perfectly as he is the shape and size most Kingsmen would be expected to be. The one I'm wearing isn't as snug as the one I left in the North Tower gym but I can get around. Given her petite size, Faith is struggling the most. She has taken a uniform from Xyalis' own guards which has been painted black. From a distance, it just about looks like the borodron of ours but no one will be fooled close-up. It is also a lot heavier than our uniforms and, although she would never admit it, she is finding the weight difficult to bear.

'I'll be fine,' Faith says, knowing I am mainly addressing her.

Soon, the light darkens as we enter the long tunnel which leads to the underground station at Windsor Castle. As the train begins to slow, I close my eyes, not wanting to see the torture chamber into which we are being driven.

Within moments, the train doors are yanked open and we hear the Kingsmen's voices discussing what to take first.

Crates scrape, guards grunt with exertion, and then we hear the sound of footsteps echoing away from us.

I move as stealthily as I can, edging around the crates until I reach the door. The platform is empty, so I wave the others towards me and then run to the front of the train, drop down onto the tracks, and then race to the other side of the train before settling in the shadows of the tunnel. Opie, Imrin and Faith are right behind and we sit and watch silently as the Kingsmen return over and over to finish unloading the food.

An hour or so passes and the only thing we can do is shuffle into slightly more comfortable positions. At first I run through everything I have to do in my head. Opie doesn't know where he's going so it is important I don't do anything reckless. Without me, he is lost, trapped here in the way I was. I try to enjoy the gentle breeze, the final vestiges of natural air billowing around us before we head upstairs. Most of all, I try to force myself not to run. After the train pulls away, it leaves a pinprick of light at the far end of the tunnel – a chance to escape from here, away from danger. We could run now, head out into the daylight and not come back. Imrin always said we could make it on our own and we have already seen the type of community my mother has helped to create. But running towards the light means Hart will likely die, that Wray and the others will never be avenged, that Colt and my mum will live the rest of their lives with a death sentence hanging over them.

And that I would have to choose: Imrin or Opie?

Is that really my motivation? While we are here, they will do what they can to help me, even if it means them working together. If it is ever over, they will look to me and want an answer.

Or is this all about revenge? Has the myth become reality? Am I happy to be the figurehead of the rebels because I want a better future for Colt and Imp? Or are all of the other motivations things I keep telling myself so that I don't have to make a decision?

As the faint light in the distance slowly turns as dark as the rest of the tunnel, we wait for one more hour and then cross the tracks towards the spiral staircase which will take us into the castle. I remember being here months ago when we first entered, Jela and Pietra slightly behind me – at that point I didn't even know their names. I'm so glad they don't have to go through this a second time.

I lead the others to the top where there is the sliding door Imrin and I spent weeks trying to find a way through. We don't need to worry about a strip of borodron any longer as we are covered in it. Whether it is for Wray, Hart, Colt or myself, my decision is made as I swipe my arm past the scanner on the wall and the door slides back, revealing the clean, fresh red carpet of hell.

None of us pauses as Imrin and Faith march away without a word. Their task should be straightforward, although it may involve waiting for a safe moment.

I remember every twist and turn of our route perfectly. Xyalis says he will take care of the cameras but I still find myself taking a slightly longer path to avoid as many as we can. Part of our route is the same journey we took back to the dormitory after Wray was killed on our first night. I try to ignore it but I can smell his blood in the air and taste that coppery scent of death drifting around us.

All of the new Offerings will be locked in the dormitories by now and we don't see anyone as we move through the corridors.

'Are we nearly there?' Opie asks as I finally stop moving and press myself against the wall.

'The King's quarters are around the corner.'

'We're going past that, right?'

'I've only been this way once. It's a long story but we had breakfast with the King. It should be straightforward but I want to make sure you know the way back, just in case anything happens.'

Even though we have had our uniforms on for hours, this is the first time I properly look at Opie. The helmet shapes his face perfectly, his thick, solid jaw completing the oval. The biggest giveaway are his eyes. Instead of the harsh grey or brown irises of a Kingsman, his glow bright and blue, hanging on my words and telling me that if anything does happen, there is no way he'll be leaving unless I do. I don't relent and finally he gives in.

'I remember the way,' he replies, although I know he is lying.

I am about to say that it is time to go when we hear a clanging of doors and an anguished gurgle of annoyance. Opie stares at me, confused, but I know exactly who the voice belongs to as King Victor staggers around the corner and looks us both up and down.

27

I straighten instinctively, standing to attention in the way I have seen the Kingsmen do before. Thankfully, Opie follows my lead.

'That's better,' the King slurs, drunk. His ginger hair has grown longer than it was when I last saw him choking on the poisoned wine, thinking he was going to die. There are some food remains matted into his beard, of which he seems unaware.

'What happened to the wine?' he bellows, eyes darting in all directions. 'There was supposed to be some on the way.'

There is a pause and I am screaming at Opie in my head, reminding him that I can't speak. We don't know of any female Kingsmen and although the uniform allows me to pass as one, anything I say would instantly give us away.

As he finally remembers, Opie stumbles over the first part of his reply. 'It's on its way, Your, er, Highness,' he says.

It is painful.

The King stares at him, eyes slanted and confused. I see the sword hanging limply from his belt and remember what he did to Wray with it. He mutters something I don't catch and then wipes his mouth before stumbling to the side.

The thought suddenly occurs to me that we could kill him now. Snatching his sword would be easy – he is drunk and unable to defend himself. One lunge, one strike and this is over. I could do it now.

Do it.

I start to reach forward but my feet are planted to the spot, the feather-light borodron so heavy that I cannot move.

Do it.

Now I cannot even open my mouth, as if my senses have deserted me. What am I waiting for?

The King stumbles towards Opie and slaps him in the chest. 'I'm the King, you know?' he says, the words falling into one another.

'Yes, Your Highness.'

'If I want wine, I should have wine.'

'It's on its way.'

His eyes roll back into his head as he falls forward, forcing Opie to hold him up. At the sight of Opie's panicked expression, my feet finally come loose. The King is unconscious, his face squished awkwardly against Opie's chest with both arms draped around him.

'What do we do?' Opie hisses.

I see his eyes shoot towards the sword in the way mine had.

I shake my head. 'Not like this – it'll mean nothing if it happens here. There are people out there who still believe in him. They need to see the truth; this will only make it worse.'

I'm not sure if Opie understands but he heaves the King up and follows me around the corner, past the room in which we once had breakfast and through a huge set of double doors. Inside are two Kingsmen, one of whom runs towards us. I wait by the doors just in case, but the guard is shaking his head disdainfully.

'Not again,' he says, reaching towards the slumped body of the King.

Opie mumbles a reply as they move him onto a bed and then we hurry away before any other questions can be asked, closing the doors behind us.

'Have you seen him drunk before?' Opie whispers as we continue past the doors towards our destination.

'Plenty of times. It's why we targeted his wine when we used the tan fruit on him. He never lets any go to waste.'

'He seems very different when he's on screen.'

'I've seen him act completely different in person. I guess it's just the wine. When he's sober, there's this way he has of saying things that makes you listen. Even if you hate him and what he says, it draws you in.'

'Like Xyalis?'

'Exactly.'

'And you.'

I stop in the centre of the corridor and grab Opie's arm, pushing him towards the wall. I am so shocked that, if it wasn't for the borodron encasing him, I would be squeezing into his flesh. *'What?'*

Opie doesn't realise what he's said. 'I just meant that people listen to you. There's nothing bad about that, is there? You're not like them. It's like the other day – we were having problems controlling Imp but the moment you wander into camp, he's all over you, hanging on your every word.'

He's not wrong but coupled with what Imrin said to me at the camp about manipulating people, I feel as if the two people closest to me are picking me apart. Opie's statement was innocent enough to the point that he doesn't even know what he's said. He stares at me, confused, wondering what to tell me to get me to focus again.

'Forget it,' I say, letting him go and continuing along the empty corridor.

I swipe through a door at the end and enter a room that is so bright Opie gasps involuntarily as the doors swish closed behind us. The ceiling and walls are completely white, the blinking red dots underneath the three security cameras in the corners of the room the only splashes of colour.

'Do you think Xyalis knows what he's doing with the cameras?' Opie asks, pointing at one of them.

'I hope so.'

When I was last here, the blinking lights meant trouble. It means the cameras must be recording – but Xyalis has a way of ensuring whatever is being broadcast to anyone watching the security footage doesn't include us. If it was me, I would have looped earlier footage.

Of everything we have to do in the castle, this is the part I am least sure about. On the map Imrin and I created when we were effectively prisoners, this area was the only one we didn't know. Xyalis told us that the old research labs are beyond the King's quarters and this is where the medical samples are kept. Although the room appears bright, there is a thin layer of dust across the counter-tops that are pressed against the walls.

I crouch and open the first freezer underneath the desk, allowing a cold blast to shoot through the material of the gloves which makes me shiver. A mist of frost billows from the unit as I hunt through the rack of virus samples.

The containers in the freezers are a mixture of square tubs, flat transparent circular containers and long metallic tubes that are sealed with thick stoppers. Xyalis insists we are safe to carry anything as long as we don't remove the top. He says the diseases are in concentrated form and although they are very dangerous, the seals can only be broken via an applicator because the metal is unbreakable. I recognise a few of the names as I scan the labels but most of them are a mystery.

Opie starts to search through the freezer next to me. 'Did he give you any idea where the sample to help Hart would be?'

'No, he just gave me the code number for the universal cure that he says will be written on the side of the container. He says there might be more than one sample, so we'll take everything we can carry. He said the other thing he needs for his device should be here too.'

I finish looking through the first freezer and move to the one beyond Opie. He is barely halfway through the second shelf and is checking each label thoroughly.

I expect another freezer as I yank the next door open but instead it is a cupboard full of empty shelves. I start to close it and move on to the next but then I see a reflection at the back of a shelf. Because of the armour, it is a struggle to reach, but I force my fingertips to close around a small spherical object and pull it out.

'What is it?' Opie asks, looking at the ball in my hand.

I turn it around but the only things I can see, other than the smooth grey metal, are three tiny holes. Given its size and metallic feel, the sphere seems a lot lighter than it should be. I put it back in the cupboard and shut the door, moving on to the next unit.

'Look out for the applicator,' I say, as Opie shuts his freezer. 'It's supposed to be long and pointy, like the syringes we have at home. Xyalis says the sample will be useless if we can't apply it. Try those drawers on the far side.'

Opie stands without question and moves across to the place I have pointed out. I don't tell him that he is working too slowly.

I am three-quarters of the way through the next freezer when I find a label that matches the formula Xyalis requested. It is not the medicine, it is for the device he wouldn't explain. It's in a thin metallic tube, unidentifiable other than by the number on the side. I slide it into the pouch on my belt and check the cylinders next to it in case there is more than one. When it is clear there isn't, I continue looking for the medicine – the thing I really want to find.

After I have looked through more samples, Opie calls me from the other side of the room. 'Is this it?' he asks, holding a cylindrical metal contraption that has a wide hole at one end and a thin one at the other. On the side is a trigger that makes it look like a gun.

'I think so. Are there any others? Keep looking and take as many as you can find.'

As I move on to the final freezer, I begin to think that Xyalis could be mistaken or, worse, he has tricked us into coming here for a reason he hasn't revealed.

'I've found two others,' Opie calls from behind me.

'I'm nearly there,' I reply, although there is also the prospect that I've been moving from sample to sample so quickly that I have missed what I was supposed to be looking for and will have to start again.

'Those red lights are still blinking,' Opie says absent-mindedly. I'm not sure if he is trying to make conversation as he is bored, or if he's trying to help. He's certainly not doing the latter. I glance around and see him standing by the door, examining one of the syringe devices in his hand. I ignore him and pull out the final rack, flicking through the first row of metal tubes. The gloves are now offering no protection against the cold as my fingers struggle to close painfully around each cylinder.

As I start on the second row, I am about to return a tube to the rack when I realise I am staring at the sample code I have been looking for. My eyes have become so accustomed to scanning the labels that I almost moved on to the next one before registering what it was. I check the tube next to it, which has a matching number, and I am about to pocket both when I hear a familiar voice behind me.

The words purr from his lips, like ice through my veins.

I turn to see the Minister Prime standing in the doorway, his mouth tight and sneering. 'Well, well, well, Ms Blackthorn. I didn't think I'd be seeing you again.'

28

I am shivering but it isn't because of my frozen fingers or the haze of frost drifting from the freezer. The sharp trans-fixing tone of the Minister Prime's voice coupled with his knife-like black eyes have me pinned to the spot. I try to stand but my knees are shaky and I have to put a hand on the counter to steady myself, hauling my body up until I am standing. The tubes with the healing virus inside roll under the freezer, out of sight. The Minister Prime looks exactly as he did the last time I was here: the living version of the colour black, from his hair to his clothes to those terrifying eyes that don't stop looking at me.

'As I remember,' he says, 'the last time I saw you, you were leaping from a window.'

My eyes flicker from him towards Opie, who is uncon-scious on the ground, his head propping the door open. The Minister Prime must have hit him as I was peering into the freezer, concentrating on the samples. He smiles as he sees me glance away. 'Which one is this?' he taunts. 'I don't recognise him as one of your little friends.'

He moves around the central counter but I edge the other way, keeping it between us.

'You weren't this quiet the last time.'

He's right. When we were face to face a few floors up, I knew what was coming. I didn't know if I was on the brink of escaping, or about to jump to my death. I wasn't bothered either way – the final outcome was that I would be away from the castle. Now I am back in the place I never wanted to return to.

He can see all of this in my face, his lips curling slightly upwards into a tighter, thinner smile that is full of derision.

'Why did you come back?'

Suddenly my voice returns, full of a confidence I don't feel. 'Wouldn't you like to know?'

We continue circling the counter as he reaches the still-open freezer. He glances towards it quickly and then kicks it shut. 'No one has been to this room in years. It took me a few seconds to even remember where the alarm was coming from.'

I see the camera light blinking behind him, wondering if Xyalis has somehow made a mistake, and then remember the sphere in the cupboard. It must be some sort of light or sound sensor. Compared to the vials, it seemed out of place.

'I bet you didn't expect me,' I say.

'Indeed not.' His eyes flicker towards the door as he realises I am closer to it than he is. I could turn and run but there is no guarantee I would get away – and I would be leaving Opie at the King's mercy. Not to mention Faith and Imrin.

I step past Opie, relieved that there is no blood pooling around him. I assume the Minister Prime took him by surprise, rather than hurt him seriously.

As I register the gap into the corridor, I realise the other reason he may have looked towards the door is that he has given away more information than he should have done. By admitting the alarm from here doesn't go off regularly – and that he didn't know it was me in this room – he has inadvertently let me know that he came alone. There would surely be an army bursting through the door if he knew why the alarm had gone off.

'All on your own?' I taunt, letting him know I am cleverer than he thinks.

His eyes flicker in annoyance, hand hovering around the sword on his belt. 'How's your brother?'

I can hear two voices – one inside of me, panicked and scared, telling me to stay calm. The other comes from my mouth, confident and strong. One is me, the other the myth.

'Don't you know? You're the one with Kingsmen all over the country looking for him.'

Another twitch of annoyance.

'He's safe and having the time of his life,' I add.

I wish I felt as confident as I sounded.

'Do you know what I'm going to do when I get hold of him?'

I try not to show him that this is how to hurt me but he already knows. 'You won't find him,' I say.

'I'll start by pulling his fingernails out one at a time.'

Stay calm.

'I'll sew his eyes open so he can see everything and then I'll kill your mother in front of him.'

He lunges around the table between us and I am so stung by his words that I almost forget to move, stumbling backwards away from his grasping hands before steadying myself on the top of the freezer. He grins, eyes narrow, stepping over Opie.

'I'll send him back to the medical wing each day so they can keep enough blood in him for me to work on him over and over.'

'You won't find him.'

'I already know where he is.'

I stumble again, tripping over the corner of the counter. 'You're lying. If you knew where he was, you'd have him already.'

'How about you hand yourself in now and I let him go free?'

I stop moving and face him, trying to see if it is a genuine offer. Myself for Colt is a sacrifice I would make in a heart-beat.

I nod towards Opie on the floor, not wanting to give away his name. 'What about him?'

'He goes free too.'

'And my mother?'

'Free.'

I think about Imrin and Faith in another part of the castle. 'My other friends?'

'Pardons for all of them.'

He takes a step towards me and this time I don't move. 'How do I know you'll let them go?'

'The King will address the nation live and tell everyone that all crimes have been forgiven. All you have to do is surrender yourself.'

I have no problem giving up my freedom for everyone else's but even if the offer was genuine, what would it achieve? There would still be thirty more scared children sent to their deaths every year, with thousands more going unnecessarily hungry. Even if he was free, what sort of world would that be for Colt to grow up in? And then there is Wray, whose death would have been for nothing.

I'm about to say no deal when I realise the Minister Prime is closer to me than I thought. He lunges across, snatching the corner of my armour and using his body weight to drag me to the floor. I try to scramble to my feet but he grabs my ankle and punches the join to my foot so hard that it twists sideways. I stumble into one of the freezers but all of my weight falls on my damaged ankle and I crumple to the floor next to Opie's limp body.

This time the Minister Prime makes no mistake. He pushes himself up and then deliberately stands on my already shattered ankle, pressing his full weight onto me.

I scream in agony but he bends over and backhands me brutally across the face. I can taste his foul breath as he hisses in my face. 'Shush . . . I don't want the guards to interrupt my little bit of fun now I've got you to myself.'

I can taste blood in my mouth and my ankle hurts so much that it doesn't feel as if my leg is there any longer.

'You've caused me so much trouble,' he says, sitting across me with his knees pinning my arms to my side, his back to the door.

'Good.'

He backhands me again, unwilling to listen any longer.

'Where are the others?' he asks.

I don't know if he means the others in the castle, the others I escaped with, or Colt and my mother. Not that I would tell him anyway – I am stalling for my life.

'Who?'

'All of them.'

I assumed he was bluffing at knowing where my family

are but it is hard to switch off when he talks about Colt or my mother. It is a weak spot I cannot ignore.

'I'll never tell you.'

'We'll find them eventually. If you tell me, I guarantee everything will happen quickly. If we have to find them then I won't be responsible for my own actions.'

For perhaps the first time, I have the feeling that he is telling the truth. He is deluded enough to think I would give away the locations of everyone I care about just to make our deaths a little less painless – as if the agony of my betrayal would not hurt enough.

'I'm not telling you and you'll never find them.'

He leans back further, digging his full weight into me and breaks into a grin. 'I was almost hoping you'd say that. If you have nothing to say, then you're not worth keeping alive.'

His hand flashes towards his belt from where he pulls out a long, sharp dagger. He twirls it in his fingers and then tosses it to one side and cracks his knuckles.

'This time,' he says, 'I think we'll do it the old-fashioned way.'

29

The Minister Prime doesn't see the blow coming as Head Kingsman Porter smashes a thick chunk of wood into his head. He crumples sideways away from me, slumping onto the floor as Porter helps me to my feet.

He looks as if he has aged ten years since I last saw him, his hair has almost vanished and there are new wrinkles across his face. His voice is frantic. 'Why did you come back?'

My ankle collapses under me and I have to use the bench to hold myself up. 'We needed something. I found Xyalis.'

Porter was the person who first told me that name and his face is full of shock. 'The old Minister Prime?'

I don't answer, falling to my knees and stretching for the tubes that rolled under the freezer. I cannot reach them, so Porter tilts the unit while I scoop them both into the pouch on my belt and then pull the bottom drawer open again to take out the final two samples.

'How did you know we were here?' I ask.

'Since you left, the security system has been updated. I

was working late and noticed something not quite right with it . . .'

'That will be Xyalis.'

He points to the cameras in the corner of the room. 'There's some sort of interference going on with the cameras that I didn't notice at first. When I spotted what was going on, I realised someone was using a backdoor to access the security system. Once I'd figured that out, I saw you here.'

I look at the Minister Prime sprawled face-down on the floor. 'You should go,' I tell Porter. 'He doesn't know it was you who hit him. Don't blow your cover.'

Porter's features relax slightly as he realises I am right. 'Are you okay? You can barely walk.'

I crouch over Opie and gently poke at his face, trying to wake him.

'Here,' Porter says, taking a small caplet out of his pocket and handing it to me. 'It's pure adrenalin.'

I run a nail along the seam, letting me pull the sections of the capsule apart, and then empty the liquid contents into Opie's mouth. Within seconds, his eyes are blinking awake and he is on his feet staring at the carnage around him.

'What happened?'

'Just get me out of here,' I say, thanking Porter one final time and telling him to stay safe.

Opie doesn't seem to have any after-effects from being hit in the back of the head and I use his shoulder to half-rest, half-hop through the empty echoing corridors as we hurry back through the castle with me trying to ignore the pain in my ankle.

Because of the time we have taken, I am expecting to see Faith and Imrin already waiting for us in the agreed place – the King's dining area. I told Imrin about the private breakfast the Northern Offerings had with the King in this room and he should remember where it is, but the room is empty.

'Wow,' Opie says, stepping inside.

I don't blame him. The room is the most impressive I saw in my time at the castle. It is elegantly lined with drapes and wall coverings in the same regal red the King usually wears, with an elaborate throne at the head of a long wooden table that is currently empty. On its own, it is memorable enough but it is the stained glass window at the far end which is truly stunning. It stretches from the floor to the ceiling and the moonlight is streaming through, sending colours glistening into the corners around us.

Although it portrays the King standing over the slain leaders of the two opposing armies, something symbolic rather than accurate, the content is almost irrelevant. The sheer beauty of the handiwork is almost hypnotic, the tiny raised portions of the glass and the subtleties in the colours from one section to the next truly captivating. It is only when my ankle collapses and I stumble into Opie that I remember what I am supposed to be doing.

'It's amazing,' Opie says, coming to his senses as I do.

'It was made by an Offering. The King cut his hands off so he could never create anything to rival it.'

Opie doesn't reply, he simply stands staring at the window.

'They should be here,' I say, checking my thinkwatch.

'Could they have gone already?'

'Neither Imrin or Faith would have been able to work the equipment. They wouldn't have gone without us anyway. We only get one shot.'

I hobble to the door and check the corridor but there is no one there. When the Minister Prime comes around, he will surely raise the alarm, so we haven't got much time.

'We'll have to go and find them,' I say.

Opie doesn't sound too impressed. 'How? You can barely walk.'

'And you don't know where you're going. We'll have to go together.'

He seems reluctant and I don't want to ask if it is because it is Imrin we are going to save. It looks as if he wants to argue but his only protest is a disapproving shake of the head before he lowers his shoulder so I can lean on it.

We move as quickly as my ankle allows, up a twisting set of stone steps towards the dormitories. When we reach the top, I see Faith rushing towards us with a row of female Offerings behind her, each looking more terrified than the last. They seem so young, most of them wearing pyjamas and still half-asleep. As everyone stops at the top of the stairs, one by one they notice who I am. I hear my name being repeated in anguished whispers flittering up and down the corridor.

'Did it go okay?' I ask.

Faith is out of breath, her uniform looking more uncomfortable than ever. 'We had to wait downstairs and then there were Kingsmen when we got up here. Imrin froze.'

I look over her shoulder towards the door that opens into the girls' dorm – the place from which I thought I would never escape – and there are two guards lying facedown on the floor. I don't ask what happened.

'What about the boys?'

'Imrin's on his way.'

I dig into the pouch on my belt and take out the sample Xyalis requested, handing it to Faith. 'You take this, I've got the medicine. It's best if I don't hold onto everything, just in case.'

She puts it in her own pouch as we hear a clatter of footsteps at the far end of the corridor, where there are two rows of boys, looking even younger than the girls, running in our direction. At the back, I see Imrin cajoling them towards us.

'Were there many Kingsmen?'

Opie heads back down the steps towards the King's dining room, the girls following behind him. Faith touches each of them gently on the back as they pass. 'None of the Kingsmen downstairs paid us any attention. Whatever Xyalis has done to the cameras must have worked because there were only two up here.'

'Can you help me?' I ask, pointing towards my ankle.

Faith is the perfect height for me to lean on and helps guide me down the stairs just as the boys arrive and follow us. The girls whispered my name as if they couldn't believe it was me but the boys seem too stunned to say anything at all.

We trace our steps back to the King's dining room, where Opie has already started to sort the girls into their Realms: North, South, East and West. I use the table to support myself until I can reach the window that stretches from floor to ceiling and then find the box in the far corner of the frame running around the glass that Xyalis told me about. It is metallic and weighty but otherwise unremarkable.

I check my thinkwatch for the list of codes Xyalis gave me as the room begins to feel full. Even though they are scared and shocked, it is hard to keep thirty children quiet – even the older ones. As the boys finish filing in, Imrin closes the heavy wooden door and wedges a long strip of wood through the handles to try to stop anyone opening it from the outside. Opie has finished sorting the boys and the girls as I quickly prise the back of the metallic box away and insert the connector that Xyalis gave me, snapping it into place as he instructed. I tap a code into the number pad on the side of the box and flick the switch. A hum of electricity confirms it is working as I use a chair to pull myself up and then sit on it as everyone turns to face me, instinctively going silent.

'I'm Silver Blackthorn,' I say, speaking too quickly but knowing we need to move. 'You will have heard a lot about me but none of that is important now. You were all brought here as Offerings a couple of days ago and you may already have realised that it isn't safe here.'

As I look from face to face, I see a few of them nodding but there are mainly blank looks. On our first night, the King killed Wray but it seems they haven't had an experience like that yet.

The hum from the box behind me gets louder as the light flickers overhead, making everyone look up in anticipation. I turn and point towards the window.

'A very clever man who used to work here began creating a teleportation device a long time ago. He was never able to finish it but neither did anyone else. This was the room where he worked and the window frame has the remnants of what he was working on. He gave me the equipment to fix it so that you will be taken back to your Realms when you step through. There will be people waiting there for you to take you somewhere safe. If you return to your families, none of us can stop you – but the Kingsmen will come for you. Tell them we forced you to do this.'

There is another roar, this time from the entire window as opposed to the box. It is humming like a swarm of furious bees.

I turn to Opie and ask him for the children from the East. They all seem scared but one of the older girls finally steps forward and says she will go first. I tell her to be brave and simply walk towards the window. She tells me that her mum talks about me all the time and reaches out to touch my arm to make sure I am real. As she strides forward into the glass, she is hesitant, expecting to hit something solid. Instead, there is an orange glow around her that shrinks quickly into the centre of her back until she is gone. There is an orange person-shaped haze against the window that quickly fades.

Around the room, there is a gasp of awe and then, having seen it work, one by one the rest of the children from the East pass through.

I have to change the codes for each Realm but the South, West and North follow until it is just Imrin, Faith, Opie and I remaining. I switch the device off and start to reprogram it. Xyalis talked me through the theory, and the code is on my watch, but my fingers have stopped obeying as I type incorrectly twice in a row. I am midway through it a third time when we all turn in unison as something smashes into the doors. They bounce inwards but Imrin's wooden barricade holds.

'Quick,' Opie says unhelpfully as I get the numbers wrong a third time.

Another almighty bang sounds as something hits the door.

I take a deep breath and start again, this time using my middle finger instead of my index. It is slow going but I put the final number in just as we hear a splintering from the door. The barrier is still holding, but it is split along the centre and will only take one more hit. Imrin runs to the other end of the room and picks up a chair, shoving one of the legs width-ways into the handles just as the loud humming sounds again around the window.

'Go,' I shout at Faith, heaving myself up and trying to balance. She asks if I need help, but I push her towards the window just as the doors clang open. Faith is looking backwards, reaching towards us as she disappears into the orange light.

Kingsmen pour into the room, the one at the front grabbing Imrin by the throat as they turn to face myself and Opie at the other end of the room.

'Go,' I say to him but he doesn't move.

From the front, the window looks normal but the hum is clear and the Kingsman holding Imrin cannot figure out what is going on.

'Where are the Offerings?' he demands.

'Gone,' I reply matter-of-factly.

'Gone where?'

'Home.'

He is confused as the lights flicker above us again. His grip tightens on Imrin.

'Are you ready?' I say loudly.

'Ready for what?' the Kingsman barks.

He doesn't realise that I wasn't talking to him but Imrin and Opie both take the cue, bracing themselves as I flick the switch on the grey and black device in my pocket that Imrin stole from Rom's office and gave to me as a Christmas present.

Xyalis invented it as a sonic weapon and the high-pitched shriek it emits sends the Kingsmen cowering to their knees in pain. The one at the front drops Imrin, reaching for his ears, although it will do no good. Xyalis gave us earpieces that block the noise. We can only hear a small whistle; they are deafened and disorientated.

This time Opie does turn, grabbing my hand and jumping into the window. As I fall with him, I switch off the sonic device, twisting in mid-air, expecting to see Imrin next to me. Instead, the Kingsman is covering one ear but using his other hand to hold onto Imrin's foot.

I try to step back into the room but it is too late. The sensation starts on the outside of my skin, as if I am being tickled. Gradually it creeps into me, seeping into my pores until every part of me is itching. I can no longer feel the pain in my ankle but realise it is because I can't feel anything other than a scraping sensation. A bright orange fills my vision and I struggle to breathe before there is a popping sound and I stumble forward into Xyalis' main laboratory under Lancaster Castle. Faith is handing him the formula I stole and, as he notices me appearing, Xyalis steps forward and slaps a button on the console.

It takes me a few seconds to catch my breath, re-adjusting to the room as I see Faith and Opie both looking beyond me. Somewhere during the journey, Opie has let my hand go. I follow their gaze and am hit by a sickening feeling in my stomach that has nothing to do with the teleport.

Imrin didn't make it and Xyalis has switched off the signal.

30

'Turn it back on,' I yell, but Xyalis is focused on the sample Faith has given him, grinning as he twists it in his hands.

'Turn what on?' he says, not looking up.

'The teleport. Imrin didn't get through.'

Xyalis glances up, narrowing his eyes and peering around the room, as if he expects Imrin to be in a corner hiding. His expression changes but it is with annoyance, not panic.

'Why wasn't he with you?'

My voice is trembling but getting louder. 'One of the Kingsmen had him. You've got to start it again.'

He puts the stolen tube in a rack on his worktop and looks towards the dials next to a keyboard. 'If you close a door, it takes time to start it again. It's going to take a minute or so to reopen and we can't risk the Kingsmen invading here, not now you've got the sample.'

I take a step towards the console myself but forget about my damaged ankle and collapse on a step. 'They'll kill him,' I say, the whimper in my voice surprising even me.

Xyalis checks the controls again. 'Did the Offerings get away safely?'

'Yes,' Faith replies. 'We told them people would be waiting on the other side.'

He nods. 'The codes were for a central point in their Realms. Now our communications are working again, I sent messages to the closest rebel groups, so they know what to expect.'

He sounds pleased with himself but that only makes me angrier. 'Why did you shut it off?' I scream.

Xyalis points to Opie. 'He said you had to use the sonic alarm, so I thought you were in trouble. I can't risk anyone finding all of this. When I saw you, I thought that was it.' After a pause, he adds: 'I'm sorry', but it is hard to tell if he is.

I sit on the step staring across the room as it begins to sink in that Imrin is at the mercy of the King and the Minister Prime. Opie sits next to me but I shrug him away, not wanting to talk to anyone, least of all him. If he had kept his mouth shut about the sonic alarm, this may not have happened.

Xyalis is tinkering with something behind me as I stare at the floor. 'Tell me how it works,' I say.

'The teleporter? It's very complicated.'

'Just tell me.'

Xyalis sighs but doesn't stop whatever it is he's working on. 'Think of it like two doors. You have the first in one place and the second in another. When you walk through one, you come out in the other. Both doors have to be connected to each other. The one in Windsor Castle was dormant because it wasn't linked to anything.'

'At any point since you left, the King and his men could have created another door to send them places,' I say.

'They didn't know what they had and probably still don't.'

'What about the doors around the country where we sent the Offerings to?'

'They aren't hard to create – you just need that initial technology. I've had that here for ages. I've refined things a little and sent a few boxes out to places I thought they might be useful – the various rebel groups – but I've always kept the method of how it works to myself.'

'Why haven't you been using it?'

He sighs again, as if I wouldn't understand. 'I've had a lot of work to do and it's mainly been just me. I've had to prioritise other things. It is pre-war tech, so many of the parts are unavailable now.'

I limp across the floor towards the spot where we arrived through the teleport. There is no door, just a box on the floor like the one by the stained-glass window at Windsor Castle. I assume that Xyalis' more recent refinements means that it works more like a portal than the earlier prototype around the window. I take a screwdriver and a hammer from a nearby bench, sit on the floor and start removing the front panel from the box.

'What are you doing?' Xyalis calls across at me sharply.

'I'm just looking.'

The cabling inside the box is tightly packed but I pull it out, separating each of the wires on the floor. I hear Xyalis tut but ignore him as I start tracing the routes to the circuit boards. He told me what I needed to know to get people out of the castle but perhaps gave away too much. I use his explanations as a starting point and begin to dig deeper into the box. The basics aren't too difficult to understand, at least for me, although the scope is what is impressive. In essence, instead of moving computer data across vast areas wirelessly, he has found a way to move people using roughly the same principle of disassembling and reassembling the information. Much of the equipment was readily available when I was working at the castle, so little of it is unfamiliar. Now I can see how he has put things together, it is not too hard to get my head around.

The brilliance isn't so much in the technology – it is in having the idea in the first place.

'I don't understand why you need two doors,' I say, looking across the room to where Xyalis is using a syringe to extract some liquid from the tube I stole for him.

'You don't,' he replies, 'at least not in theory. The problem is that you need to give an exact location that you want to go to. If you get that wrong – for instance if you shifted yourself a couple of centimetres too low – part of your body would materialise within the matter.'

Opie puts it best. 'So you could end up half inside a tree?'

'Perhaps, but you'd never be inside it. You can't both occupy the same space, so there would be an explosion. Your instructions would have to be perfect enough to get you to materialise in an open space slightly above the land. Too low and you'll explode, too high and you'll fall to your death. That's why I created the doors, because it is much safer.'

'Have you ever tried it without a second door?'

Xyalis is annoyed, his tone of voice like my mother's when she tells me off. 'Of course not. I told you, I've had more important things to do.'

I have other questions but Xyalis bangs the desk in frustration, cursing. 'I've been locked out of Windsor!' he cries, pointing at one of the monitors on his desk. 'They obviously found the backdoor I was using to monitor their system. I have no way of knowing what they are working on any longer. Getting you around those cameras must have been too obvious.'

The accusing tone in his voice has me furious as I hobble across the room. 'We risked our lives to get that sample for you. Imrin's stuck there. You haven't even told us what you needed it for.'

I drag myself up the steps towards where he is and snatch the tube away. He growls and reaches for it, his eyes fiery and furious in a way I haven't seen before.

'What is it?' I demand.

Xyalis arches his body as if he is about to attack but Opie quickly steps to my side. As Faith edges to my other side, he stops tensing his muscles. I'm not sure he was going to do anything anyway but I suspect the aggression comes from getting his own way for a long time. If he was serious, he could call his guards to deal with us. Instead he pulls a chair across and sits facing his equipment, away from us.

Xyalis' tone is softer when he speaks next. 'How many samples of the cure did you get?'

'Four.'

'Did you get the applicators we talked about?'

Opie reaches into his pockets and takes out the three devices he found, placing them on the counter.

'I'll show you how it works,' Xyalis adds, picking up the first one.

He flicks a mechanism at the top of the applicator and I hand him the metal cylinder, which he slides inside. It looks straightforward, but he shows me a number of checks that need to be done before the trigger can be pressed. Without them, if the tube isn't correctly aligned, it could cause serious harm to the person being injected. I fit the tubes into the other two applicators, leaving us one spare.

'That should help to cure whatever is wrong with your friend,' Xyalis says wearily. 'Now can I have the other one back?'

'What is it?'

'It's a sample of the King's blood.'

For a moment, I am not sure how to react. I'd assumed it was some sort of chemical, or ammunition. I reluctantly roll it across, my fingers only letting it go as he starts to pull it from me. 'Why did you want us to steal that?'

'You said you wanted revenge. This is something I've been sitting on for a little while. It will help you get what you want.'

I shake my head. 'I've changed my mind. If I wanted revenge, we could have killed him this evening. It's not about that – it's about making life better for my brother and everyone else younger than him.'

Xyalis stares at me but doesn't seem bothered what my motives are and I realise he has manipulated me again. It was never about my revenge – it was about his. He sent me to get the blood because he didn't want to risk his own life.

He turns back to the desk, taking a few drops of the King's blood and placing them into a solid-looking metal box that has a timer on the front. 'What do you need it for?' I ask.

Xyalis reaches under his desk and presses his thumb to a scanner on the front of a safe. When it pops open, he reaches inside and takes out a thin black metal tube that looks like it is made of borodron. On the top is a thick metal cap with a push-down button.

'Now I've got his blood, I can separate the cells and the plasma until I have the component parts. That will give me the data I need and then all I have to do is pour his blood into this and press the trigger.'

'What will it do?'

Xyalis licks his lips, his hands flashing around the worktop before they return to the keyboard. 'One of my specialities before the war was biological attacks. Pressing the button will cause a chemical reaction. You'll have to be close enough to him – perhaps within ten metres or so – because it is his blood. Combined with the substances already in the tube, it will enable you to literally boil his body from the inside.'

His tone is perfectly steady, no hint of remorse that he is talking about doing this to a fellow human – no matter who that might be.

Opie shuffles uneasily next to me. We can both see Xyalis is holding something back.

'What else?'

He peers away from the bench, looking into my eyes as if asking why I'm so concerned. 'Everyone who shares his blood type within a twenty-mile radius will die in the same way.'

I feel a shiver rock through me and can barely get the words out. 'But that will be thousands of people . . .'

He looks away and shrugs, dismissive and unconcerned. 'This is a war, Ms Blackthorn. There will always be casualties.'

31

I cannot sleep, lying awake and staring at the ceiling with the knowledge that I have put a weapon in the hands of someone who is willing to kill thousands of people just to settle a score. The fact that I ever uttered the word revenge as my motive disgusts me. This isn't about me; this is about Colt and Imp – and everyone else who will come after them.

Time crawls as evening becomes night and then early morning. Opie and Faith played along wonderfully as I told Xyalis that I was with him – that sacrificing so many people was a price worth paying. He was delighted, beaming with joy, telling me that we would plot more in the morning. This is the man who didn't even notice Imrin had been left behind and is now a prisoner in Windsor Castle, a place he was so instrumental in getting us away from. He went back for me and I failed him.

But at least I care. Xyalis is concerned for no one but himself, joyously saying how he didn't know the King's blood type and that this is the only way he could ensure that his plan works.

As everybody sleeps, the electrical hum of power drops as my thinkwatch signals that it is the early hours of a new day. I don't know if they have been sleeping but, after an hour on low power, I whisper loudly for Faith and Opie to get ready. Within seconds they are on their feet, bags on their backs. The uniforms are gone and we are dressed for a night of walking. Two more people willing to do anything for me.

We creep through the metal corridors as quietly as we can until we reach the quarters that Xyalis' guards share. There is a sensor next to the door but it is not as sophisticated as the ones in Windsor Castle. It could be because Xyalis doesn't have the materials, or perhaps because he doesn't feel under threat. Either way, I lever the front panel off and pull out the cables, using my knife to slice through them all. The only way the guards will be able to get out is by crawling through the air filtration system – or, if they can manage it, brute force through the sheet metal door. Whichever option they take, we will be long gone by the time they figure it out.

Faith has strapped my ankle as tightly as she can, blocking off much of the pain, but it is still hard to walk on as we move as quickly as we can through the corridors until we reach Xyalis' sleeping quarters.

Opie can be as soft as the tortoise I gave to Imp but here he is fearlessly brutal, wrenching Xyalis out of his bed throat-first. He is shocked and angry as he is dragged kicking and screaming along the corridor. We tell him that we have taken care of his guards, so the shouting counts for nothing, but it doesn't prevent him howling non-stop.

As we reach his lab, Opie hurls Xyalis up the stairs with such force that his head bounces off the top one and lulls to the side. He is still conscious but only just.

'Open the safe,' I order.

He stares at me, confused, pale and panicked. 'What are you going to do?'

'I'm taking the weapon.'

'Are you going to use it?'

I am furious he could even think I would, but keep my voice calm. 'Of course not. You're barbaric.'

'You said you wanted revenge!'

'I was wrong – killing all those people isn't right, even if I did want vengeance.'

I can see in his face that he doesn't understand. For him it is about defeating the King and getting his own way – nobody else matters. We are pawns in his plan.

Like Opie's father was in mine.

I suddenly understand what Imrin was trying to tell me – that manipulating Evan in the way I did is the way things like this start. Before you know it, everyone else is just someone you can use to get what you want.

Xyalis tucks his thumbs into his fists and pushes himself against a wall. 'I'm not opening it.'

I look towards Faith but don't need to say her name before she marches towards Xyalis and wrenches his arm forward.

Be the myth.

I speak harshly and coldly: the way he did when talking about killing thousands of people. 'If you don't open the safe voluntarily, we'll cut your thumb off and open it anyway.'

Faith tugs the knife from her belt and places it on the ground so Xyalis can see it. He splutters in fear, trying to shuffle away before Faith grabs him again. He tries to kick her away but Opie steps forward menacingly. I can see the gash on Xyalis' head from where he hit the step as blood seeps into his hair.

'It's your choice,' I add.

He doesn't move, sniffling and sobbing on the floor until Faith reaches forward and picks up her knife. As she tosses it from one hand to the other, he yelps in self-pity and crawls to the safe before pressing his thumb to the sensor on the front. The door swings open and he pulls the black cylinder out.

'It's already primed,' he says, cradling it to his chest. 'All you have to do is get close to Victor and then press the trigger.'

'Give it,' I demand, holding my hand out.

He continues to cradle it until Faith stands and takes a step towards him. The fact he is so terrified of a girl half his height would be laughable if he wasn't holding a weapon that could cause such destruction. Before she can take another step, he pushes it into my hand.

'You know what he's like. You can still use it. There's a safety catch on the bottom and then you press the trigger.'

I take it from him and put it in my pocket. 'When we're away from here, I'm going to take it apart and destroy it. You're an evil man.'

I take a step towards the door but he wails after me. 'You can't go!'

I walk away with Faith on one side and Opie on the other, ignoring him. We are about to pass through the door and leave for good when it slams down in front of us, sealing the room. Xyalis is crumpled over the control panel, madness in his eyes. He has spent years planning his revenge and isn't about to let us walk away like this.

'You've lost, Xyalis,' I say forcefully. 'Open the door or we'll make you do it. None of us wants to hurt you.'

'I thought you wanted what I wanted?'

'I don't.'

'But you want to kill him?'

'Maybe. Not like this. If that's all you want, why would you do it this way? You have guns, knives and swords – plus access to his security system. When I connected the teleport doors, you could have sent your guards through to try to kill him.'

He shakes his head, tearing at his hair. His reply is a mixture of laughter and despair. 'It wouldn't have hurt him enough. Can you imagine the agony of feeling your body boiling from the inside?'

He breaks into a grin, showing his teeth and the insanity that has gripped him. I should have seen it before; the signs were there.

'Why is it so important to hurt him?'

Xyalis spreads his arms wide. 'Because this is the life he's left me. Hiding underground, trying to link together tinpot nobodies. I should be running an empire.'

It has taken all this time but then it dawns on me. 'The reason you left wasn't to do with Victor, was it? You'd helped install him as King because *you* wanted to be in charge. You thought he would be a puppet and that you'd be running things. You weren't offended by what he was doing, you were offended that he wouldn't listen to you.'

He shrugs and kicks the floor, not bothered that I know. 'You wouldn't understand.'

It is true – I don't have that need to control other people. I haven't craved the life I now have. I never wanted to be followed by people that listen to what I say and still don't know how I can cope with the responsibility that brings. My bad decisions put an evil weapon in the hands of someone willing to use it – and left Imrin at the mercy of the King and Minister Prime. When Xyalis says I don't understand, he is right – I don't know why anyone would desire that power.

'Open the door now,' I demand.

He looks away from me dismissively. 'You're so brave with your soldiers at your side.'

At first I am too shocked to reply. Is that what Opie and Faith are to me? Henchmen? Cadets? People who get their hands dirty?

I stumble over a reply but Faith cuts across me. 'I make my own decisions.'

Opie sounds even more forceful. 'I'm here because I want to be. Imrin wanted to be here too.'

It feels strange hearing Opie say Imrin's name.

Spurred on by his taunts, I am suddenly an afterthought as Opie and Faith take charge. They move towards Xyalis, who looks nervously from one to the other and holds his hands in the air. He sidesteps along the console, his hand hovering over the top of a green button.

'It's that one,' he says.

'Press it then,' Opie replies.

Xyalis steps away, grinning. 'You do it.'

Faith strides forward up the steps and starts scanning the console. 'It does say "door" over the button,' she calls, turning to face me. I watch Xyalis, trying to read in his face if this is some final trick. He is staring at the ground, hands behind his back.

'Press it,' I say.

Faith leans forwards and pounds the button with the palm of her hand. Instantly the door hisses upwards. Opie and Faith turn to head towards me but, as they do, Xyalis suddenly comes alive, launching himself sideways with an agility I would never have imagined. No longer is he snivelling and begging for us to reconsider, he has been waiting for his moment.

I try to shout but the words catch in my throat and it is too late anyway. Xyalis skids across the metal floor and grabs the knife from Faith's belt. She turns, primed and ready to react, but he is already ahead of her.

No warnings, no threats, no second chance, no emotion and no mercy.

Xyalis strikes the knife into Faith's chest and then kicks her viciously, sending her bouncing down the cold, hard steps as blood sprays onto the floor, the knife still embedded in her chest. Xyalis launches himself towards the safe as Opie and I are frozen.

The whites of Faith's eyes stare across the room at me and then, as her eyelids flicker closed, Xyalis rolls away from the safe with a gun.

A drop of Faith's blood dribbles from his hand to the

floor as he extends the weapon until it is pointing at me. His words are calculated, the madness gone. 'It's time you gave that back, Ms Blackthorn.'

My eyes switch from him to Faith's limp body as blood begins to ooze from her chest. It is my fault this has happened. As I turn back to Xyalis, his hand tightens around the gun, twitching but without hesitation.

And then he pulls the trigger.

32

The bang is so loud that I instinctively crouch, covering my head. The bullet bounces around the metal walls until it lodges somewhere I cannot see. My ears are still ringing as Xyalis focuses the gun back on me. 'It's loaded,' he says needlessly. 'Now give me the tube back.'

I want to move but my legs feel as if they have lead tied to them. My throat is raw and as I try to speak, I only manage a cough. Imrin is captured and Faith is dead – both because of me. Out of the corner of my eye, I see Opie step forcefully towards Xyalis but he twists to cover him with the gun.

'Don't be stupid, boy,' Xyalis spits, walking down the first two steps away from his console. 'Throw your weapons over here,' he adds.

Opie glances towards me but I can barely even see him; Faith's limp body is the only thing I can focus on. There is a clatter of movement as Opie tosses his knives to the ground in front of Xyalis.

'Good,' the man says with a nod. 'You too.'

It takes me a moment to realise Xyalis is talking to me.

Without looking away from Faith, I try to pull the knife from my belt but it sticks on the leather catch. I wrench as hard as I can until it pops free and, for a second, enjoy the feel of the hilt in my hand.

'Drop it,' Xyalis demands, turning the gun back to me.

I wonder if there is any chance I could fling the weapon across the room towards Xyalis. Is my aim that good? I know it isn't and that I would probably end up getting Opie or myself shot. I toss the knife on to the floor, where it slides and rests against Opie's weapons close to Faith's body.

'And the other one.'

I crouch and take the knife from my ankle holder, flicking it towards the others. The only weapon I have now is the one that will also kill everyone who has the same blood type as the King within twenty miles of here. I don't know if that includes Xyalis, let alone me and Opie – if it works at all.

Xyalis takes another step forward until he is on the bottom step. His gun is fixed on me. 'Now give me the weapon.'

'No.'

I feel the bullet fizz past my ear a fraction of a second before I hear the bang echoing around the room. This time I don't crouch.

'I'll happily use this to take it from you.'

'Do it then.'

He edges closer to me, until he is level with Faith. I stare towards her body, consumed with despair at the people I have let down. We were all she had left and look at where it got her.

Xyalis' finger tightens on the trigger.

'I'm not bluffing, Ms Blackthorn.'

He takes two more steps forward and is close enough for me to see the individual hairs on his finger. I can sense Opie watching, wondering if he should move but I know anything he does will be suicide. I try to think if there is a way I can get him out of here, even if I'm stuck.

Xyalis adjusts his aim until the pistol is pointing at my head. 'Last chance. Hand it over.'

'I'm not giving it to you.'

'I'll take it anyway after I shoot you.'

'Shoot me then. You've already left one of my friends in Windsor and killed another.'

He doesn't falter. 'I'd rather not have to kill you.'

'If you want your weapon you're going to have to.'

I cannot read his expression; it is fixed and emotionless and yet he hasn't pulled the trigger. Perhaps he is wondering if I am more use to him alive or dead.

I spread my arms and open my palms showing him I am no threat. If he wants to kill a second teenage girl then he can.

I breathe in through my nose, enjoying the feel of the air

as it fills my throat. Before I can take my next breath, it feels as if time has stopped again. Faith's eyes pop open, a pained gasp sticking in her throat. Xyalis turns in surprise at the sound but Faith is too quick for him. She scoops up two of our discarded knives, slamming the first into Xyalis' foot and slashing the second across his throat as he keels over.

He is dead before he hits the floor.

Time speeds up as I rush towards where Faith is trying to sit up. Opie has an arm around her, supporting her weight, but he doesn't know what to do any more than I do.

Faith's eyelids are beginning to droop but she musters enough strength to pull the knife out of her chest and drop it to the floor. I press my hands to her skin, trying to push the blood back into her but it is like a torrent.

She puts her hand over mine but there is no strength behind it.

My words don't sound enough. 'I'm so sorry.'

Faith smiles but there is blood in her mouth and she gurgles for breath. I lean in and hold her close, her final breaths whispering delicately across my ear.

'You make it worth it.'

With that, the life seeps away from her body. Her arms flop to the side as I cradle her the same way I did when we were hiding underneath her bedroom. I start to weep, an anguish building deep in my stomach. It's not just her but everyone else we have lost too.

I have no idea how much time passes before Opie scoops me into his arms. 'We have to go,' he says. My body doesn't feel as if it can move but Opie puts both hands on my face, his thumbs cupping my chin. 'We're not going to get Imrin back if we stay here.'

Imrin and Opie.

I wipe the mess of blood and tears from my face and grab our knives from the floor, before helping Opie to lift Faith's lifeless body.

33

The beautiful orange glow wraps itself around the horizon as the remnants of black sky slowly turn blue. There are no clouds and the only sounds are the winter songs of the few birds who haven't escaped the cold. Their whistles dance into one another, creating a perfect melody as we lower Faith's body into the hole we have spent the night digging.

I throw in the first handful of dirt before Opie and I cover her with the rest. With my knife I carve the name 'Faith' into the closest tree and then we sit against it to catch our breath.

'Are you okay?' Opie asks, snaking an arm around me and passing me a flask of water.

I can't stop staring at the mound of dirt Faith is now buried under.

'I killed her.'

'You didn't.'

I drink greedily but my throat is still raw. Opie tells me to change my clothes but Faith's blood feels like a badge of shame I deserve to wear.

'What are we going to do next?' he asks, fingers tightening around my waist.

I allow him to pull me closer to him until I can feel his warmth and listen to the rise and fall of his chest. His question is one of the few things I know the answer to.

My voice doesn't sound like my own. It is strong but I feel broken, as if there are two of me. For now, I have to be the myth that so many people are desperate for me to be. I take my time, meaning every word I say: 'First, we get this medicine to Hart, then we get Imrin back, then we take down the King.'

Opie breathes in through his nose. 'Just like that?'

Sunlight sears through the trees, the birds sing louder, the breeze is cold but I don't even feel it.

'Just like that.'

Author's Note

Out of everything I've written, *Renegade* is perhaps the book I had the most fun writing. That's despite the fact it's not the story I thought it would at first be. After finishing the first novel in the Silver Blackthorn trilogy, *Reckoning*, there were always elements I knew would form the basis of this second story.

The biggest change between my early notes and the finished book is the way in which Silver's companions become such a large part of the tale. Opie and Imrin were always going to be around, but Jela, Pietra, Hart, the Cotton clan and Faith—*especially* Faith—almost seemed to write themselves at certain points.

As such, *Renegade* ended up being far more a story of friendship and trust than I ever intended and, I think (and hope), a lot better for it.

There are all sorts of people to thank for the fact that this book is in your hands. First among these, as ever, are Natasha and Nicola—my editor and agent—who have been big supporters of Silver ever since I submitted the first draft of *Reckoning*. Without them, if this existed at all, it would be in a poorer form, hidden away somewhere that you, as a reader, would likely never have stumbled upon.

Then there's Susan, who makes my clumsy meanderings a bit more graceful; Trish, a marvellous and constant bastion of support; the rest of the Pan Mac crew: Jodie, Stuart and the ever-wonderful Sam. Lastly, not leastly, there are those across the pond working to do the same: Sara, Alicia and Michelle. They all have worked incredibly hard to make this series a success and I thank them for it.